SO-AII-087

THE BEAST IN CAÑADA DIABLO

THE BEAST IN CAÑADA DIABLO
A Western Trio

LES SAVAGE, JR.

Five Star • Waterville, Maine

First Edition

First Printing: February 2004

Published in 2004 in conjunction with Golden West Literary Agency.

Set in 11 pt. Plantin by Liana M. Walker.

Printed in the United States on permanent paper.

Library of Congress Cataloging-in-Publication Data

Savage, Jr., Les.
   The beast in Cañada Diablo : a western trio / by Les
   Savage, Jr.—1st ed.
     p. cm.
   Contents: The brand of Señorita Scorpion—Queen of the
   long rifles—The beast in Cañada Diablo.
   ISBN 1-59414-044-8 (hc : alk. paper)
   1. Western stories. I. Title.
PS3569.A826B43 2004
813'.54—dc22
                                           2003061272

THE BEAST IN CAÑADA DIABLO

Table of Contents

The Brand of *Señorita* Scorpion

Les Savage, Jr., narrated the adventures of Elgera Douglas, better known as *Señorita* Scorpion, in a series of seven short novels that originally appeared in *Action Stories*, published by Fiction House. She was, by far, the most popular literary series character to appear in this magazine in the nearly thirty years of its publication history. The fifth short novel in this series, "The Brand of Penasco", is included in THE SHADOW IN RENEGADE BASIN: A WESTERN TRIO (Five Star Westerns, 2000). The seventh, and last, story in the series, "The Sting of *Señorita* Scorpion", is collected in the eponymous THE STING OF *SEÑORITA* SCORPION: A WESTERN TRIO (Five Star Westerns, 2000). The short novel that began the series, "*Señorita* Scorpion", can be found in THE DEVIL'S CORRAL: A WESTERN TRIO (Five Star Westerns, 2003). That story so pleased Malcolm Reiss, the general manager at Fiction House, that he wanted another story about her for the very next issue. Savage titled the sequel "*Señorita* Six-Gun". The author was paid $300 for it upon acceptance in January, 1944, but Malcolm Reiss changed its title to "The Brand of *Señorita* Scorpion" when it appeared in *Action Stories* (Summer, 44).

I

The snort of a horse outside brought Elgera Douglas up out of her wooden-pegged chair by the stone fireplace. Texas sunlight streamed in through the west windows of the big room and caught the momentary shimmer of her blonde hair when she turned nervously toward the creak of leather that was men dismounting. She was a tall girl, a pleated white camisa serving her for a blouse, tucked into Mexican *charro* leggings of reddish buckskin with big silver bosses down their seams. Her full red lips compressed as she heard the pound of boots across the flagstone porch, and she wondered for the hundredth time that day if she had made a mistake, trusting an outsider with this thing.

Then the heavy oak door was shoved open, and the first man entered with a swift, catty stride. His eyes met Elgera's, and she drew a sharp breath with the sense of a staggering physical impact. They were set deeply beneath a heavy black brow, those eyes, and a savage violence seemed to emanate from the brilliant little lights flaring and dying again in their jet black depths. A feeling of suffocation crept over Elgera as she was held there. Then the man's white teeth flashed in his swarthy face, and he bent forward in a bow. The inclination of his dark head took his eyes away. It snapped the spell.

Elgera realized she had been unconsciously holding her breath. She expelled it with a small hissing sound, only then becoming aware of the other two men who had entered. One was her brother, Natividad Douglas, lean and young in the same reddish *charro* leggings as worn by Elgera. His angular face was burned deeply by the sun. He removed his flat-topped Stetson, introducing the men.

"Elgera, this is *Señor* Ignacio Avarillo, the mining engineer," he said, indicating the swarthy man with the strange eyes. "And this is *Señor* Thomas. Gentlemen, my sister, Elgera Douglas."

Thomas was skinny and dour; his face seemed like an ancient satchel. With one claw-like hand he clutched a briefcase of brown leather up against his dusty tail coat. Elgera was drawn again to the swarthy man. *Señor* Avarillo wore a *cabriolé* of blue broadcloth, the short Spanish cape still affected by some men in this border country—but even its loose folds failed to hide the hulk of his great shoulders. He was looking around the large room with its *viga* poles for rafters above the fireplace, blackened by the smoke of generations. His glance stopped at the rawhide-rigged saddle that hung from a peg to one side of the door, its hand-stamped skirt marked with the Circle S brand that had been used by the Douglases ever since they had come to the Santiago Valley.

"Ah, yes," said Avarillo, and his voice held a deep vibrancy. "The *Circulo* Ⓢ, the mark of the fabled Lost Santiago Mine. You can imagine how I must feel, *Señorita* Douglas, after hearing the thousand legends of the mine, to be standing here in your house in this lost valley, knowing I have at last found what men have hunted for two centuries. And those Dead Horse Mountains . . . *Santa Maria!* I can well understand why no one has ever discovered the mine before this. Without your brother to guide us in from Alpine, *Señor* Thomas and I would be buzzard bait right now."

His faint smile suddenly disturbed Elgera. She was surprised at the impatience in her own voice. "You brought your papers?"

"*Naturalmente,*" he said, inclining his head toward the dour man. "If you please, *Señor* Thomas."

Thomas glanced around the room, chose the ponderous, wooden-pegged table by the far adobe wall. He set the cheap oil lamp to one side, put the briefcase on the sleazy, fringed satin cloth. Elgera saw the gilt letter **A** inscribed on the flap before he unlocked and opened it.

"I don't want to seem rude, rushing it this way," said the girl. "But you understand why I want to be so sure of you."

"Your brother told me about some trouble with this Hawkman," said Avarillo. "He owns all the land around you, I understand, and is trying to get yours away from you."

The girl spoke bitterly. "The only reason we're still here is that Hawkman hasn't been able to find us yet. He owns land in these Dead Horses, but he's never seen most of it, never been able to hire men who would ride in and survey it for him. It's the worst badlands in the Big Bend. Our valley is the only spot capable of supporting cattle. The Indians have avoided these mountains ever since they began passing them in their raids down the Comanche Trail into Mexico. Few white men have penetrated beyond the first ridges and lived. Even if it weren't for the mine, though, Anse Hawkman would still go to any lengths for our spread."

"What a boundless greed the man must have," murmured Avarillo. "*Sí,* what a boundless greed."

Thomas glanced at him sharply, then went on taking papers from the case. A shadow entered Elgera's blue eyes. She looked from one man to the other.

"What I can't understand," said Avarillo, "is why you didn't develop the Santiago Mine before."

Natividad answered: "That tunnel by which we entered

the valley is the original mine shaft. It leads right through the mountain from the outside and is the only way in or out. It was the mine that brought *Don* Simeón Santiago and George Douglas here in the first place. They had worked it about six months when the Comanches and Apaches raided. The Indians killed Santiago and all the others except Douglas and a woman who hid in the bottom level of the diggings. When the Indians left, they caved in a portion of the tunnel behind them, leaving Douglas trapped on the inside. We are the descendants of that George Douglas, *señor*, and it was only fifteen years ago that we succeeded in digging back out."

"There were some of us who wanted to stay cut off, to have the peace we had known," said the girl. "Others wanted to begin working the mine again. It has been a continual argument among us. But Hawkman has been closing in, and our hand is forced. The mine is all we can fight him with. If we can get it working before he discovers our whereabouts. . . ."

"*Sí,*" murmured Avarillo, and his voice held a sibilance. "Before he discovers your whereabouts. *Ahora,* my papers. You have the diploma from the *Escuela de las Minas* in *Ciudad Méjico,* the sheepskin from Columbia School of Mines, letter of recommendation from the Apex in Colorado, letter of introduction from *Señor* Hopwell at Alpine, and so on . . . you see them, they are all there."

Elgera glanced perfunctorily at the gilt-edged diplomas with their fancy scrolls. She picked up the letter of introduction from Hopwell's land office in Alpine. They had been reluctant about trusting even him, although he had run the office there for many years. But they had to trust someone, and Natividad had asked Hopwell to recommend a competent, trustworthy mining engineer. Hopwell had communicated with Avarillo in Colorado. When the man arrived at

Alpine, Natividad had gone up to meet him and bring him back to the Santiago.

"And now," said Avarillo, "if everything is in order, might I presume and ask to see your papers."

"My papers?" asked Elgera.

"Legal aspects," stated Thomas in his dry voice. "Deeds, will, mortgages, anything you have. That's why Avarillo brought me. After all, he doesn't want to start digging on any mine unless he's sure you own it."

Elgera frowned, hesitating, and Avarillo spoke softly. "Of course, if you have nothing here, we could check the county records. *Pues* that would take time. And Anse Hawkman. . . ."

The name goaded Elgera. She turned toward the fireplace. "I have papers."

She drew a heavy stone from its place, took a packet wrapped in greased buckskin from the cavity. She handed it to Thomas. He unwrapped the soft hide, rustled through the papers.

"Last will and testament," he muttered, waving one.

Avarillo turned to the girl. "Your father?"

"Made out before we took him to the hospital at Alpine," said the girl. "He. . . ."

"Ah, sick, how unfortunate," broke in Avarillo, something impatient in his voice. "Did you hear that, Thomas? The old gentleman is sick."

Thomas held up another document. "Quit-claim."

"Is it what we want?" asked Avarillo quickly.

" 'This indenture, made the . . . ,' "—Thomas paused in his reading—"no date. We can fix that. 'This indenture, made the blank day of the blank month, Eighteen Hundred and Ninety-Two, between John Coates Douglas, cattleman, Santiago Valley, Brewster County, Texas, party of the first part, and' "—he paused again—"no name there, either. We

13

might as well see to it all right now."

He drew a bottle of ink and a quill pen from the briefcase, bending over the table. Elgera heard the scratch of pen on paper and stepped forward.

"What are you doing?"

"You," said Avarillo, and his eyes caught her, "you must realize how dangerous that deed might be in Hawkman's hands."

"My father made it out," she said. "No matter how hard the small *rancheros* fought Hawkman, no matter what they did, Hawkman got their land sooner or later. Dad saw him closing in around us like that with nothing stopping him and thought it would be useless to fight. He wanted to spare us the pain and bloodshed and loss the others had suffered. He made arrangements to meet Anse down at the Smoky Blue line camp, had the quit-claim drawn up. My brother found it before he left and stopped him."

"Hawkman, then, might know about this deed?"

The girl shrugged. "Dad might have told him he'd have it. What does it matter?"

Thomas straightened, clearing his throat. "How does it sound now? 'This indenture, made the fifteenth day of March, Eighteen Hundred and Ninety-Two, between John Coates Douglas, cattleman' . . . so on, so on . . . 'party of the first part, and Anse Herald Hawkman, Boquillos, Brewster County, Texas, party of the second part. Witnesseth . . . that said party of the first part, in consideration of twenty thousand dollars' . . . I made it a tidy sum, you see? . . . 'twenty thousand dollars lawful money of the United States, paid by the party of the second part, do hereby grant and release unto said party of the second part, heirs and assigns, forever, the land lying between Dead Horse Peak. . . .' "

14

"Never mind the rest," snapped Avarillo. "That do the job?"

"It does," said Thomas. "I made the date as of today, you see. We can register the transfer when we get back to Alpine."

The girl was looking from one man to the other, trying to grasp what she had just heard. It was simple enough. Yet she couldn't believe it. Her voice was faint.

"You. . . .You signed Hawkman's name?"

"You're sure it's legal now?" said Avarillo swiftly to Thomas. "You can put Hawkman's handle to it like that?"

"I have power of attorney," said Thomas. "If no one contests this, it's as good as the gold in the Santiago Mine. And that's your job, Valeur, to see that no one contests it."

It must have taken Natividad that long to understand. His boots made a sharp rasp on the earthen floor as he stepped forward, hand slipping to the butt of his old-fashioned Remington.

"Valeur?" he said.

The swarthy man's hand slid upward to the lapel of his coat and he smiled. "*Sí*, Jan Valeur. . . ."

The pound of someone's feet across the flagstone porch turned them toward the door. It burst open, and Elgera's younger brother, Juanito, stumbled in, white cotton shirt tails flapping around his buckskin *chivarras*.

"Elgera," he gasped. "It's Bickford. He must have trailed Natividad and Avarillo in when they came. He was waiting in the mine with Hawkman's *vaqueros*."

"Juanito!" cried Elgera, taking a step toward him and reaching out to keep him from falling.

Bick Bickford's huge form was skylighted for a moment in the doorway as he came through after the boy. Juanito Douglas was still stumbling forward when Bickford caught up with him and slugged him behind the neck with a big black .44.

The boy fell against Elgera without a sound, hands clawing down her leggings as he slumped to the floor. Her horrified eyes rose slowly from the still form at her feet to Bick Bickford, standing there with his thick legs straddled one on either side of the kid he had struck down. The round bore of his gun covered the room.

The swarthy man's voice startled Elgera, coming in harsh anger from behind her. "You fool, Bickford. I told you not to show till we gave you the high sign!"

He was a big bull of a man, Bickford, with a heavy-boned forehead that lowered over close-set eyes, a week's stubble of yellow beard on his ugly, bulging jaw. He tucked his freckled left hand into a cartridge belt that was pushed down low beneath the sag of a growing paunch.

"This kid heard us waiting in the cave," he growled to the man behind Elgera. "I tried to cut him off, but he got away. No use staying after that, was there? Did you get the quit-claim?"

The girl turned to Natividad. His face was white and twisted. He opened his mouth helplessly, closed it again. She whirled back to Bickford.

"You . . . !" she choked.

"Yes," he said without smiling. "Me. Did you think Anse wasn't going to find you sooner or later? Everybody in the Big Bend knew he's been hunting for this valley, knew how much he'd pay for any information about it. Hopwell kept his mouth closed, but he had to get in touch with Avarillo by mail, and he made the mistake of sending his Mex handyman to the stage with the letter. The Mex guessed it had something to do with the Santiago. He'd seen Natividad in the land office. The letter went to Avarillo all right, but we found out what was in it before we sent it on."

The girl's pale face turned slowly back to the swarthy man.

16

Bickford went on heavily: "You knew me and the rest of Anse's boys. The only one you didn't know was Thomas. We brought Valeur, here, in from New Orleans to do the job. He made a right nice Avarillo from the looks of things."

"Yes," said Thomas dryly, crackling the deed. "A very successful deception. Too bad you didn't see what the real Avarillo looked like, though, Bick."

"We got his papers, didn't we?" said Bickford. "That's all we needed."

"And left him running around free as air," snapped the swarthy man whose real name seemed to be Valeur. "You were a fool to jump him at night. And not even getting a look at him before he vamoosed, that was the payoff."

"Let's not quarrel," said Thomas. "It's done now, and we have what we want. We found the way to the valley, and the Santiago belongs to Anse now."

The girl heard her own choked sob. Yes, the Santiago belonged to Anse Hawkman. She couldn't believe she had just stood there and let them take it away like that. Yet what could she have done? How could she have known? Fists clenched, she looked at Natividad again. He held his hand out in a small, helpless gesture, eyes blank and stunned. And how could he have known?

The girl shuddered suddenly with a wave of terrible, impotent anger. She whirled back toward Bickford, taking a jerky step toward him. The man snapped his .44 up.

"Hold it, Elgera," he said. "Valeur, you better take care of this girl right now."

Elgera felt the insistent pound of a little pulse in her throat. Her body was still rigid with the impotent rage, but the first sense of her utter defeat began to creep through the anger. She looked from Bickford to Valeur, and suddenly she wanted to cry very badly.

"We'll take care of all the Douglases right now." The swarthy man smiled. "You leave it to me. Especially the girl."

It was an odd thing that came to Elgera's mind then. Yet, not so odd, in a way. A certain man had helped her once before. Through all her anger and fear and stunned surprise, the name began to take form. It was a singular name Bickford would know or Hawkman. Chisos Owens.

II

The Del Norte Mountains cast purple afternoon shadows into Alpine, huddled at the base of their western slope. The town had been founded twelve years before with the coming of the railroad. The Southern Pacific's brick depot and loading platforms fronted on the tracks at the north end of the main street. The Alpine Lodge took up half of the first block, a paint-peeled frame hotel with a sprawling porch that looked across toward the dilapidated row of business houses on the other side. The Mescal Saloon squatted forlornly on the southwest corner of the next block, the blank windows to the assayer's office staring from its second floor. Beneath the warped overhang of the pine oak lounged a dusty idler, leaning against an unpainted *soporte* to one side of the saloon's batwings.

His Texas-creased Stetson cast a shadow across blue eyes holding the narrowed, wind-wrinkled look that comes to a man spending most of his time on the range. He was rolling a wheat straw with a deftness that seemed odd, somehow, for his blocky, rope-scarred hands. He finished with the cigarette and lowered his free hand to tuck a thumb inside the cartridge belt of his oak-handled Bisley, its scarred holster slung indifferently against his brass-studded Levi's.

Three horsemen had just turned in past the depot and were cantering toward the Mescal. The man in front of the saloon glanced at them disinterestedly. He could already see

19

that none of the three was the girl, and he found himself wondering if she would ever come riding in. Then he took an impatient puff on his wheat straw. *Chisos Owens*, he told himself, *you are a fool*. He allowed gray smoke to stream from his nostrils. All right, so he was a fool. That was the only reason he kept drifting back to Alpine, though, because of the girl. She would be opening the mine about now; rumors of it had already reached this far north. Alpine was where her ore would come for assaying. It was in the back of his mind always, the hope of seeing her again.

The first dry, gritty feel of dust raised by the riders came to Owens, blown by a vagrant gust of wind. He took small notice of it. He was still thinking of Elgera Douglas. It seemed a long time ago that he had followed her into the Santiago. Yet it was only a few months. He was sorry now that he had ever left the valley. He knew it was only his stubborn pride that prevented his return. Even when he had discovered she was heiress to the Santiago, he still had asked her to leave with him. And she had asked him to stay. But it just hadn't seemed right, somehow, for a man to live off a woman when he felt that way about her. It still didn't seem right. Staying there, or taking her away, he should have something to offer. And he had nothing. . . .

"Hell!" It was but a whisper.

Owens shrugged, dropping his cigarette to grind it out with a scarred heel of his Justin. The three horsebackers had passed him and were pulling up at the hitch rack farther down where a covered stairway went up the rear of the saloon to the assayer's office on the second floor. Owens couldn't help marking the size of the man who forked the chestnut mare. It wasn't so much his height, although he must have stood over six feet without his patent leather boots. It was the tremendous bulk of his chest and shoulders that not even the loose hanging folds of his short blue cape could hide. In a land where most men were as lean and drawn as a rawhide dally from spending all their time in the saddle, this man stood out like a Brahman bull in a bunch of range-gaunted Mexican *ladinos*.

He pulled the chestnut to a halt and swung down, alighting with an easy grace that was surprising in such a large man. He spoke swiftly to the other riders. The tall, dour one in a dusty frock coat climbed off his nag stiffly. The plank walk groaned as he stepped onto it, popped beneath his boots as he turned southward toward the newly erected municipal building. He held a brown briefcase under one arm.

Slung across the chestnut's withers were leather *alforjas*. The man in the blue cape slipped one arm beneath the high pockets of the Mexican saddlebags and bent in under, heaving them off onto his shoulder. Their weight was evident in the way he leaned forward when he stepped to the walk and disappeared up the stairs. Owens got the impression that few other men would have been able to carry the *alforjas* without help.

The third man was dismounted now, and he stood there with his sharp face turning nervously up and down the street. Owens was about to look away when something on the man's horse caught his eye. It was a blocky dun, flanks caked with sweat and dust of a long ride. On its heavy rump was a very evident Circle(S) brand.

"Ees a strange mark to see in the Big Bend, no?" said a soft voice at Owens's elbow.

Owens turned sharply. He hadn't heard the man come up. He was Mexican and he couldn't have measured much more than five feet tall, or much less than five feet around. His moon face was the color of a coffee bean and his big, sad, bloodshot eyes reminded Owens of a hound dog's. Providing striking contrast to his English riding boots and gray whip-cords was the broad sash of a violent red bound around his singularly prodigious girth.

"What's so strange about it?" asked Owens warily.

The Mexican took a *cigarro* from the pocket of his white silk shirt, bit off the end, spat it out. "The *Circulo* S. A very ancient brand. Used by the House of Santiago in Mexico. It was *Don* Simeón Santiago, was it not, who discovered the Santiago Mine, and who subsequently disappeared along with that mine?"

"Are you asking me?"

The man lit his *cigarro*, chuckled. "Maybe I should ask you. I think you could probably tell me things about the Santiago no other men in the Big Bend know. Then, again, maybe I could tell you things about the Santiago that even you don't know. Monclava was the old capital of the combined provinces of Tejas and Coahuila when Spain held this country. Simeón Santiago was *adelantado*, entrusted with the visitation of the mines in New Spain, when he discovered the Lost Santiago. The church at Monclava still has the official documents. I have had access to those documents. They contain things which would be interesting . . . even to you." He cut off as Owens glanced at him sharply, then chuckled. He took a complacent puff on his *cigarro* before speaking. "Chisos Owens, isn't it?" he asked. Then: "*Señor* Chisos Owens who owned the Smoky Blue until the creek dried up and one Anse Hawkman forced you out. *Señor* Chisos Owens who might know what it could mean to see a man like our friend out in the street riding a horse with the ancient *Circulo* S brand, which hasn't been seen in existence since the House of Santiago was confiscated during Santa Anna's time in the old country."

"You seem to have a fund of information," said Owens.

"Upon discreet inquiry by me, the barkeep in the Mescal was glad to oblige. He seemed to think you were the only man who had bucked Hawkman and stayed around to talk about it."

"I don't talk about it," said Owens. "Two things generally happen to *hombres* who buck Hawkman. Most of them give up and go to work for him, sooner or later. Hawkman has a man named Bickford who takes care of those that don't give up in a permanent way, sooner or later."

"*Si.*" The Mexican grinned. "Only you are the exception which proves the rule. That *hombre* standing by the horses? He strikes me as being a stranger here. Perhaps brought in by somebody for something . . . ah, special . . . as it were."

The man by the dun had his gray vest buttoned up tightly about a skinny chest. Owens hadn't missed the way he slung his gun around low in front, because there were always men in such towns as Alpine who wore their guns in that manner. He might, as the Mexican said, have been brought in by somebody for something special. Men of his type had reasons for coming and invariably had even better ones for leaving. Owens shook his head. "I'd say he isn't a native."

"And not being a native, he wouldn't know you, perhaps?"

"No," said Owens. "I don't think he'd know me."

"*Excelente.*" The Mexican laughed and suddenly he held a pack of tattered cards in one pudgy hand. "Now, *Señor* Chisos Owens, has it ever struck you what a big majority of men who, shall we say, have a certain skill with their guns which they use in a professional way also have an irresistible passion for gambling? You couldn't say that almost every gambler was a gunman, *pues* you could say with a reasonable certainty that almost every gunman was a gambler. No . . . ? *Si.*"

While talking, he had begun to do tricks with the deck,

turning slightly so his manipulations would be visible to the man in the street. Black *cigarro* in his mouth he flipped the cards back and forth between his fat fingers, made them leap from one hand to the other as if alive. His voice became louder than before.

"*Dios,* what a dull *día* this is. No *compadres* in the *cantina,* no friends to play cards with. I would give my right *brazo* for another *hombre* or two. A man's money can only stay in his pocket a little while before it begins burning holes. . . ."

Owens caught the small shift of the skinny man in the gray vest; something intent came into the tilt of his head. The Mexican went on talking, moving toward the saloon door.

"What could be more enjoyable after a long dusty ride than a bottle of mescal, a *compañero* or two, and a deck of cards, eh?

"What's the game?" Owens asked, and he wasn't talking about the cards.

"Anything you like, *amigo,* keno, chusa, poker," said the fat man in a tone still loud enough to reach the man in the street, then he had reached the batwing doors, and he lowered his voice. "Many men have heard the rumors that the Lost Santiago had been found again, *Señor* Owens. But who was beside the quaking asp on Saltillo Peak when it whispered to the wind that Anse Hawkman had branched out of the cattle business into mining? Eh, *señor* . . . who?"

Still playing with the cards, he shoved through the doors. They creaked shut behind him. Owens could hear his bland chuckle diminishing inside.

The three of them sat around a scarred deal table at the rear of the Mescal. Chisos Owens had been the first to follow the Mexican in. The skinny man had held out a few moments, then swung through the door almost defiantly. He had gone to the bar first, had a drink beside the other two men there. But the light slap of cards drew him irresistibly, and now he was sitting across from Owens, gray vest still buttoned tightly. The Mexican leaned back in his chair, grinning expansively.

"What shall we call you, *señor*," he chuckled, "what shall we call such a good *compadre* who has come to drink with us and play with us and win all our money?"

The thin man glanced nervously toward the door. "Hoke. My handle's Hoke. You?"

"Me?" The Mexican chuckled. "*Por supuesto,* you could call me Felipe, and that would be my name, or Juan, or Amole, and those would be my names, too, and yet none of them would quite be my name entirely, if you understand what I mean."

Hoke seemed to appreciate that. He laughed shortly. "Yeah, I understand. You?" His glance swung to Owens inquiringly.

Owens shoved the cards to him. "No thanks," he said. "You deal."

Hoke looked at him sharply, then down at the cards. He grinned, shrugged, took up the deck. As he began to shuffle, the Mexican looked at Owens and laughed softly. Owens shifted uneasily in his chair. He knew he had been drawn into this by the Mexican, who sat calmly smoking the *cigarro,* and wondered just how much he knew about the Santiago Valley and the *Circulo* S and Anse Hawkman.

Owens hadn't much skill with the cards and wasn't surprised when Hoke took the first pot. He got the impression, though, that the Mexican did possess a skill and that he had let Hoke win deliberately. Hoke seemed to relax a little. He took a long pull at the clay jug of mescal. It was growing dark outside and the bald-headed barkeep dragged a chair beneath the single overhead light, climbing up to turn the lamp high.

It was stud—two down and three up—and by the third hand Hoke was showing his liquor. Trying to focus his eyes, he put down a pair of aces with two kings turned up on the table. Felipe slapped his cards into the center disgustedly.

"*¡Santiago!*"

Hoke jerked up. "Whassat?"

"Santiago," said Felipe with a bland grin. "An expression. A war cry, really. Originated when the Spanish were trying to rid Spain of the Moors, you understand. *Santiago y cierra España,* they would cry, Saint James and clear out of Spain."

"Oh," said Hoke, and he seemed relieved. "Oh."

They went through another hand. Hoke finished the jug. He was perspiring. His ratty eyes were dull. Felipe leaned back in his chair.

"*Por Dios,*" he said. "My pockets are light again. My *dinero* is disappearing. And I have no mine to fall back on like you, Hoke."

"When those diggin's begin turning out yellow, I'll play cards every night and lose an *alforja* full of gold pieces every game and still be able to buy me a spread ten times the size of Hawkman's mangy pasture . . . "—the skinny man hiccoughed, then he raised his head with a jerk, suspicion flickering into his eyes. "How'd you know?"

The Mexican leaned forward, plunking a stack of yellow coins.

Hoke's glance fell on the stack of yellow coins. "Yeah, yeah. I'll take this hand, too."

Understanding what the Mexican was pointing at now, Owens dealt. He hadn't enough skill to plant the card. He knew the Mexican named Felipe would keep Hoke drinking and all the beans would spill out sooner or later.

The narrow-faced gunman bent over his cards, underlip

slack. The Mexican perused his hand, grunted almost under his breath.

"You know, I'm not sure whether to believe these stories about the Santiago or not. I don't think Anse Hawkman has found it at all. Not when men have been hunting it for two hundred years."

"Who says Hawkman found it?" grunted Hoke, pawing for the empty jug. "Valeur did all the work. Those damn' Douglas coyotes would've rec'nized Hawkman or any of his riders. It was Valeur fooled the gal. It's him working the mine now."

Chisos Owens stiffened. The girl? Then he caught Felipe's eyes on him, a warning in them. He relaxed, allowing a heavy breath to slip from him, glancing dully at his cards. They were crumpled in his fist.

Felipe held up a fat finger for the barkeep, turned back to Hoke. "It seems to me a *hombre* of your caliber would ride a better horse than that crow-bait dun."

"My hoss went lame," muttered Hoke, looking blankly into the empty jug. "I was going to take the Douglas gal's palomino. Bick wouldn't let me, wouldn't even let me take any of the others in the Circle S remuda. Hell. Think I was gonna stove up my animal riding him up here lame? I snuck the dun out."

Felipe took the fresh bottle from the barkeep, shoved it to the center of the table. "There you are, Hoke, *compadre,* more paint remover, so to speak. This Bickford must be a very unco-operative *hombre.* I'll bet he wanted the palomino himself."

"He didn't want the blondie," snarled Hoke thickly. "Bick's just spooked by this Chisos Owens, that's all . . . Bick and Thomas and Anse, the whole bunch of 'em. They said Chisos Owens was still around and might spot the palomino.

They was even skeery of him seeing me forking any other Circle S animal." He tipped the full bottle up and his Adam's apple bobbed when he drank.

Felipe flourished his *cigarro*, knocked ashes from it, gave Chisos a sidelong glance. "This Chisos Owens must be quite a *diablo* to have a man like Anse Hawkman afraid of him," he said.

"I dunno," said Hoke, head sinking toward the table. "Anse's getting old. Maybe he is afraid of Chisos Owens. He told us to finish Owens's tortillas for good if he showed at the valley. Seems Owens is sweet on the gal. He followed her in from the outside. The only one who knows where the valley is . . . at least he was the only one. Now, Valeur and me, yeah, Valeur and me. . . ."

His voice trailed off as his face pressed into the table. Felipe shoved the bottle into his hand again, smiling slyly at Owens.

"*Sí,* you and Valeur. And I'll bet you're the only one who isn't afraid of this Chisos Owens. I'll bet you're the one who gets him if he comes. No . . . ? *Sí.*"

"Bick's the one who knows him," said Hoke, trying to raise his head for another pull. "Valeur and me came in from New Orleans for the job. I don't see why they're all so skeery of one *hombre* like that anyway."

Felipe was still looking at Owens. "Neither do I. *Pues,* maybe Hawkman knows this Chisos Owens better than we do, Hoke."

He stopped, turning toward the sound of boots coming down the walk outside. Owens saw the batwings swing open suddenly and the big, swarthy man in the blue *cabriolé* burst into the room. He came on in with that swift, rolling walk, like a savage jungle animal pacing its cage. For a moment his eyes swept to Chisos Owens and their glances locked.

Owens felt himself recoil as if he had been struck. The force of personality emanating from the man's eyes was almost physical. They were jet black but lacking the opaque quality of an Indian's eyes, and all the unbridled violence boiling inside the man seemed to burn in the brilliant little lights flashing through their depths.

When his glance left Owens and jumped to Hoke, it was like snapping a cord between them. Owens straightened in his chair, realizing how tightly his hand gripped the table. The big man stopped beside Hoke, grabbing the edge of his vest in a hairy fist, jerking him up.

"Damn' fool, Hoke," he snarled. "I told you to stay clear of this place. I told you not to get drunk this time."

" 'Sall right, Valeur," mumbled Hoke. "These *hombres* already knew Hawkman was working the Santiago."

His words ended with a gasp as Valeur's arm straightened, shoving him violently over backward. Even before Hoke hit the floor, Valeur was turning.

"You pumped him!" he almost yelled, and his hand slipped beneath the blue cloak. "Nobody knew Hawkman had the Santiago. You got him drunk, and you pumped him."

Owens kicked his chair back from beneath him and tried to rise and draw. But before his hand touched his Bisley, he saw Valeur's fist flashing back out of his cloak, the butt of a gun gleaming between taut fingers.

Then a bulk was thrust in between Owens and Valeur. It took that instant for Owens to realize Felipe had leaned over the table with his burning *cigarro* held outthrust in one pudgy hand. The swift deftness of the Mexican's whole movement made it seem almost ludicrous. He jammed his *cigarro* against Valeur's gun hand. The big man bellowed with pain, hand pulling away spasmodically. His shot went wild into the ceiling instead of hitting Owens.

Valeur whirled toward Felipe, face twisted savagely. Owens had his Bisley out by then. He drew down on Valeur. Someone shot out the light.

With the tinkling crash of the wrecked oil lamp following the thunderous shot, Owens fired blindly into the sudden darkness. The flame that stabbed out ahead of him might have been Valeur, shooting at Felipe. Someone pounded in through the door.

"Valeur?" he shouted. "You in here, Valeur?"

Owens lurched forward, cocking his gun. He slammed into a man before the hammer was eared back. Anyone else would have been staggered by his hurtling weight. This man stopped him like a stone wall.

Owens struck upward with the barrel of his gun, heard a pained curse. He threw out his hand to ward off the return blow. Then the man's arms were about him. He felt the terrible, driving surge of strength in that awful bear hug, knew his first shot had missed Valeur, and knew who held him now. He tried to free his Bisley and strike again. His right arm was pinned. He twisted, jabbing in a left. He struck a belly like an oak plank and wondered if his hand was broken.

The scuffle of their feet was sharp and swift on the bare floor. Owens jabbed again with his left. He choked on the pain it caused him. They slammed into a table.

"Damn you!" gasped Valeur. "Damn you."

His arms flexed, and Owens felt himself levered backward. He fought for solid footing, breath exploding from him. Someone struck his head from behind. With sound and smell and pain suddenly slipping from him, Owens sagged against Valeur. He heard a dull thud, and Valeur cried hoarsely. The man's arms relaxed. Owens went on down against him.

Hands slipped beneath Owens's armpits, jerking him free of Valeur. His boot struck a table leg as someone dragged him across the floor. A man groaned to his left. Hoke, maybe.

Owens's last coherent thought was to wonder who had hit him from behind. The man who had come running in, shouting for Valeur, hadn't had time to reach them. Hoke had been on the other side of the table. Felipe?

Chisos Owens's first sensation upon regaining consciousness was the fetid, gagging smell of decaying food. He rose to an elbow and was very sick without opening his eyes. Then he looked and was sick again. It came to him finally that he was jammed down between two boxes of refuse in the alley behind the saloon. A month-old New York *Sun* poked moldering headlines in his face. Empty bottles clinked beneath him when he moved. Shoving the trash off, he got to his feet, staggered toward the rear door of the Mescal.

The barkeep was a pot-bellied little man with a fringe of reddish hair around his baldpate. He stood on a deal table in the center of the room, putting up a new oil lamp. Owens weaved to the bar.

"Who conked me last night, Irish?" he wanted to know.

Irish climbed down, circled behind the bar. He poured Owens two fingers, flipped the jigger across the scarred mahogany. "Dunno, Chisos," he said. "I make it a practice to duck behind the bar when things like that begin. I do know those jaspers spent about an hour hunting you before they left."

"Somebody tucked me away for the night beneath a pile of your trash," mumbled Owens, tossing off the drink. "I don't wonder they couldn't find me. You tell 'em who I was?"

"The big gent in the blue *cabriolé* asked me your name," said Irish, "but I just couldn't seem to remember. That fat Mex had asked me about you earlier in the day, and I figured I'd blabbed enough to him. He has such a way of asking things, though, you don't know you've told 'em till they're out."

"That," said Owens, fishing for a quarter, "is the truth."

He put the coin down and turned toward the door. His buckskin was standing at the rack. Owens unhitched a pair of old apron chaps from a tie string on his saddle skirt, slipped them on over his dusty Levi's. He would need them where he was headed. He didn't feel like breakfast. There was some coffee and flour in the fiber *morral* slung from his saddle horn that would do when he got over being sick. There was something decisive about the way he swung aboard the buckskin and turned it toward the brick depot. His destination was clear in his mind now and he felt better than he had in a long time, somehow. An early morning freight was halted by the loading platform. He rode by the puffing engine and on out across the tracks without looking back at the town.

In all Texas there was no more wild, rugged country than the Big Bend, and in all the Big Bend the wildest, least-known, most desolate section was the mysterious badlands encompassed by the *Sierra del Caballo Muerto*—the Dead Horse Mountains. White with alkali of the Rosillos Basin, Chisos Owens turned into the Dead Horses late the second afternoon out of Alpine. He had followed the ancient Comanche Trail through Persimmon Gap and hugged the western flank of the Santiagos for the better part of the day. Irish had said Valeur and the other two had left Alpine after their hour's search for him. Often now he could see their trail. Sometimes, too, he caught the sign of a fourth man's track. It was hard to tell whether he rode with Valeur, or alone, but Owens didn't need their sign to tell him the way.

He had a forward lean to his seat in the saddle that humped his shoulders into a dogged line, giving a stubborn quality to the weariness that lay in the sag of his blocky torso.

Grinning mirthlessly, he urged the flagging buckskin up the first barren slope of the mountains.

Topping the ridge, he was struck by a wind that was dry and yet cold, a cutting wind that made him hunch deeper into his denim jumper and wish for a Mackinaw. The gaunt *alamos* arched past him as he dropped down the opposite slope, their foliage sere and sparse. A hoot owl heralded the coming night. Memory of his other trip into this lonely place served Owens now. Ridge after ridge lay behind him when he finally dropped down a shaly barranca into the bottom of a valley, turning northward along the dry course of a river. There was absolutely no water and a man not knowing the way would face sure death, turning on into unknown land that way. Owens could already feel his cutting thirst as the valley narrowed, becoming a cañon. Brush began to thicken in the bottom, clawing at his apron chaps, ripping at his *tapaderos*. Finally the chaparral became practically impenetrable, and he dismounted, cursing the pop and snap of mesquite as he forced his way through. A hundred yards beyond he hitched the buckskin to a growth of nopal and began to move forward alone. He stopped finally, pulling out his gun, staying there a long time, listening.

It was a box cañon and ahead of him the brush thinned out until an oblong clearing lay beneath the towering walls of red sandstone blocking off its end. The cliff here had more slope to it than the part behind Owens. He searched the hovering shadows formed by the boulders and uplifts until his eyes ached. Nothing moved up there. He shrugged. There was only one way in and he would have to take it sooner or later. His figure made a square blot against the pale-yellow parch of sand, moving out in a solid-footed stride.

Halfway across he stopped abruptly. His head jerked upward toward a small, scraping sound. His gun swung in a tightened fist when he saw the man on the rocks above him. Then it stopped its swift upward arc. Owens turned part way toward the other wall of the cañon and he was too dog-tired to feel his defeat very sharply.

There was another man across the way there—the noise he had made climbing down was what had stopped Owens. Both men had rifles that caught the moonlight in fitful metallic glints, and they were in a position to cut Owens down with a crossfire. He realized suddenly how confident they were to have allowed him that instinctive upward swing with his gun and still hold their lead. They didn't even ask him to drop his Bisley now. They moved down the steep wall, sliding from boulder to boulder.

One wore slick batwing chaps that made a faint slapping sound against his extremely bowed legs as he moved. A steeple sombrero cast his face into deep shadow. He seemed puzzled by Owens's dull acceptance of this. He tipped his head sideways and regarded Owens for a long moment.

"Think you could walk right in?" he said.

Owens shrugged, and the other man spoke from where he stood in the sand at the base of the cliff. "Got a handle?"

"Not one that sticks out," said Owens.

The man in batwings stiffened, motioning with his Winchester. "Don't act smart. Hand over that iron and tell us your name."

Apparently they didn't recognize him. That didn't mean they weren't Hawkman's men. Many of the *vaqueros* on the northern AH pastures knew Chisos Owens by name only. Owens handed the gun over, oak butt first. The man waited a moment, breath harsh.

"I'm Bick Bickford's brother," said Owens finally. "Anse sent me to tell Valeur everything's set."

The bow-legged man bent forward sharply. "Whaddaya

mean, everything's set? What's set?"

He must have gotten it then. He broke off and took a vicious step forward, rifle bearing on Owens's belly. The other man made a move in the sand.

"Hold it, Pinky," he said. "You know what Valeur told us."

"Bickford's brother, hell!" spat Pinky disgustedly. "I say we dust him, Drexel. I said we should have dusted him first off."

Drexel was a big, lanky man, *chivarras* greasy on skinny legs. "I'll go get Valeur. Ventilate this *potro* before I get back, and you know what Valeur'll give you."

Pinky spat again. Drexel went to the thicket of black chaparral that climbed up the rock wall of the cañon. He pushed his way straight into the thicket. Pinky was watching Owens closely. Perhaps he expected surprise. Owens kept any expression from his dust-grimed face. He knew what lay behind the chaparral. Apparently anyone going in through it would meet the abrupt wall on the other side, but Owens had been through it himself once. It covered the mouth of the Lost Santiago Mine.

Evidently they had staked horses inside the shaft. Owens heard one snort, caught the creak of saddle leather. The dull thud of hoofs faded away, and there was silence. Owens's hand moved over to the makings in his jumper pocket.

"Keep 'em free," snapped Pinky.

Owens let his hand drop away from the cigarette papers. The other man sat cross-legged in the sand, facing him, rifle across his lap. Owens must have dozed. He didn't know how much later it was when the snap of bushes jerked his nodding head up.

The first man through the chaparral leading into the mine was Drexel. After him was Valeur, blue *cabriolé* swirling around his great shoulders. His teeth flashed white in his dark face when he saw Chisos Owens.

"Well, if it isn't our inquisitive card player." He laughed. "Or is it insistent, like your Mex *amigo?* Might've known you'd be trailing in."

Pinky stood up. "We kill 'im?"

"Why not?" said Valeur—then a strange, sly expression crossed his face. He looked at Pinky, at Drexel, his smile growing. He looked at Owens and began to chuckle. It held a sibilant menace. "No," he said finally, "no, on second thought, no. I have a better idea." His chuckle grew. Pinky's boots made a soft sound shifting uncomfortably in the sand. Owens felt a sudden clammy sweat breaking out on his palms.

"Yes." Valeur laughed. "I have a much better idea."

III

Elgera Douglas sat on her bed, gazing absently at the weather cracks in the adobe wall of her bedroom. *They should be plastered again soon,* she thought dully. Then she shook her head, blonde hair shimmering. What was the use of torturing herself with thoughts like that? They wouldn't be plastering walls again, or bringing in the cattle from the outer draws again, or eating together in the living room. They wouldn't ever be doing the normal, happy things they had done. It belonged to Hawkman now. She looked up as sounds from the other part of the house reached her, the clink of dishes, a man's harsh laugh. Valeur had returned from Alpine that evening. He had taken up a load of ore in his *alforjas* to check on the assay. That wasn't his only business in the town, though. Thomas had registered the transfer of title. He had registered it with the same county clerk who had helped her father draw up that quit-claim and who had been expecting it to come in under Hawkman's signature as had happened. It had all been so simple. It gave Elgera a sick sense of utter defeat.

She straightened a little as the door opened. Ed Walker stood just outside, one of Valeur's men, tall and raw-boned with a single gallus holding up his tattered jeans. He spoke to the old woman who came in past him. She carried a bull-hide pail of water, and her shapeless shift of cotton flapped dismally about the torn rawhide *huaraches* on her feet. It might have been weathering that turned her seamed face the yellow-tan color, or it might have been her great age. María Douglas was her name, but they all called her Granny. Valeur had kept her at the house to cook and serve for them. Elgera rose, helped her lift the bull-hide pail to the white china crock on the crude side table.

"You've got to escape tonight," hissed the old woman beneath the gurgle of water. "Thomas and Bickford left just as soon as Thomas and Valeur got back from Alpine. They've gone to Boquillos for Anse Hawkman. You know what that means."

"I can't leave you now," said the girl. "Even if I could get free, do you think I'd run away? It would be like . . . like betraying you."

"Hurry up," snapped Walker from the door.

The old woman turned. "You've got to, Elgera. Chisos Owens is somewhere on the outside. He's our last hope. The rest of us are helpless down there in the mine. If we don't do something before Hawkman gets back, we'll never be able to do it. You're the only one, Elgera. . . ."

The scuffle of boots at the door cut her off. Hoke had come down the short hall and was shoving past Walker, snarling at the man.

"You know Valeur told you not to let 'em talk like that, Ed. Get out of here, Granny, and next time you act funny, we'll put you down in the mine with the rest of 'em." He gave the old woman a backhand shove as she went past, then turned to Elgera. "Valeur wants to see you."

Elgera rose slowly, fists clenching at her sides. There had been no trouble with Bickford during the time Valeur had been at Alpine, perhaps because Bickford was the older man, or because his heavy indifference to most things included women. Whatever it was, there had been no trouble. But Valeur was a different kind of man. And he was back now.

He sat at the big center table in the living room, leaning back a little in his chair. A scattering of empty plates lay before him, some cold pan bread left in one, a coffee pot beyond that. He turned as Elgera entered. During the first few days Valeur had stayed at the house, before he had left for Alpine. Elgera had learned that those strange little lights flickering through his eyes could reveal whatever emotion was passing through him at the moment. She had seen them blaze in anger at Hoke, or dance mockingly at Granny, or smolder with contempt for Bickford. Now she could see them kindle instantly with a certain cruel, hungry eagerness.

"Elgera," he said softly.

Hoke laughed shortly, sidled across the room. Walker stood yet behind the girl. Valeur rose, and she couldn't help mark the easy grace of his movement. Her own eyes narrowed, becoming opaque.

"Don't look like that." He laughed. "Bick said you were a wildcat, didn't he? Do you know how long we'll be here now? Do you know how long we'll have to tame wildcats?"

Still laughing, he moved toward her. Valeur's boots made a soft noise against the earthen floor, coming on.

The knock on the door sounded like a thunderclap.

Valeur took a heavy breath, turned. "Yeah?"

Hoke opened the door, and a man took a step inside, blinking in the light. "Some *hombre* just showed up at the cave."

"Who?" asked Valeur impatiently.

The man shrugged. "He gave us a line about being Bickford's brother. Pinky wanted to kill him. I thought you'd better know first."

"You didn't bring him on through?" asked Valeur, swinging around to get his *cabriolé* from the back of the chair.

"No," grunted the man. "But I don't see why. . . ."

"Too many *hombres* know about the mine already. After that business up at Alpine, nobody even sees the shaft or this valley till I'm sure about them, understand? Hoke, you watch the girl . . ."—Valeur stopped in front of Hoke, grabbed him by the vest, jerked him close—"and don't pull another botch like that at Alpine. I think I'd kill you if you did."

He glanced once more at Elgera, inclined his head toward Walker, went out the door. Walker followed. Hoke stood there a long moment, blood returning to his pale face slowly.

Elgera suddenly felt sick. The fingers of her right hand twitched slightly, and she realized how tense she was. She forced herself to relax, moved toward the table. Then she became aware of Hoke, watching her. She turned sharply toward him.

"I saw you," he said, his laugh shaky and forced. "Yeah. You would 'a' scratched Valeur's eyes out. I saw your hands. Like Bick said. Reg'lar wildcat."

There was something rat-like in his narrow face, his weak, unshaven chin. It revolted her. Yet she continued to watch him, a speculation entering her blue eyes. Granny had been right, of course. Elgera knew she did her own people no good here. And Chisos Owens was on the outside somewhere, the man who had bucked Hawkman before. Elgera measured the weakness in Hoke carefully. Then she rubbed her arm, shivering a little. "It's cold," she said. "Why don't you light the fire?"

Hoke's smile was sly. "Think I'm gonna turn my back on you that way? Think you're smart? *You* light it."

She let her lips pout, turned toward the fireplace. Hunkering down on the hearth, she began to strip kindling from a length of jack pine. There was a poker lying beside the big kettle to one side of the hearth. She placed it in her mind without looking in that direction. She muffled her voice deliberately. "What happened in Alpine?"

She heard Hoke's automatic movement toward her. "What?"

"I said . . . what happened in Alpine that made Valeur so angry?"

"Nothing," he muttered. "I got high with a couple of *hombres* and talked a little."

She turned without rising. "Got a match?"

He fished in his hip pocket, came toward her with several matches in his sinewy hand. Then he stopped suddenly, that sly smile revealing discolored teeth. "Think I'd hand 'em to you?" He laughed.

Still hunkered down with one hand flat on the hearthstones beside the kettle, she felt her lips twist with contempt. She held her other hand out. "Oh, no, Hoke," she said, "you're very clever. I wouldn't think of trying to put anything over on you. Give me the matches, please."

He stood two or three paces from her, boots shifting nervously. He laughed again and tossed her the matches. She moved while he was still bent forward slightly. With a savage little cry, she bent sideways and scooped up the fire iron and threw herself upward at him. Hoke's mouth opened, and he took one clumsy step to the rear, trying to drag at his gun. Elgera swung the poker viciously. It struck Hoke's right arm. He shouted hoarsely with the stunning pain of it. His gun clattered to the floor.

Still going forward, Elgera swung the iron out with a jerk and brought it in again at Hoke's head. The sound of the blow was dull and fleshy. He hit the table, slid down to the floor, and lay there.

Elgera stopped herself and stood above him a moment, panting, wiping a lock of blonde hair absently off her wet forehead. She dropped the poker finally and bent to pick up the six-shooter. It was a Smith & Wesson, and the black butt was smooth in her palm. The reaction to what she had done was coming now. She began to tremble. With a hoarse breath she stepped past the man toward the hall door. She was almost running by the time she reached it, and she turned right to the end of the south wing. The rear door was unlatched. Night enfolded her, dark and chill and protecting.

She headed toward the split-rail corral a hundred yards behind the house, tore at the rawhide tie on the let-down bars. There was a whole remuda inside, but she wasted a precious moment getting a coiled dally from a peg and cutting out her own horse. It was a perfect palomino Morgan, hide the color of newly minted gold, mane as blonde and as silky as Elgera's own hair. She had trained it herself, and all it needed was the dally tossed across its back to stop it running the rail. She was moving toward it, looking for a saddle hanging from the rail, when Hoke appeared from the house in a weaving run that carried him from the black shadows thrown by the sprawling building into the yellow moonlight.

"The gal's got away!" he shouted feebly, holding his head as he ran. "The gal's got away! Somebody stop her . . . !"

Knowing there would be no saddle now, Elgera hackamored the palomino with a swift half hitch around its lower jaw. Holding the rest of the forty-foot dally coiled in her hand, she twined fingers in the creamy mane, swung her body with a leaping twist that carried her up and onto the horse.

Hit bareback like that, the palomino spooked and reared. She jerked the hackamore, forcing it out through the gate. She lay forward along the horse, feeling the breath heave through it as the hill steepened across a clearing of curly grama. Ahead were the shadowy motes of juniper climbing up on either side of the mine. She could see the mouth of the tunnel, a dark blot in the upthrust of jagged hill. Hoke was yelling louder now.

"The gal," he shouted, "get the gal!"

There was a dim movement in the trees above the mouth of the mine, another to the side. Elgera pleaded more speed from her animal as the first man showed between two junipers. The horse gathered itself perceptibly, sweat beginning to warm its flanks beneath her legs. The second man scrambled down from over the cave.

"Hoke?" he shouted.

"That's not Hoke! Can't you see that's the girl's horse?" yelled the other man as he quartered toward the cave, turning to call to Elgera. "Stop your animal. I don't want to shoot you. Don't make me do it!"

The moonlight glinted on his Winchester as he jerked it from the crook of his elbow. Elgera ducked low on the Morgan and let go a loop of the hackamore to give her slack, reaching for the Smith & Wesson in her waistband.

With the gun fisted, she caught up the loop again, bunching the rawhide tightly on the horse. The men levered their Winchesters. One of them yelled again, then their shots made two flat detonations. Something tugged at the girl's leggings, clipping off one of the bosses with a metallic ring. Holding hackamore and gun in the same hand, she threw her first wild shot. The rawhide was taut, and the buck of the gun jerked the horse's head around.

Elgera thundered straight for the first man. He tried to jump back and lever and shoot all at once. He tripped and went down with the gun exploding into the air. The other man yelled crazily and threw himself out of the way, dropping the rifle. The palomino's right front hoof struck his boot as it raced by. Elgera pounded into the blackness of the cave, the only way in or out of the Santiago Valley.

The palomino was heavy set, even for a Morgan, and not trained for bareback. It was all she could do to drive on through the Stygian gloom of the tunnel. Suddenly she heard a yell from ahead.

"Who is it?" shouted a man. "Don't come any nearer. Who is it?"

She didn't answer. A gun began to thunder from ahead, then another. The palomino whinnied shrilly, squatted like a jack rabbit. Elgera was almost thrown off by the mount when it wheeled, heading back the other way.

The guards she had passed must have followed her in, because guns began to blaze from that direction. Screaming its fright, the Morgan slid to a halt again, lunged back around the other way. There were men on both sides of her, then, and she was trapped. Desperately she tried to drive the Morgan on. But the guns began pumping ahead of her again, throwing a veritable wall of viciously stabbing flame up in front of her, and she realized she couldn't hope to get through alive. Lead forming its high whine about her, she was swept with the reasonless panic of a cornered animal.

She leaned forward on the palomino, giving the terrified beast its head. The horse wheeled once more toward the mouth of the cave and broke into a wild gallop. The two guards began firing again, and the Morgan tried to slide onto its haunches. But whatever happened, Elgera knew this was her last chance to break through, and she was determined not to be taken alive. Sobbing bitterly, she jerked the Morgan's head from side to side and drove spiked boot heels into its sweat-soaked flanks. The animal reacted instinctively, quit sliding, gathered itself, and plunged with a wild whinny back through the cave.

Elgera sensed the dim movement of men throwing themselves aside. She snapped a shot toward them. There was a yell, a last, deafening gun thunder. Then the palomino crashed out through the mouth of the cave and back onto the moonlit slope. Hoke was a dozen paces ahead. She turned the animal sharply, catching the surprise in his white face. Then she was clattering into the trees, low branches clawing at the camisa serving for a blouse.

Finally she broke into the open on the other side of the motte. Behind her she could still hear the men shouting to one another. She turned the palomino up the rise, fighting back her sobs, and she didn't know whether she was crying from that or from her utter failure to break through.

On the peak of the rise she turned the horse a moment, trying to quiet it, sitting there rigidly as she fought to control herself. Below her, past the trees, was the house, a dim U-shaped sprawl, *viga* poles thrust from its walls at rafter height and casting an uneven shadow pattern across pale adobe. Elgera caught movement in the corral, heard the faint nicker of a horse. They were saddling up to follow her by then.

She wheeled her palomino, looking at the forbidding ridges of the Dead Horses ahead. Another attempt to get through the cave was no good. The only other way to the outside was through the mountains themselves. More than one Douglas had been lost in those jagged uplifts, never to be seen again. It was a mysterious, unknown barrier that had kept outsiders from finding the Lost Santiago all these years, holding secrets no man had seen and lived to tell. Yet it was the only way.

She straightened a little on the horse and turned it down the other side of the rise and into the black shadows puddling the bottom of the draw. Then she rose again onto the moonlit slope opposite, heading straight into the *Sierra del Caballo Muerto*.

IV

Chisos Owens didn't know how many miles he had ridden through the mine shaft behind Valeur when the first two shots came to them, flat and muffled. Valeur leaned forward on his chestnut, cursing beneath his breath. Pinky sat a line-back mare behind Owens, carrying the buckthorn *entraña*, its weird light throwing their shadows black and monstrous across the ancient hand-hewn timbers forming the *soportes* and beams of the shaft. There were more shots. Valeur turned to Pinky.

"Hold this *hombre* here," he said. "Walker, come with me."

The raw-boned man named Walker urged his horse into the blackness after Valeur. The last thing Owens saw of him was the buckle on his single gallus, winking in the torchlight, then it disappeared. The buckskin snorted dismally beneath Owens. There was no sound for a moment—then the noise of a running horse in the dark somewhere in front of them and Valeur's voice.

"Who is it? Don't come any nearer. Who is it?"

The pound of hoofs became louder. A sudden volley of shots stiffened Owens. A horse whinnied in high fear. The noise of galloping hoofs ceased abruptly. There was another crash of gunfire. Owens couldn't help his instinctive forward move.

"Watch it," snapped Pinky, and the torchlight wavered.

The horse must have started back the other way, because it began running again, and the sound diminished swiftly. Owens caught a muffled yell, a final pair of gunshots. He barely heard the horse whinny this time. Then it was silent.

Finally Valeur's voice came impatiently: "Pinky. Bring him on."

Thrown by the flickering light, Owens's shadow undulated across the rolling sides of the tunnel and the sagging timbers as they went around a turn. Valeur was waiting for them, dismounted.

"What happened?" asked Pinky.

"I don't know," said the swarthy man. "Some fool on a horse. Maybe one of the Douglas bunch got loose. When he saw he couldn't get by us, he turned around."

Valeur had put his gun back in the holster underneath his brown coat. He pulled the short *cabriolé* over that, lifting a foot to his chestnut's stirrup. He stopped that way. Someone was stumbling through the cave toward them. Hoke weaved into the circle of light, head raising at the sight of them. Valeur put his foot down again, turned a little.

Hoke took his hand away from a bloody weal that ran along the side of his head. He was looking at Valeur, and his face grew pale. He choked his words out. "I couldn't help it, Val. She took me by surprise. You stopped her in here, though. She came back out the tunnel and scooted into the hills. I already put Smith and Tommy on her tail. . . ."

Valeur almost yelled it: "I told you what would happen if you pulled another botch like Alpine, Hoke!"

Hoke's mouth opened. He took a step backward, trying to say something. He must have seen it coming. "Val, I couldn't help it . . . !"

Owens didn't see Valeur's hand when it moved. He only knew the big man took a vicious step forward, and the gun was suddenly in his hairy fist, bucking. The dust puffed out of Hoke's gray vest, and he stumbled on back with a hollow grunt. He fell over, clawing at the top of his empty holster.

Valeur's heavy breathing was the only sound for a moment. The flush faded slowly from his face. The revolver he held was a double-action .38. When he slipped it back beneath his cloak, it made no perceptible bulge. He turned and climbed onto his chestnut. "Let's go," he said.

Face pale, Walker urged his mount after Valeur. He glanced momentarily at Hoke's body as he passed it, then looked away quickly. Owens clucked his buckskin forward, lips compressing until the flesh around them was whitened. He had a sick, hollow feeling inside, and he didn't know whether it was from seeing Hoke killed that way, or from realizing fully, perhaps for the first time, just what kind of man Valeur really was.

A hundred feet back of where the tunnel opened out into the Santiago Valley they came to a railing of split juniper that surrounded a large vertical shaft, sunk to one side of the tunnel. The shaft itself was topped by a framework of fresh-cut timbers supporting a large winch. Suspended by a thick hemp rope from the spindle of the winch was a four-by-four platform that dangled over empty space. Valeur turned slightly in his saddle.

"Get on the elevator," he told Owens.

Owens dismounted, moved toward the railing. He put a hand on the top bar and looked over it into the shaft. It fell away beneath him, bottomless as far as he could see. Pinky and Walker had dismounted. The bowlegged man thrust his *entraña* into the earthen wall, then went with the other to the crank. Valeur's voice was sharp. "Get on, I said."

Owens ducked beneath the rail, leaned out, and caught the rope. He had to pull the platform a little. When he stepped on, it swung back out and continued swinging, back and forth, like a pendulum. The shriek of the winch startled him. He gripped the rope with a certain desperation as he began to go down. The last man he saw was Jan Valeur, sitting his chestnut behind the railing. Their glances locked for that moment. In the brilliant lights that flared through his jet black eyes, Chisos Owens could see all the ruthless violence and unbridled savagery of the man's nature. Again, it gave him the sensation of a staggering physical impact. Then the lip of the shaft cut off his view, and he went on down into the darkness.

Spinning around and around in the black emptiness, swaying back and forth in that pendulum motion, bumping now and then against the earthen sides of the shaft, Owens lost all sense of time or distance. It might have taken an hour, or a day. It might have been a hundred feet they lowered him, or a thousand. His hand on the rope became cramped with the force of his grip.

Finally the downward motion seemed to cease. The swinging elevator knocked against something. A flare of light blinded Owens momentarily. Then he could make out a stationary platform built into the side of the shaft. From it led a tunnel, and in that stood a group of shifting, muttering people. The one holding the torch stepped out onto the boards.

"Chisos," he said sharply. "It's Chisos Owens."

There was defeat in the haggard lines of Natividad Douglas's angular face. His blue eyes regarded Owens dully. Raising the burning *entraña,* he reached out and helped Owens onto the platform. Eddger Douglas was there, too, Natividad's uncle, a tall, spare man with stringy gray hair and bony shoulders bent wearily beneath his torn shirt of homespun. Juanito Douglas had blood splotching the cotton bandage around his head, the dirt smeared on his cheeks as if he might have been crying. The women stood farther back among the other men; one of them let out a hopeless sob.

Natividad put a clumsy hand on Owens's shoulder. "Somehow, we didn't think we'd see you . . . down here."

He trailed off, and Owens moved into the tunnel with them, not knowing what to say exactly, seeing how he had failed them. He tried to hide his own bitter sense of defeat, speaking gruffly. "Hawkman?"

Natividad stuck the torch into the wall, nodding. He told Owens how it had happened.

"I know it sounds stupid, Chisos," he finished. "It *was* stupid. I'll never forgive myself. Hopwell sent for him, and I was to meet him at Alpine. When I met Valeur instead, with all Avarillo's papers and Hopwell's letter of introduction, how was I to know the difference?"

Eddger grasped his nephew's arm. "You couldn't know, Natividad. Don't blame yourself. We were all taken in. I'm as much to blame as you. I was up here at the mine with Juanito and should have stopped Bickford. . . ."

"It was the only way they could find the valley," said Juanito hotly. "Bick and his riders must have trailed Natividad when he brought Valeur back from Alpine. I guess they were supposed to wait in the cave until Thomas and Valeur had located the quit-claim."

"Hawkman knew about that, then?" grunted Owens.

"He must have," said Natividad. "Either Dad told him he had it made out when he got in touch with Hawkman, or Hawkman found it out from the county clerk who helped Dad draw it up. Thomas had it witnessed and then transferred the title up at Alpine. I guess it went through without a hitch. There wasn't anybody to protest it."

For a long time Owens had been aware of the man

standing slightly apart from the others, farther back in the cave. He had the feeling he should know him, yet couldn't remember anyone so small and fat in the Douglas clan. Now the crowd was shifting apart and the torchlight fell across the pudgy figure fully. The man's legs were thick as post oaks and seemed to stretch his English riding boots to the bursting point. His white silk shirt and gray whipcords were turned incongruous by the broad sash of violent red bound about his imperious girth. In one side of his mouth he held a black *cigarro,* and his fat lips twisted around this to form an expansive grin.

"*Buenas noches, Señor* Chisos," he said. "You are late."

A series of burning buckthorn *entrañas* thrust into the wall cast a weird red glow over the Douglases, picking at the sides of the tunnel with the tools Valeur had packed in. Owens stopped work for a moment, leaning wearily on the splintery handle of his pickaxe. There was no telling night from day down here, but it must have been sometime in mid-morning. After a fitful slumber Owens had been awakened with the others by Pinky and Walker, who came down on the elevator with a breakfast of soggy pan bread and cold coffee.

Beside Owens the fat Mexican named Felipe pried at the pay streaks running down the tunnel. His white silk shirt was soaked with sweat and it clung to his pudgy torso like skin, revealing a gross roll of fat that bulged over his tight red sash every time he bent forward. Owens reached automatically for the makings in his jumper pocket, opening the sack of Bull Durham with his teeth.

"No!" cried the Mexican, straightening, putting up a protesting hand. "*Dios* no, Chisos. Light a *cigarrillo* now and you blow us down to *el diablo.* Can't you smell the gas?"

He sniffed loudly to emphasize his question. Owens

sniffed, too. All morning he had been aware of the faint, cloying odor in the tunnel. It was heavier now, gagging. He put the tobacco away.

Felipe flourished his cold cigar. "Gold forms along faults, understand, fissures that reach to a profound depth. In a volcanic formation like this, you are bound to find gas. It seeps up through faults. And where you have a fault, you have a possibility of a slide. No . . . ? *Sí.*"

"Felipe," grunted Owens, "who conked me on the head that night in Alpine?"

"I've seen cave-ins started by no less than a sneeze when there is such a fault," said the Mexican, glancing up at the ancient beams above them, puckering his lips. "And look at those shorings. Dry rot. Touch them with a horse feather and they collapse. *Pues,* I hope nobody makes a loud noise in here. I hope nobody sneezes."

"Was it you?" asked Owens.

Felipe turned to him, chuckling. "*¡Caracoles¡* What an insistent fellow you are. Maybe that is why Hawkman fears you so, eh? Beware of the man with the single-track mind. Of course, it was I who hit you on the head. Who else? I knew that fight wouldn't finish until everybody was dead. That's the kind of *hombres* you are, you and Valeur. Did I want everybody dead? *Dios,* no! Why do you think I seduced you and Hoke into the Mescal in the first place? He might have known what was going on down here, but we didn't. You might have known the way down here, but I didn't. And if you killed each other, I would have no one to follow down here, would I? No . . . ? *Sí.* I shot out the light. I tapped you on the *cabeza*. I had to tap Valeur to get you free. I hid you beneath the garbage in the back alley. When Valeur and his two *amigos* left, I was the sinister character trailing them."

"Why?" asked Owens. "Who are you? What's your stake in the Santiago?"

"*Por Dios,* how can you ask that? What is any man's stake in the Santiago? Look at that bench gravel . . . ?"—the Mexican waved his *cigarro* at the streaks of yellow in the sides—"a thousand dollars to the ton at least. And not only the pay streaks. After all, think of what an achievement it is merely to find this fabled mine. Do you know how old these diggings are? It was originally worked by Indians for centuries before Santiago found it. In that shaft above I saw pieces of pottery bearing the distinct imprints of the paddle-and-anvil methods of thinning walls which were used in the Second Pueblo period."

"That isn't mining," said Owens, grinning faintly.

"Did you think my accomplishments were limited to cards and gold?" said Felipe, waving his *cigarro* excitedly. "That is archeology. Upheavals thrust the Dead Horses up and around this valley sometime in the Mesozoic era . . . and that is geology . . . cutting it off completely from the outside. Those Indians weren't deliberately trying to open the valley, understand, they were just following a vein through the mountain, that's all. Can you guess how many generations it must have taken them to drive the shaft in from the box cañon on the outside?"

Natividad was coming toward them, a leather strap around his head supporting the *zurrón* on his back—a bag of woven fiber of the same type the Indians had used for centuries in which to carry their ore. He set the *zurrón* down, glanced backward. Farther down were more Douglases, a little group of three or four digging under each burning torch. Beyond them Owens could see Pinky and Walker.

"Chisos," said Natividad, "you've got to get out of here. Bickford has come with Hawkman!"

Owens straightened, hearing the silence that had fallen over the tunnel farther on. His rope-scarred hands closed more tightly about the pick handle. He could hear Valeur talking from beyond Pinky and Walker.

"You'll have to pack the ore out on mules, Anse. There isn't any other way. The less men we bring in from the outside the safer it'll be. We might as well work these Douglas coyotes instead of importing any peons."

Anse Hawkman spoke in a harsh, grating voice. "I didn't want it this way, Valeur. You know that. You can't just turn people into slaves. I always gave a man a chance to work for me. I never stepped outside of the law."

"You mean they never caught you stepping outside the law," corrected Valeur. "And you never did nothing this big, Anse. You're in the Lost Santiago. Men have been hunting this place ever since they put an x in Texas. Maybe the Douglases didn't know what they had. I do. . . ." His voice trailed away.

They were coming into the light now. Hawkman, a tall, spare man in a dusty frock coat, wore his gray trousers tucked into cavalry boots. A black Mormon cast his bony face into shadow, hiding its features, but there was something greedy in the way his sinewy hands hung at his sides, grasping fingers curled a little like talons.

"Chisos," whispered Natividad. "You can't stay here. You know what'll happen if he recognizes you."

"You told me yourself this was a dead-end tunnel," said Owens. "Where can we go? What's the use in running?"

"In *Méjico*, we call them *yalotis*," snorted Felipe. "Little birds what sit on a branch and let *hombres* come along to knock them off with a stick."

Anse Hawkman was still talking: "I know, Valeur. But this . . . !"

54

"What else?" snarled Valeur suddenly. "I told you what you were putting your loop to when you started out to get this valley. Thomas got the deed on the legal side. Far as the law goes, you own this fair and square. That's as far as it does go. Any of these Douglases get out, and you'll have more troubles than you had in the big freeze. It's kill 'em or work 'em. Which'll you have?"

"Listen," whispered Felipe, pulling at Owens, "at least be moving when they kill you. I never did like to die standing still."

Hawkman stopped suddenly, stiffening. Valeur followed his gaze to Chisos Owens where he stood in the light of the torch, his square, blocky figure humped forward a little, eyes gleaming from the gray mask of dust and sweat that was his face.

"That's the *hombre* I told you about." Valeur laughed. "I thought I might as well use him in the diggings. Maybe this is worse than a good quick slug through the brisket anyway."

"You fool!" yelled Hawkman, his voice cracking on the last word. "That's Chisos Owens! Bick. That's Chisos Owens!"

Bick Bickford lurched out from behind Anse Hawkman, his face expressionless as he pawed with a freckled hand at his gun. Owens crouched in a jerky, instinctive way. Valeur's voice was high in surprise.

"Chisos Owens?" he yelled, and his mouth stayed open after the words were out.

Hawkman was pulling a six-gun from beneath the frock coat, but he threw himself backward at the same time, leaving Bickford out in front. Owens already had the pick swinging upward in both hands. Bickford's gun came out. Owens grunted with the effort of heaving the pick. It struck Bickford fully in the face. With a wild scream the heavy man staggered backward, dropping his gun, pawing at his smashed features. Felipe must have yanked the *entraña* out of the wall from above Owens. They were suddenly standing in darkness. Owens felt the fat Mexican's pudgy hands pulling him. He had to turn to keep from falling.

"*¡Santiago . . . !*" cried Felipe lustily. "Saint James and clear out of Spain, you *ilegítimos* blackamoors!"

Out in the light the Douglases swarmed at Hawkman and Valeur, picks and stakes in their hands. Pinky and Walker clubbed viciously with their Winchesters. There was a shot. Eddger Douglas fell away with a cry of pain. Valeur burst through two more men, face dark with rage. He came pounding down toward Owens, gun flaming.

The shots echoed, and the echoes multiplied, until the whole tunnel seemed to tremble and rock with the deafening sound.

"*¡Dios!*" howled Felipe, "and I was afraid of someone sneezing."

Stumbling through the blackness, trying to fight free of the Mexican's hands, Owens heard a groaning, slipping noise, louder than the shots. He brought up suddenly against the resilient pudginess of Felipe's body, clawing at the thick shoulders to keep from falling. Then he knew why the man had stopped.

"There it goes!" shouted Felipe.

Whatever else he said was silenced by the terrible, all-enveloping wave of sound that covered Chisos Owens. Rocks and earth rained down on him in an ever-growing hail. He went to hands and knees beneath the crushing avalanche of dirt and rock, head ringing, mouth filled. A rotten beam fell across his legs, pinning them. A *soporte* hit him over the ear. He reeled sideways, arms slipping from beneath him. He thought all the Dead Horses had fallen in on his body.

After a long time the terrifying sound began to die. A last chunk of rock thudded down somewhere to Owens's left. There was a creaking groan. Then a silence that was worse than the noise had been. He tried to raise himself weakly. The beam held him helpless. He heard someone moving. Whoever it was kept on making small, grunting sounds. Finally Felipe spoke.

"That's it, I guess," he said heavily. "The main portion of the cave-in was between us and the others out there. Maybe they didn't get it. We got it. We are trapped!"

V

Beneath the sun of mid-morning the Dead Horses lay cruel and empty and desolate around Elgera Douglas. *Cenizo,* like its name the color of ashes, blotched the barren slopes; sickly gray-green *palmilla* squirmed feebly from cracks in the lava formation. The gun in Elgera's waistband pressed coldly against her stomach as she leaned forward wearily on her palomino. A rider could make it from the outside to the valley with a bare margin of safety, if he knew that route in through the narrow box cañon and the mine. But Elgera knew she had been wandering, and as yet she had found no water. She knew that it was the only thing that would save her now.

They were still behind her or on her flank. That was the way they had followed her—not by tracking, for that would have been next to impossible during darkness, but by keeping her below them so they could see her whenever she crossed the open slopes and moonlit meadows. She had tried to hide in timber where she wouldn't be visible from above. But she saw, whenever she did that, they would stop and wait on some hogback, and she knew that whenever she chose to move again, they would spot her, and in desperation she had ridden on. The only thing that kept her ahead of them was the superiority of her Morgan. But the palomino was caked with lather and alkali now and was blowing most of the time.

She was nursing it through scattered prickly pear when something glinted in the sun on the ridge lying across her

right flank. Her blonde hair shimmered as she turned sharply
that way. It took her a moment to make out the rider quartering down the slope. The muted crash of mesquite on her
other side jerked her back. From an angle the second man
was cutting toward her through the brush. This was it, then.
They were riding the ridges. They were going to finish it.

She bent forward on the Morgan, plunking a boot into its
flank. The horse responded sluggishly, broke into a flagging
gallop. She heard the shout from her left. Then came the gunshot, flat and ugly across the dry air. Reddish sandstone
kicked up a length in front of the Morgan. Bareback that way
it would have been deadly to release either hand. Her control
over the animal lay in the hackamore she kept bunched tightly
in her right hand. If she released her grip on the mane with
her left, a sudden turn would unhorse her. She shook out
some slack to give her length enough for reaching the Smith &
Wesson in her waistband. Then she caught up the loose rawhide till the dally was tight again. She turned toward the man
on her left because he was the closest. Holding gun and
hackamore in her right hand, she watched the rider come on
in. He forked a blazed-face sorrel and he had his gun out, too.
He let go another shot that went over Elgera's head before she
fired.

Every time her Smith & Wesson bucked in her hand, the
palomino shied to the right, head pulling that way to the jerk
of the taut rope. On her third wild shot, Elgera saw the sorrel
stumble and veer sharply. Instead of quartering in down the
slope now, it was running parallel to her own mount. The
man jammed his revolver back in leather and started jerking
back and forth on his horse. Dust rose thickly around him. It
was a moment before Elgera realized what was the matter.
The sorrel was still going ahead, but its gallop was twisting
and lurching. She had hit the animal. The rider was trying to

kick free. His boot must have been caught, because he was still jerking wildly when Elgera heard his sharp cry and saw the running sorrel go down onto its face. Both horse and man disappeared in the cloud of dust they had raised.

Elgera cast a look behind her. The second man had cut too sharply down his side, evidently expecting the other rider to block her off. He was at the bottom of the slope now, far behind. It gave Elgera a faint stab of hope. Their success in following her had depended on their team work, keeping her down in the draws and gullies by blocking off whatever attempts she made toward the ridges. Now there was only one of them. The palomino hadn't been trained for bareback. Any chance she had now to outride that second man lay in her getting a saddle. It was worth the few precious moments. She turned the Morgan into the prickly pear.

Hawkman's rider lay beneath the dead sorrel. Elgera couldn't tell whether he lived or not. She slid off the palomino, untied the latigo on the dead animal's saddle, then she jammed her dusty Hyer boot against the sorrel's barrel and tugged the broad hair cinches from beneath it. A moment more and she had the hull on her own horse, cinching up front and flank of the Texas rig with swift surety. The Smith & Wesson had one bullet left unfired. It was a .44 while the man who lay there packed a .45. She dropped Hoke's black-butted Smith & Wesson into the sand, unstrapped the gun belt from around Hawkman's rider. She drew it around her slim waist to the last notch and still it hung far down her thigh.

When she mounted again, the man on the ground was stirring feebly. The palomino seemed to take out with more eagerness under saddle, and the leather was a relief to Elgera's sore, weary legs. She didn't have to fight the animal now and she free-bitted it, cutting across the bottom of the valley, turning into a narrow cañon that cut through high sandstone cliffs. Behind her she could see the second rider halt his horse on the opposite slope, where the dead sorrel lay among the prickly pear. He dismounted and helped the other man to rise. She could see them standing there, ant-like figures that grew smaller in her vision as she rode on into the gunsight notch. Finally they mounted tandem on the remaining horse and turned after her.

She found a brackish sinkhole of water a hundred yards on and had a hard time keeping the Morgan from foundering itself. She took a few careful sips herself, keeping an eye behind. When the men showed at the mouth of the notch, she mounted and went on.

The walls of the cañon rose steeply, and soon the sandy bottom of a dried-up watercourse was the only space between. At first she thought a cloud had swept over the sun. The cañon had darkened perceptibly about her. Then she felt the hot, biting sensation in her lungs and saw that it was a haze, that darkness, a red haze that thickened as she rode forward. It gave her an eerie feeling.

She came to the end of the notch abruptly, finding herself looking out into a vast amphitheater over which the haze hung like a mysterious curtain, shredding here and there to reveal mountains on the opposite side, rising harshly and nakedly into the thin blue sky. Elgera turned sharply in the saddle. They were still behind her. She could see them making their way up through the cañon. There was no way to go but forward.

She gave the horse its head once more. The Morgan picked its way down a shelf of sandstone that crumbled incessantly beneath nervous hoofs. Finally they reached a gentler slope and dropped into a stretch of timber. Elgera recognized cottonwoods and aspens and a scattering of juniper, but none of the trees had foliage. Their branches reached out, naked and gray, like malignant, clawing hands. When a slight wind sighed down from the rim rock, they rattled in hollow, mocking echo.

Elgera wiped a lock of blonde hair off her flushed forehead. It was damp with perspiration. The horse began to shy and snort. The girl felt the heat then, striking out at her in waves. Farther on it was like coming up against a solid wall of it. The palomino whinnied. Elgera jerked it around, out of the furnace blast, breathing swiftly. Filled with nameless apprehension, she wheeled her horse and trotted it through the trees a quarter mile to the north. Every time she tried to go back down, the wall of heat stopped her dead. Finally she brought up against a sheer cliff of sandstone and had to turn back. It was the same thing on the other side of the round valley. At any spot she chose, she could only ride so far into the haze-covered grove of seared trees, then the awful heat rose up impenetrably.

Cliffs on either side too sheer for the horse, the heat before her—Elgera realized the only way out was to go the way she had come. She turned the palomino uphill, panting with exhaustion.

Hawkman's men stood in the mouth of the notch. They must have been there all the time she had ridden back and forth down among the trees, must have sensed something had stopped her, must have realized how they had snared her. With a hoarse pant, she tried to keep the Morgan in its gallop upslope, running it directly toward the men, savagely wanting it that way now. The horse might have been good for a level run. Uphill it was no use. It began to blow and stumble. Finally the gallop slowed to a walk, and nothing Elgera could do would speed it up again.

The wild, heady excitement of going at them full tilt

faded from her. It was a different thing, walking into it. It was certain death. Dully she halted the wind-broken horse and slid off, stumbling to a pothole amid the crazy cottonwoods, sinking into it. The men began to move down toward her.

All right, that was the way it would be. She cocked the .45 and shoved it over the lip of black rock forming her scant cover. The man who had ridden the sorrel showed first, working down through the trees. He was tall and skinny, greasy *chivarras* belted around his middle with a piece of mecate. He must have borrowed the other man's six-gun. He held it out before him, searching the red haze for Elgera. The second man came through the trees with his saddle gun. Brush crackled beneath his boots.

The man with the short gun saw Elgera then. She had waited that long, wanting it sure. Her full lips twisted, and her gun bucked hard with the shot. The man in *chivarras* jumped backward with a sharp cry, dropping his weapon.

She couldn't see him then. She could hear the brush rattle as he crawled away. The man with the rifle stayed out of range, shifting back and forth indecisively. Then he disappeared, too. After a time they showed again above the haze, moving back toward the notch. The one with the saddle gun was helping the wounded man. She could barely see what they were doing. They seemed to stand by the horse a moment, talking. Finally the wounded man mounted and turned the jaded animal back into the narrow cañon. The other one settled down on the limestone bank, rifle across his knees.

Elgera could guess well enough where the rider was going. Perhaps the two of them hadn't found the heart to face her gun. Half a dozen could finish it without too much risk. Half a dozen led by Valeur.

The one thing they hadn't wanted was to have a Douglas escape to the outside. She knew how far Valeur would go to protect what he had hold of. She sagged wearily into the pothole, rocks hard against her limp body. Her choked sob was small, somehow, in all the vast desolation of that weird place.

VI

It was silent in the mine shaft now. Chisos Owens lay where Felipe and Natividad had dragged him, after digging the earth off his back and prying the fallen timber off his legs. At first he had been numb from the knees down, but now a tingling pain was beginning to seep through. He hoped dully that it didn't mean his legs were smashed.

"The whole thing was caused by the fault," said Felipe, making small, scratching noises in the darkness. "The gas had to leak in from somewhere. I was in a cave-in at Virginia City just like this. . . ." He broke off, sniffing. "*Sí*, just like this. We located the fissure by smelling for the gas. Then we followed the fissure out. There is a chance, a small chance."

"What's the use?" choked Natividad. "There's a dead end behind us and a million tons of earth in front. We're through."

"*Pues,* maybe not a million." Felipe chuckled, crawling around Owens, sniffing like a dog on the scent. "Ah, here it is. Chisos, over here."

Owens struggled across smashed timber. Felipe's body was hot and fetid beside him. He sniffed, choked. Natividad came crawling to them. Together they tore at a beam, clawed earth free. The smell of gas became stronger.

The fat Mexican began to laugh. "The fault," he said. "We have struck the fault. They are caused by earlier displace-

65

ments of earth, understand? It might lead down. It is the chance we take. The gas will asphyxiate us if we stay in it too long. I will go first. I am the bulbous one, and, if I can get through, you most certainly can. May the gods of chance smile upon us this *día, compadres*. No . . . ? *Si*."

His voice was muffled on the last words. Owens crawled forward tentatively, found the narrow hole in the wall. The surface, pressing into his belly, was smooth and slick. He worked against an upward slant, clawing, digging, trying to hold his first breath as long as possible. Finally he had to empty his lungs and suck in the gas-laden air.

He buried his face into the earth for a terrible moment, fighting the paroxysm that threatened to sweep him. His ears began to ring and there was a pounding in his head. He would never be able to remember the rest clearly. It was one hell of crawling a few feet, expelling air, drawing in another breath that had more gas than oxygen, fighting to keep from choking on it, crawling on. Once, as if in a nightmare, he heard Natividad coughing mutedly behind him. Then the sound stopped.

The earth began grumbling. The whole fault shook and trembled. Owens fought down a wave of panic. At the end of an interminable period he felt pudgy hands slipping beneath his armpits, drawing him out into a larger space that was filled with deliciously cool, fresh air. He lay on his belly for a long time, sucking in great gusts, sobbing. Finally he sat up. Behind, he could still hear the ominous, rumbling sound. The earth began to tremble beneath his legs.

"Felipe?" he wondered.

"*Si*," answered the Mexican weakly. "I think we have reached one of the old tunnels dug by the Indians. They must honeycomb these mountains. It has a definite slant feel. We take the upward way, and . . . *¡Sacramento!* . . . we are out.

Pronto now, before the whole *negocio* caves in on us."

"Natividad?" said Owens.

No one answered. For a moment they sat there in the dark with the earth groaning and slipping all around them.

Felipe let out a hissing breath. "We cannot be *pendejos* now, *Señor* Chisos, we cannot be fools," he said swiftly. "We must look at it coldly. It would be better for two of us to live than all of us to die. It is the expedience, Chisos. It is hard, but it is the expedience."

Owens made a small, scraping sound crawling back toward the fault. The rumble grew louder. The tunnel rocked suddenly with a violent tremor. Owens took a great breath, jammed himself into the fault. He heard Felipe shout after him.

"You won't stand a chance. If the gas doesn't finish you, the whole Santiago Mine will cave in on you. Come back . . . !"

Again it was that crawling, fighting, digging madness, trying to breathe where there was no air, battling with a terrible panic and violent horror of being buried alive, clawing at earth that shook and roared beneath his hands, squirming like a doomed slug deep down into its own grave.

Then he felt the limp body of the boy. Somehow he got twisted around so he could shove Natividad back out ahead of him. There was a shaking roar, drowning out the smaller groanings of earth. He kicked, clawed, drew in a spasmodic breath—and felt a horrible suffocation grip him.

Consciousness began to leave him for long moments at a time. He would come to, realizing his legs and arms were still working in a desperate, instinctive effort of self-preservation. Earth filled his mouth and eyes and nose. Natividad was a dead weight above him. Sound threatened to burst his eardrums. He didn't know exactly when he shoved the boy out ahead of him into the tunnel. He crawled out himself in a flaccid, exhausted way. He heard Felipe's voice dimly.

"Damn' *pendejo,* damn' fool . . . !"

He remembered laughing. Then he let himself sink into unconsciousness without a struggle.

Felipe was right about the upward slant of the old diggings leading them out. He had revived Chisos Owens, and, carrying the boy between them, they staggered up through the terror of that thundering darkness. Hours, days, years—it was all the same. Light reached them from the mouth of the cave finally, and they stumbled toward it with a pathetic eagerness, sagging down in the black brush. Behind them the rumblings died slowly.

The shaft had led them onto the slope far to the south of the main tunnel. The house lay behind several intervening rises. They worked toward it through a grove of Mexican persimmons and approached a compound that seemed strangely silent. Circling around the mouth of the large mine shaft, they finally stopped at the fringe of juniper to the left of the house, halfway up toward the corral. An old woman appeared at the rear door of the building's right wing. She seemed to be crying. Natividad leaped forward, and Owens barely caught him before he was in the open.

"Careful!" Owens warned, but the boy yanked free of the heavy hands.

"Granny," hissed the boy.

The woman's seamed face turned toward them. She glanced back up toward the cave, then walked around the house. She appeared a moment later with an empty bull-hide pail and walked away from the adobe wall toward the river that coursed through shadowy motes of cottonwood in the bottom of the valley. Her route was circuitous and carried her past where the three men stood, hidden from above. She set the heavy pail down as if to rest, speaking without looking directly at them.

"*Gracias a Dios,* you are alive," she murmured. "Hawkman thought you had been killed in the cave-in . . . no, don't show yourselves. There are still a couple of guards at the mine."

"The cave-in missed them, then?" grunted Owens.

"It was between you and them," she said. "Hawkman's men all escaped. And Chisos . . . Elgera is trapped back in the mountains somewhere. She was trying to get through to you when they holed her up. The two men who had followed her didn't have the courage to go in after her by themselves. The one named Tommy came back with a bullet in his shoulder. They left him here. But the rest of them have gone back, Valeur and Hawkman and Bickford and two or three of the AH *vaqueros.* I heard Valeur tell Hawkman they couldn't take any more chances, heard him say they were going to forget she was a woman. Chisos, they've gone to kill Elgera."

VII

Chisos Owens's buckskin was jaded now. Lather caked its flanks thickly. All three men had driven their horses at a cruel run through the heat of noon and afternoon. Granny had saddled the mounts and brought them to the men in the timber. Then she had attracted the attention of the guards at the mine with her cracked wails, while Owens and the other two circled the house and used the cover of the stream lower down till they were out of sight.

They all carried gum-pitched *morrales* of fiber, full of water. But even that didn't save their horses, the way they forced them. Owens knew he was two or three hours behind Hawkman. All he could think of was Elgera, and he knew it would have to be a dead run every step of the way if they expected to save her. They were cutting down through a slope of prickly pear when they passed the dead sorrel with the blazed face.

"Hawkman's first casualty," puffed Felipe, "and that's what will be happening to our *caballos* soon if you don't ease up."

"That sorrel's been shot," said Owens.

"Shot or not, you can't run a horse all day through heat like this," said Felipe. "Let him drink and you founder him. Don't give him water and he dries up and blows away beneath you."

Owens bent in his saddle to study the plain trail they were

70

following. "That's Valeur's chestnut . . . couldn't miss a Tennessee Walker in this country. They weren't pushing as hard as we are. Intervals between hoofs aren't as long as ours. Passed here two, three hours ago. That grama's already beginning to rise up in the tracks."

He put a boot into his buckskin, and the animal lurched forward. Owens's face was caked with alkali. His heavy shoulders were humped beneath the faded jumper in terrible weariness. The heat was draining the men as well as the animals. Natividad almost slid off his horse when they veered at the bottom of the slope.

Owens reined over, caught the boy's arm, yanking him back into the saddle. They rode on that way, Owens holding up Natividad. Maybe it was a mile past the dead sorrel that Owens's buckskin began to quiver beneath him. He halted it and slid off, standing there a minute with his big, rope-scarred hand on the lathered rump, a certain faint grief entering his glazed eyes. Then he jerked a Barlow knife from his jumper pocket. The muscles across his face tightened until cracks appeared in the thick cage of dust. He took a hoarse breath, jabbed the knife into the buckskin's haunch.

"*Santa María,*" groaned Felipe weakly. "What good will the death jab do? So you bleed him, and he goes another mile, so what then? So he dies anyway."

"Shut up," said Owens harshly. "I've had the General six years. Shut up."

A strange expression crossed the Mexican's face. Perhaps he was beginning to realize what a grim thing was driving Chisos Owens. Some hands would rather kill themselves than deliberately ride a horse to death they had owned that long.

Owens climbed back on, and leaned forward. What he said into the animal's ear was not audible. The horse twitched a little, staggered into a heavy trot, then a gallop.

The other two men followed. They were passing a bunch of clawing agrito when Natividad jerked straight in his saddle, kicking his boots free of the *tapadero* stirrups with a weary curse. He hit the sand to one side of the lurching animal, staggered two or three steps, then went onto his face. The horse went down to its knees before it stopped, then keeled over on its side, put its foam-flecked nose into the sand, and died.

Natividad began to sob from utter exhaustion. "That's all, Chisos. That is the end of it."

Owens almost fell when he dismounted. He stumbled over to the boy, bent down, and grabbed him by the shirt collar. "Get on my hoss. We aren't through with it yet."

He had Natividad standing on his feet finally and turned him toward the buckskin. Then he stopped. The buckskin was down, too, and the blood trickling from the wound he had made was thin and watery. He looked at it dully for a moment, wishing he could feel something. A man should feel something when his horse died. Maybe he was too tired for emotion now. He didn't know. Felipe tried to get his mount moving again, but it stood dispiritedly beneath his curses and feeble kicks. Finally he got off, leaning wearily against it.

"This *caballo* is *solado*. No . . . ? *Sí*."

Natividad sank to the earth again. Lips thin, Owens went to his dead animal, slipping the *morral* off the saddle horn. He slung the fiber canteen over one shoulder and moved heavily back to the boy, pulling him to his knees, to his feet, shoving him forward.

"Think I'll let you quit now?" he said, and the utter lack of expression in his voice made it more terrible. "Think I pulled you out of the mine to bring you out here and let you die? We've got a long way to go yet. We'll finish this if it's on our bellies, see . . . ?"

Like drunken men they staggered away from the two dead

horses and the one standing on its feet, glazed eyes unseeing. Their footprints left a weaving, meandering trail behind them. They reached a stunted cottonwood. Felipe staggered into it, low branches giving before his weight with a popping sound. He could hardly speak. "Listen, I know when I'm done. At least let me die in peace. *Por Dios, un hombre* has that much right. *Por Dios. . . .*" He trailed off, panting, sweat darkening his white silk shirt.

Owens grabbed him, yanked him feebly away from the tree. He bunched the soft white collar of the shirt in one fist, slapped the Mexican's fat face with a callused palm. "Damn you," he gasped. "I told you how it's going to be. You've got a lot of *pasear* left in you!"

The glaze lifted from Felipe's eyes. He fought feebly. Then he stumbled on around the tree, tearing free of Owens's grip, going on forward. "I am beginning to see," he panted. "I am beginning to see why Anse Hawkman should fear you enough to want you killed on sight."

Beating them, kicking them, Owens drove the two men down the valley. Sometimes he didn't feel it when his hand struck Felipe or the boy. His legs were numb and flaccid beneath him. The sun seemed to be inside his head, burning his very brain. Finally Natividad fell on his face in some mesquite. Owens bent to get hold of his collar. He tried to lift the boy's weight, failed. With a dry sob he let him sink back into the sand.

"Oh, hell," he said, and staggered on past. "Oh, hell . . . !"

His tongue was swollen in his mouth. He stopped once to sip at the *morral*, spilled most of the water anyway, and then dropped the bag clumsily. He started to pick it up, knew he would fall if he bent over, and knew he would never get up again if he fell. Felipe must have given up somewhere behind him. He couldn't see him any more. He went on like a blind man, hands out in front of him, crazy sounds coming from his cracked lips.

Then the shot came to him, small and thin and far away but distinctly a shot. His head jerked up. His glazed eyes went to the narrow cañon that cut into the high cliffs of sandstone. The thing that had driven him this far flamed anew down inside him, blotting out all weariness and thirst and pain, and he began to run in a tottering, stumbling way toward that cañon.

At first he thought it was something wrong with his eyes, the sudden darkness that swept over him. Then he saw that it was a reddish haze emanating from the other end of the notch. Horses stood there, too. And beyond them was a man, squatted down in the purple shadows at the base of the cliff, a rifle across his knees. Owens's hand brushed absently across his own empty holster.

He began to climb the cliff on that side of the horses, seeking a bench higher up. He must have risen several times his own height when his hand slipped across the shelf formed by the strata of eroded porous rock. Crawling along the flat on his belly, he passed above the mounts.

Patently Hawkman had taken it easier on his horses. Just as patently he had driven them hard enough to stove them up. Seeing those ruined mounts, Owens realized how much Anse Hawkman must have wanted to stop the girl. Or was it Hawkman? Valeur was here, too.

Cracked lips thinning, Owens moved ahead with a sudden, awkward kick of his legs. He could see the end of the cut through the cliff now. It opened out onto a slope grown over with a weird spread of leafless trees, their dead gray branches clawing up to form an insane pattern against the reddish haze that hung over the bowl-shaped valley.

He must have made a small noise, rising up above the man

below. The man turned toward him with a grunt. It was Bickford. Most of his heavy-boned face was covered by a white bandage where Owens's pick had hit him. Bickford had always been a slow-moving, enigmatic man, and Owens had almost expected the lack of surprise or anger or fear in his thick voice.

"Chisos," he said as if they might have been meeting on the street, and his Winchester swung upward in freckled hands.

Owens jumped, and the rifle exploded in his face. His head jerked backward to the stunning blow of the bullet, and he couldn't see Bickford any more, or the haze, or anything.

VIII

Elgera stiffened when the gunshot came to her from the cañon. She stayed that way for a moment, one hand gripped tightly over the upthrust of rock in front of her. She wondered why the shot had sounded from there. Then she sagged back into the pothole. What was the difference? They had come, and they were all around her now, out there in the red fog, spreading through the grove of trees, or they would approach her from all sides. Valeur. Hawkman. Pinky. No telling how many more.

The wind, blowing down off the rim rock, rattled through the dead trees like mocking laughter. Elgera changed her revolver from one hand to the other so she could wipe sweat from her palm. When she changed it back, the butt was still sticky in her fingers.

Her blonde head bent forward slightly as she tried to pierce the haze. Her circle of vision was growing smaller and smaller as that mist swept in. She wondered dully why she felt no fear. She should. They had come to kill her. It struck her suddenly that maybe she wanted to die. Maybe she wanted that relief from all this exhaustion and thirst and waiting, waiting, waiting. . . .

The crackling sound to her left was louder than that of the wind. She grew rigid, gun swinging that way. Then someone called.

"Valeur?"

Valeur's voice was husky, tense. "Yeah. Anse?"

"Where are you?" said Anse Hawkman.

"How do I know?" snapped Valeur. "Over this way."

Elgera's fingers cramped on the gun butt. Her eyes ached with trying to pierce the dark haze. There was the crackling of dead branches as someone moved through them, then the voices.

"Did you run into that heat?" Hawkman almost whispered.

"Yeah," grunted Valeur. "Must be what stopped her. She can't get away. All we have to do is find that hole. . . ."

"You're talking too loud," hissed Hawkman.

"She can't hear us," said Valeur. "Smith said that pothole was over on the other side. He's working in from there. We'll know when we're near if we find her palomino."

"You won't let her get away this time?" said Hawkman, that high pitch to his voice.

"What about you?" answered Valeur contemptuously. "You've got a gun. What about you not letting her get away?"

"I won't, but. . . ."

"But you hope it's me who comes to her first," said Valeur. "You want her killed, but you don't want to do the dirty work."

"She's a girl. . . ."

"Chisos Owens wasn't a girl," snapped Valeur. "Lucky you let Bick have that crack at him in the cave, or it would have been your face that got smashed. You've just been letting other men do your gunning so long, you've forgotten how yourself. Or can you be afraid, Anse?"

"Afraid!" said Hawkman shrilly. "You know it isn't that."

"Do I, Anse?" said Valeur. "I think you're afraid of Chisos Owens."

"Damn you, Valeur."

Hawkman's voice cut off to the crackling sound that must have been Jan Valeur crawling away. The girl tried to hold her breath, listening. She couldn't tell if it was the wind now or a man, that eerie popping of the dead trees. It seemed to be all around her. Valeur had said the man named Smith was working in on her from the other side. She turned her head that way, and she drew a choked breath, biting her full underlip.

Smith was the chunky little man with the saddle gun who had stayed behind when Tommy had returned to the house for Valeur and Hawkman. He wore a buckskin ducking jacket and patched *armitas* for chaps, and, when he materialized out of the fog, he was even more surprised to meet Elgera than she was to see him. It gave her the chance to haul her gun up and fire.

Yelling sharply, Smith threw himself to one side, firing a wild shot from the hip. Desperately wanting to keep him in sight, the girl half rose from her protection, jumping over the lip of rock, firing again and again after the dim figure staggering back into the fog and the trees. She heard him cry again, heard a heavier crash of snapping branches. She didn't realize he had quit shooting until her own gun clicked on an empty chamber. In the following silence she began punching madly at the exploded shells. They dropped to her feet with small, pattering sounds. She thumbed the first fresh cartridge from the loop in her belt. Maybe she was turning anyway, or maybe it was the scraping noise of a man's boots on the rocks behind that turned her.

The haze shredded around Anse Hawkman as he stepped into the open. He saw Elgera, standing helplessly there with that single fresh shell still held between the thumb and forefinger of her left hand and the empty gun in the other. A sudden triumph glittered in his cold blue eyes. He brought up his own gun.

Elgera threw her iron from where she held it beside her hip, a scooping, underhanded throw, casting her own long slim body after it. The heavy weapon struck Hawkman's gun arm below the elbow, and his own six-shooter blared on an upward cant, the slug whining harmlessly into the smoky sky. Then Elgera's weight struck him and carried him back, and he rolled to the ground beneath her. She felt her nails rake the man's flesh, saw the thin, red tracks appear on his weathered cheek. With a bitter curse he pistol-whipped her.

Head rocking to the blow, she felt herself rolling off Hawkman. She tried to hold him, but the blow had stunned her, and she couldn't control her muscles. A heavy lethargy held her. Unable to rise, she saw the man lurch to one knee, free hand held across his bloody face. His thumb around the hammer of his gun, it made a sharp, metallic sound as he cocked it.

In that last moment Elgera didn't know why she should say the man's name because he was somewhere on the outside, far away from this insane place in the Dead Horses where she was going to die. "Chisos," she mumbled, and saw Hawkman's gun twitch to her.

He stopped like that, with the black bore of his weapon aimed at Elgera's head. He was looking past her toward the trees. His face was dead white. He said the same thing the girl had, only his voice held a sudden, shaking fear.

"Chisos . . . ?"

The man came stalking through the dead trees in a hard, swift, bent-forward stride that looked as if it might be hard to stop. The set of his dust-caked face was made more terrible by the red furrow that ran from the corner of his eye back through his hair above the ear, deep and bloody. The Winchester he held across his square belly had **BB** carved into its stock. He just kept right on coming, levering a shell into the chamber with an ominous snap.

Anse Hawkman's lips worked around words that wouldn't come out as he tried to jerk his gun toward Chisos Owens. Owens pulled his trigger without any expression and without breaking his stride, and Hawkman took the bullet where the buckle of his gun belt glittered against his spare middle. He bent over with a hollow cough. His revolver slipped from his hand. He fell on his face.

Elgera rose to one elbow, trying to retain consciousness. Owens stepped over Hawkman's body, looking at something beyond Elgera, levering again the .30-30 with **BB** on its stock.

Elgera could see Valeur then. He was coming in out of the fog and gathering dusk and dead gray trees, coming in a hard, pounding run, that .38 in his hairy fist. The gun flamed. Wood splintered from the stock of the Winchester, deflecting it upward in Owens's hands. Owens fired anyway.

Valeur yelled and jerked halfway around, .38 leaping from his hand. It didn't stop him. With his bloody hand knocked out to one side, he came right on in. His boots made growing sounds in Elgera's ears. Owens was levering another shell into the carbine. Before he could shoot, Valeur's body slammed into him. They went back into a tree with a dull, fleshy thud, limbs snapping and breaking beneath them. Then they rolled to the ground and flopped away into the fog like a couple of big cats, slugging, kicking, cursing.

Elgera got to her hands and knees, head still spinning from Hawkman's blow. Painfully she scooped up Hawkman's gun. She could still hear them, fighting on the ground, just out of sight back in the haze. She crawled toward the noise.

She thought she would faint for a moment. Her hand went to her blonde hair, came away bloody. She shook her head, and it made her sick. She reached a tree finally, caught a low branch, pulled herself up. It was all she could do to stand there, trying to keep the gun from slipping out of her lax fingers.

The two men came rolling back through the trees. They had the rifle in between them, both with their hands on it, each struggling to get it free of the other. Valeur came on top, and only then did Elgera see how big a man he really was. Owens was larger than average, with a bulk to his solid torso that gave him heft without actually being fat. Somehow, though, he looked small and helpless beneath the swarthy man.

Heavy shoulders bunching, Valeur yanked the .30-30 upward. With the same movement he smashed the butt end back down into Owens's belly. Owens collapsed.

The girl tried to raise her six-gun as Valeur jumped to his feet, reversing the rifle, white teeth bared in a snarl. But a fresh wave of nausea swept her. She saw Owens roll over, one of his hands pawing feebly for the rifle barrel as Valeur jerked it around toward him. Then the girl felt herself going over on her face. She couldn't see the men any more. She only heard the shot.

Lying there, half conscious, it was Valeur's bitter curse that raised her head. Somehow Owens had thrown himself at Valeur, knocking the gun aside so that the slug had gone out between them. He was on his knees now, doggedly trying to hold onto the rifle.

Cursing, Valeur jerked it free, clubbed it. Elgera groaned with her inability to move. Pain and lethargy and nausea held her powerless. Owens launched himself from his knees, bloody face set in an awful mask. Valeur swung with a vicious grunt. The rifle caught Owens on his shoulder between the arm he had thrown up to ward off the blow and his neck. The sound of it hitting him sent a fresh wave of sickness through Elgera.

Owens stumbled a little to the side. He didn't go down. He didn't stop.

Valeur took another step backward, rifle swinging again. It slammed into Owens's head. Owens's hoarse sob held the awful pain of it. His arms pawed out, and he staggered forward with his head down, and the girl thought he was going over on his face for good this time. He didn't.

Something desperate came into Valeur's blazing eyes. With a panting yell, he took another swift step backward, swinging the rifle behind his head for a third murderous blow. That was all.

Stumbling forward blindly, arms out in front of him, bloody head down, Owens went into Valeur. They crashed to the ground again, rolling away into the fog, the branches of a dead cottonwood setting up an echoing crackle. Elgera could see the dim movement of them farther on. Valeur still had the rifle. He jammed it upward into Owens's face.

Elgera saw Owens's head snap back, saw Valeur take that moment to claw at the rifle's lever, cocking it. The sudden movement of Owens's body cut off whatever happened next. Elgera heard Valeur gasp. She saw one of his arms thrust out to the side with the rifle. The gun slipped from his grasp. He made a spasmodic series of jerks with his arms and legs. The dull, fleshy noise came to the girl for a long time after that before she realized what it was. She saw Owens's bulk lunge to one side, then the other, straddling Valeur, and each movement was punctuated by the sodden sound.

Slowly she got to her hands and knees. She grabbed hold of the tree again. She stood there a moment, eyes on Chisos Owens, still swerving from one side to the other, grimly, silently. Finally she gathered herself and staggered to him, almost falling when she reached out to clutch his shoulder.

"Stop," she panted. "Chisos, stop it. Can't you see it's done now. He's . . . dead!"

Owens stopped beating Valeur's head against the rocky ground. He straightened, taking his fist out of the man's long, black hair. Finally he got to his feet, looking at his hands as if realizing for the first time what he had done. The girl sagged against him, face buried in the dust and blood and sweat of his torn jumper.

"Don't," she sobbed weakly, "don't look like that. He would have killed you. . . ."

"Yeah," said Owens dazedly. "Yeah. I guess I went sort of loco. It was a long ride up here. I had plenty of time to think about what they were going to do to you. I guess I went sort of loco."

She might have asked him to explain the miracle of his coming to her call, but somehow it could wait. She only wanted to feel his arms slipping around her, to know it was all over. Then she stiffened.

"Chisos! There's another one. Pinky . . . ?"

"Pinky," said the pudgy, little Mexican who was walking in out of the fog, "sends you his regrets. He will not be coming this evening."

The girl turned toward him, eyes widening a little. The fat man smiled blandly, looked at the rocky formation by his feet, kicked at it.

"Volcanic tufa," he said. "Irregular masses of igneous rock permeated with vitreous matter and encased in black, scoriaceous crust of basic lava. Placed with some force against a man's head, it renders him *non compos mentis*, as it were. I found Pinky wandering around in the fog. I placed it against his head with some force."

"I thought I left you on the other side of the notch," said Owens dully.

"The shots spurred me on, as they did you," said the Mexican. "I came to the *morral* of water you had dropped. It revived me. Farther on I found Bickford. You left him in poor condition, Chisos."

He chuckled as Owens passed a hand across that furrow in his head, muttering: "Bick's shot caught me here. Knocked me out for a minute. But I was already going down on top of him. I came to in time."

"Apparently." The Mexican laughed, turning to sniff at the haze. "Oxidation of ferruginous constituents. Causes the red color. We stand in an extinct crater, *señor y señorita*. I wager it is rather hot farther on, where the shell is thinnest. I never expected to see the Lost Santiago, either. One finds many strange things in the Dead Horses." He caught the girl's eyes on the briefcase under his arm, and smiled.

She spoke hesitantly: "Who are you?"

"I found my case in the saddlebags on Valeur's chestnut, where I presumed it would be," said the Mexican. "You could call me Felipe, if you chose, and that would be my name, or you could call me Amole, or Juan, and that would be my name, yet none of them would quite be my name, either, if you see what I mean. *Porque*"—he flourished one of the gilt-edged diplomas from the brown case—"as it says here, I am Ignacio Juan y Felipe del Amole Avarillo, mining engineer *extraordinario*, archeologist *magnífico*, consultant on business matters and affairs of the heart, or whatever you happen to require at the moment."

"I might've known," grunted Chisos Owens.

"*Si*, and so might have Bickford, except that neither one of you knew me," said Felipe. "You see, they found out about me in the first place when Hopwell's letter was sent to me.

84

They read the letter before sending it on. Thus must they have intercepted my letter back to Hopwell in which I identified myself by this briefcase I always carry. It was the only way Bickford knew me. The night was black as a *negro* bull. They met me on the road to Alpine beside the cottonwood grove north of town, knocking me from my horse. Recognizing caution as the better part of valor, I escaped into the grove. I hadn't recognized any of them or any of them me. That is why I could go to Alpine and wait, *señor*. Everything comes to him who waits. No . . . ? *Sí!*"

"If you are Avarillo, you're a little late," said the girl, looking up at Chisos Owens, "and somehow I can't seem to care much."

"Late?"

"Thomas was Hawkman's lawyer," she said. "He had the deed . . . I saw him sign it and date it as of this month in our own living room. They registered their transfer. The Santiago is now a part of the AH spread. I'm glad Father never had to see that."

"He's . . . ?"

"Dead," said Elgera. "We took him to the hospital at Marathon about six months ago. He was an old man. They couldn't do anything for him."

Felipe began to chuckle.

Chisos Owens looked at him angrily, growling: "What's so funny?"

"Six months ago he died," said Avarillo, "and she saw Thomas sign and date the quit-claim as of this month. A fine lawyer, that Thomas. Didn't he know your father was dead?"

"I only got as far as taking Father to the hospital when Valeur interrupted," said Elgera. "I guess he was in a hurry to get the deed. He was an impatient man, anyway."

"You have the death certificate?" asked the Mexican, and,

when she nodded, he began to chuckle again. "Then your valley is most certainly not a part of the AH. As in the case of Oliver versus Lynn, EMMET AND EMMET, volume three, page twenty-seven, the delivery of a deed after the grantor's death is not effective. Thomas rendered the quit-claim invalid himself when he dated it. You have your proof in the death certificate."

Perhaps Chisos Owens had seen too much already for more than the slight surprise that showed through the dust and blood caking his face. "You . . . ?"

"Oh, *sí, sí.*" Felipe chuckled, taking out a black *cigarro.* "Did you think I would pass up the overcrowded practice of law. I was an *abogado* in Mexico City for a time. As I say, whatever you might require. Mining, archeology, affairs of the heart. . . ."

"Yes," said Elgera, looking up at Chisos Owens, "affairs of the heart."

But even Avarillo's talents in such matters failed when it came to Owens. Using Hawkman's horses, they returned to the valley, picking up Natividad beyond the notch. The boy was delirious but began to recuperate soon. The guards Anse Hawkman had left at the cave were glad enough to leave when they learned that Hawkman was dead. Owens let them go, knowing there would be no more trouble from that direction. He stayed at the Santiago a week or so, helping the Douglases get back to normal. Then Elgera began to notice the small, restless signs in him.

It was early morning when the three of them stood beneath the portal that formed the roof of the flagstone porch: Elgera, Chisos, Felipe.

Chisos Owens spoke uncomfortably. "It's like I told you before, Elgera. It's hard to explain. Maybe it sounds loco to you. But if I stayed here, I'd either be living off you or

86

working for you. I won't be a kept man. And do you think I could hire on like an ordinary thirty-and-found 'puncher when I feel like I do about you. If I had anything to offer, I'd ask you to come away with me. I haven't even got a hoss now. Thomas has power of attorney for Anse. He's no cattleman, and maybe he'll open up things to the outside again. Maybe I'll be able to get my Smoky Blue back. If I had that. . . ."

"I understand," she said, trying to keep the tears back. "Maybe this just isn't the time."

"There'll be a time," he murmured, "sooner or later. Meanwhile, you're in good hands with Felipe. And if there's anything he doesn't know about, just call me again. *Adiós*."

Elgera and the Mexican stood there, watching the blocky man ride up the hill on the gelding the girl had given him from her remuda. Avarillo took his *cigarro* out with a flourish. *"Sí,"* he said, *"adiós* . . . which is only a corruption of 'go with God' and doesn't literally mean farewell at all."

The girl smiled wistfully. *"Adiós,* then, Chisos Owens."

Queen of the Long Rifles

The author's original title for this story was "Lobo King of Beaver". It was sent by Savage's agent to Malcolm Reiss, general manager at Fiction House. He bought the story in late November, 1943, paying the author $330 upon acceptance. It appeared as "Queen of the Long Rifles" in *Frontier Stories* (Winter, 44).

I

An Apache sat cross-legged on the ground with the sweat dripping off his hatchet face and beat a feverish tattoo on a tom-tom, and Jacinto, the Mexican, drew an abandoned rhythm out of his madly strumming *guittara*, and Portugee Phillips's daughter whirled in a crazy fandango with a great, shaggy, drunken trapper named Terry McNary. The mountaineers were in! They had come out of the Big Horns and the Wind Rivers and the Shoshones to the Portugee Houses here on the Powder, to sell their spring harvest of beaver pelts and spend a week of drunken debauchery, trying to forget that, when it was all over, they would be drawn back to their lonely trade as surely as the geese were drawn south in the winter. With them had come Bateau Severn.

In 1798, Ian Severn had left his Scottish highlands to seek his fortune in the New World. He had trapped for Hudson's Bay Company in the British Territories, and had taken a French girl for his wife, and from their union had sprung Bateau, all the moody, violent wildness of his French mother and the grim, harsh strength of his father mixed up in him to produce a restless wanderer who had finally drifted into the vast, uncharted wilderness known then as the Louisiana Purchase.

Leaning now against the rough wall of white pine logs that formed the Portugee Houses, Bateau's shoulders stretched at his red wool shirt with a rolling bulk that came to a man who had won his name poling buffalo-hide *bateaux* on the Missouri before he took to trapping. Above the fiery flash of his black eyes, his brow was a heavy, dark line. He wore no hat, and the sun had burned golden streaks through his brown hair and short beard. Hairy, trap-scarred hands were tucked into the broad black belt that supported his grease-slick buckskin leggings as well as the brass-studded sheath of his Green River skinning blade. He had been away on the trap lines for two months, and there were no women up where the beaver built their lodges, so when Severn's eyes fell on the dancing girl for the twentieth time, little lights began to come and go behind their narrowing lids.

What a woman! Mira was her name, Portugee Phillips's daughter, with long, black hair that shimmered like a wet beaver pelt and cheeks flushed as red as prairie indigo. She was wild and untamed like an unbroken Spanish mare, and she flirted and coquetted with every trapper who came to the Houses, yet none could claim her.

The blood-stirring thump of the *guittara* grew louder as Jacinto sidled over toward Bateau. He wore tight leggings with silver *conchas* down the seams, Jacinto, and his bandy legs looked totally incapable of supporting his prodigious torso. There was still some argument among the mountain men as to whether it had been two feet or two and a half that the Taos saddler had added to Jacinto's gun belt in order that it might girt his incredible *estómago*.

"You been watching Mira." He grinned hopefully at Bateau. "Maybe you marry her, no?"

"Pourqois?" spat the French Canuck. "Because I look at a squaw, does it mean I want to marry her?"

"If you get married, then we won't have to work any more," said the Mexican. "She would make camp and cut wood and build the fire, even trap your beaver."

"Hyacinth," said Bateau, "take a look at Squawman Samuels over there, take a good look."

Jacinto's glance passed through the crowd of shouting, cavorting trappers and on by the mountain men sitting cross-legged about a game of Old Sledge, and down to the last of the half a dozen Portugee Houses set in a line facing the Powder River. Before the door of that last cabin hunkered Squawman Samuels. He had been a big, strapping man once, ready to get drunk or fight or hunt a grizzly at the drop of a wolf-skin hat. Now the fat was beginning to push at his buckskin jacket where it crossed his belly; there were no fresh trap scars on his hands, and their flesh had a pale, soft look. Standing beside him was his Crow squaw, enigmatically possessive in a bright red blanket from Chimayo.

"That's what happens when a man gets hitched to a squaw," growled Bateau. "He stays down at the Portugee Houses when he should be out on the trap lines. He gets fat and lazy and soft. He might as well be dead. I've danced with every woman between here and Saint Looey, Hyacinth, but I'll never marry one of them."

He trailed off, realizing that the Apache's tom-tom had ceased and that Mira Phillips had quit dancing with McNary, her buckskin skirt settling about bare legs as she turned toward the river. Jacinto's *guittara* subsided with a final, abortive thump, and he, too, was looking past Bateau toward the Powder. In the sudden strained silence, Bateau shifted so he could see what they were looking at.

There in the tramped wheat grass just off the riverbank was the tallest man, sitting the tallest mare, that Bateau had ever seen. He must have been a good six foot eight in his moccasins, and the horse stood eighteen hands high if it stood one. The man's hair hung, thick and yellow, down about the shoulders of a dressed deerskin jacket. Sun-bleached eyebrows uptilted over strange, pale blue eyes, and his ears were slightly pointed, and it gave his narrow reddish-brown face a sardonic cast. Across the silver-mounted pommel of a huge double-rigged saddle he held an exceedingly long rifle. His mount was glossy wet from the river, and behind him were a dozen other men forking horses wet to the hocks.

"I," said the man as if it were the most important thing in the world, "am Benjamin Longbit, and I come from Saint Looey town, and I can shoot a Jake Hawkins gun better than any man living."

Bateau raised his head to make his voice carry. "I'll accept those first two statements, *m'sieu.*"

Bateau's strength went infinitely deeper than the mere evident power of his lean-shanked, broad-shouldered figure, and Longbit must have sensed this, for, as his glance shifted to Bateau, a certain grudging respect showed in his strange pale eyes momentarily.

"Ah," he said, "you don't think I'm the best shot in the world?"

"How could you be," asked Bateau, grinning, "when I am?"

Someone chuckled.

"Down in Saint Looey, I heard about a man up this way who had the name of being the craziest, wildest, braggin'est coot in the Big Horns," said Longbit, easing forward in his huge rig. "You must be Bateau Severn."

"If you heard that, by gar," said Bateau, moving forward, "then you must have heard how I can shoot a Hawkins gun."

"Hearing is not necessarily believing," said Longbit. Then he turned back to the free trappers who had begun to gather before his riders, Mira Phillips in their front ranks. "I feel I should introduce my associates. This travesty on my left is known as Gotch Ear. He is a simple soul. He likes to eat and sleep and make love and juggle knives. I've come to believe he takes his greatest delight in the last."

The man toward whom Longbit waved his hand surveyed the crowd with a sullen, animal indifference. His right ear had been cut and mashed into an indistinguishable pulp, and his unshaven, pockmarked face would have been ugly enough without that gotched ear. Through the broad belt of Cheyenne wampum strapped around his thick waist were thrust half a dozen assorted knives. The score of trappers were tight-pressed in front of Longbit now, shifting around, not knowing exactly how to regard the yellow-haired man and his riders. Portugee Phillips had been drawn from his main House at the sudden silence and was coming toward the crowd. Longbit waved his free hand to the man on his other side.

"Here we have an *hombre* whose enjoyments in life seem even more limited than Gotch Ear's. He eats, apparently, only because he would succumb if he didn't. Sleep is a necessary evil. Women don't exist. Gentlemen, Danny Gunn."

Gunn's face might have been carved from the January ice that formed on the Missouri; his eyes were black, opaque, dead. Bateau's glance was drawn to his small hand, hanging closely above the silver-chased butt of a Paterson cap-and-ball holstered about his slim hips. There was a definite, habitual curl in the fingers of that hand, and Bateau read it as he would a beaver sign.

Portugee Phillips stepped through the free trappers gathered around Longbit. He had been appraising furs and still held a soft, brown pelt. He was a dark, hawk-faced man from Portugal, with jet black hair like his daughter, and flashing eyes. The huge, golden earrings dangling from his lobes gleamed brightly from incessant polishing. It was legend among the trappers that when Portuguese Phillips stopped polishing his earrings, the beaver would disappear from the Big Horns forever, and it would be time to put the Lecroix traps back in their trap sacks for good.

"If you have furs," said Mira's father, "bring them in. You are welcome to Portugee Houses."

"Does it look like I have furs?" said the tall, blond man, jerking his head toward the horsebackers behind him.

There were a few led horses at the rear, no pack animals. Half a dozen of Bateau's own breed sat directly behind Longbit, great-shouldered French-Canadian *voyageurs* in dirty-white blanket coats and wolf-skin hats, armed with the favored London Fusil, short-barreled and smooth-bored and deadly in a close fight. Behind the Frenchies were a handful of tall, unshaven Yankees, long rifles held, tight-fisted, across saddlebows. Most men would have taken them for trappers in their greasy buckskins and old felt hats. But Bateau looked closer, and he didn't take them for trappers. The fringe on a mountain man's leggings was not ornament; he cut it off whenever he needed leather whangs to repair worn moccasins or broken pack saddles or frayed hacka-mores. Not a whang had been cut from the leggings or jackets of these men, and, if their hands bore trap scars, none of them was fresh. Mira was appraising Benjamin Longbit boldly with her dark eyes. He smiled down at her, and she asked him: "Why have you come to the Houses, then?"

"Hudson's Bay has Prince Rupert's Land in the British Territories," said Longbit. "Ashley and Astor put their fur brigades above the Missouri. Nor'west Company holds everything west of the Rockies. I heard this land above the Platte sadly lacks any such organization."

Bateau had come in close then, and, when he spoke, his voice was loud enough to make some of the trappers turn toward him. "I never went to school, *m'sieu*. Make that a little plainer."

"Yes," said Longbit deliberately. "I want to make sure everyone understands. I have come, you might say, to take over."

For a moment there was an intense silence. A horse snorted somewhere behind Longbit. Then the free trappers about Portugee began to mutter, and shift.

"We've been drinking heavily here, *señor*," said Portugee. "It is not a time to joke."

Terry McNary was Irish and he came from Black's Fork of the Green where Bridger had built his fort, and beneath the new buckskin jacket he'd bought from Portugee Phillips he was as big and hard as a pig of Galena lead. He pushed his way to the front. "Portugee," he shouted, "I don't think this kyesh is joking!"

"I'm glad someone realized that," said Longbit. "I like to be taken seriously. You and I will form a partnership, Mister Phillips. We'll form the trappers into brigades, like Ashley did on the Mizzou. Our men will work in pairs and cover every stream in Longbitland."

"Longbitland!" burst out Bateau. "By gar, that's too much. . . ."

"Wait a minute, Bateau," said Douglas Fowler, one of the older free trappers. "This feller might have something. We ain't been making enough as free trappers to put a dollar in our jeans after we finish getting our new outfits every year. I was in Saint Looey town when Ashley's men came back in 'Twenty-Two, and they was all jingling silver in their possible sacks."

"And they all belonged to Ashley, body and soul!" shouted McNary. "They weren't free trappers. They couldn't get drunk when they wanted. They couldn't pack their mules and shuck out when they took a hankering. They couldn't even have a good fight when they wanted."

"That's right!" roared Bateau.

The other free trappers were still filled with their liquor. They began shouting, pushing, swearing. Gotch Ear took a Bowie from his belt and threw it into the air, letting the black handle slap into his palm.

"Longbitland extends from the North Platte as far up as Prince Rupert's Land," called the tall, yellow-haired Longbit, "and from the Missouri River as far west as Nor'west's holdings. There'll be no trapping in Longbitland except by my own men. . . ."

"By gar!" roared Bateau. "I've harvested plews in Prince Rupert's Land and no *homme* from Hudson's Bay chased me out. I poled a bullboat through Nor'west Company's country and they couldn't keep me from trapping. Longbitland or no Longbitland, you can't keep me out of the Big Horns!"

Gotch Ear slipped a bright-bladed machete from his wampum belt, and there were two knives flashing in the air.

Longbit surveyed the milling crowd coldly. "I'm forming my brigades now," he said. "If there's anybody here who doesn't want to work for me, I'll give them a chance to leave. They'd better get out of Longbitland and stay out."

"Longbitland, hell!" roared Bateau. "Free trapper land it is, and free trapper land it stays."

"That's right," bellowed Terry McNary, reaching out to grab the silver cheek piece on the headstall of Longbit's great mare. "It's you had better get out and stay out."

He yanked viciously, and the mare danced halfway around. A third knife slipped from Gotch Ear's belt, and he juggled all three of them without looking, his eyes on the crowd. The riders behind leaned forward a little in their saddles. Bateau saw the men who had no fresh trap scars on their hands pull their reins in tighter. Thin anger slipped through Longbit's self-assurance as he tried to jerk the mare's head-stall free of McNary's grasp. But the big Irishman hung on and pulled the horse on around.

"Ah," moaned Jacinto, slinging his *guittara* around on his fat back, "it's going to be a fight. I know it."

Bateau elbowed his way through the press of sweating, drunken free trappers toward Longbit, and the Mexican took a step after him, grabbing at his arm.

"No, Bateau, don't do anything loco. Look at all the *hombres* Longbit has. Please, Bateau. . . ."

The other trappers were surging in around McNary, shaking fists at Longbit. Bateau saw, however, that there were enough of them who hung back. More than Douglas Fowler were inclined toward the fur brigades of Benjamin Longbit. The yellow-haired man jerked his reins once more, mouth twisting. McNary laughed and kept pulling the mare on around. Suddenly Longbit quit trying to yank loose. His thin head nodded sharply toward the man who forked a horse on his left.

"Danny," he said.

Danny Gunn took out his Paterson cap-and-ball and shot Terry McNary through the belly.

The big Irishman from Black's Fork opened his mouth, but no sound came out. His hand dropped from the silver-plated cheek piece on Longbit's headstall. He took a stag-gering step backward into the crowd of free trappers, held erect for a moment by the press of bodies. Then he sagged to the ground.

It was as if Longbit had set a match to the fuse on a keg of Dupont, and it had taken that long for the flame to reach the powder. Bateau was one of the howling, shouting, cursing, drunken free trappers who flung themselves blindly at Longbit and his riders.

But there was a lethal deliberation to Longbit, and he might almost have planned McNary's setting it off that way. He raised up in his stirrups and shouted, and his whole compact body of horsemen spurred forward into the free trappers.

Gotch Ear's mount leaped in between Bateau and Longbit, throwing the red-shirted French Canuck off its pounding flanks. Staggering, trying to keep from falling on his face, Bateau was dimly aware of the battle about him. Longbit was raging through the men on foot, wielding his huge Jake Hawkins gun like a club. He swung far out to one side and caught a big, white-haired trapper named Cotton across the chest and shoulder. Cotton doubled over and grabbed at a smashed arm. Longbit swung over to the other side and hit a man from Lake de Smet in the face.

The horseman behind Gotch Ear thundered into Bateau. The French Canuck hurled himself from in front of the deadly hoofs, catching blindly at a stirrup leather as the horse swung by him. Dragged across the ground, he caught the man's downswinging rifle and yanked. The rider tried to keep his gun; he was pulled from the saddle. They rolled into the dust together, and, before they came to a halt, Bateau had both hands on the rifle. He rammed it up into the twisted face above him. A sick cry came from the man, then his weight was gone. Bateau rose shakily, still holding the long-barreled weapon.

From the dusty tumult ahead, Danny Gunn wheeled his black gelding, throwing down on Bateau with that Paterson cap-and-ball. Bateau pulled the rifle in close and squeezed the trigger. There was a hollow click, and it didn't surprise him much, because no good hand rode with a Jake Hawkins loaded.

Then Gunn's six-shooter flamed, and Bateau bent forward, grunting in the hollow, involuntary way of a man whose breath had been knocked from him. He sat down heavily, because Gunn's bullet had driven through his leg, and it wouldn't support him any more.

It was over as quickly as it had started. The shouting faded and died. Three men lay sprawled beneath the settling dust; a fourth sat holding his broken head, moaning. Portugee Phillips had dragged his daughter free, and stood cursing Longbit violently in four languages, gleaming earrings shaking with each foul epithet. Squawman Samuels stood indecisively before the main Portugee House, face pale, mouth working a little. His gun lay directly behind him; he had made no move toward it.

"Squawman!" spat Bateau disgustedly, holding his leg.

Standing where they had scattered, forming a loose circle around Longbit's riders, fifteen or sixteen trappers were left. A big mountain man pulled Gotch Ear's Bowie knife out of his shoulder, and blood leaked from the wound. Another who had been kicked in the stomach by a horse was being very sick.

"I'll repeat what I said before," said Longbit, quieting his immense mare. "Anybody who doesn't want to work for me can go now. But they'd better get out of Longbitland, because this little work-over was a mild taste of what will happen if I come across them in my holdings again."

Jacinto came up from behind Bateau; his face was bloody. "All this fighting, all this violence. I won't be able to eat for a week. . . ."

"Help me up," snapped Bateau.

Plump hands slipped beneath his armpits, and the prodigious Hyacinth lifted him like a child. He put an arm across the sloping roll of fat that passed for Jacinto's shoulder. The other free trappers were gathering into a group now; the liquor was out of them and they had a sullen, defensive air. Bateau turned to Phillips, trying to keep the pain from his voice.

"You going to lick this yellow-haired weasel bear's moccasins now, Portugee?"

Phillips's eyes still flashed angrily, but his voice was heavy. "What can I do, Bateau? These have been my Houses for twenty years. I'm getting old. I can't leave them now."

"I'm glad you look at it that way," said Longbit, smiling thinly. "I couldn't let you go even if you wanted to. You have a certain name up here, a reputation. I wouldn't want to lose either."

Bateau's heavy brows lowered, and he turned to Douglas Fowler. The older trapper wouldn't meet the French Canuck's eyes. He pulled at his scraggly beard.

"Ashley's men made money in them brigades," he muttered. "It's worth a try, ain't it, Bateau?"

Bateau's disgusted gaze swept on. "Cotton?"

The big, white-headed mountain man held his broken arm, pain twisting his mouth. "Hell, Bateau, we'd have to go south to get out of Longbitland. There ain't enough beaver left below the Platte to keep our stomachs full, much less buy us enough traps to make our living. I ain't in no fix to buck that with a busted wing."

"It looks," said Benjamin Longbit sardonically, "as if you are the only one, Bateau Severn. I'll let you collect your outfit. I'll give you a week to get out of Longbitland."

II

Jacinto had a penchant for naming things and he had called it Vallejo Escondido, because it was somewhat of a valley, and because it was so well hidden by the surrounding peaks that not even an experienced mountain man would have dreamed of its existence. A spring rose on the north slope, forming a creek that flowed through the bottom of the cup-like valley. No telling how many eons it had taken for that creek to wear away the rock of a saddle on the south side and form the gunsight notch that was the entrance and exit to the place. The only other way in was over the towering mountains, and they were so high it was unlikely anyone would reach their ridges.

Spring lay on the Big Horns and the beaver were cutting aspens for their dams and the buffalo calves were dropping in the bluegrass down by the Big Horn River. Bateau had made his camp beside that spring on the north slope of Hidden Valley. A month had passed since Benjamin Longbit had presented himself at the Portugee Houses and Bateau still limped from that ball Danny Gunn had put through his thigh.

The French Canuck had just begun to trap again, and the score of dead beaver constituting his first harvest lay piled beneath a dirty Navajo saddle blanket behind Bateau. He sat cross-legged by the skinning frame, taking a pelt off with his Green River. Jacinto hunkered against the blue hole of a pine, his mountainous girth forming a pleasant rest for his beloved *guittara.* He strummed idly at the instrument, humming:

Tu eres mi paloma blanca. . . .

"Why don't you learn to skin and flesh and grain?" Bateau grinned. "Then I could spend all my time on the lines and we would have twice as big a harvest."

"Thou art my white dove . . . ," sang Jacinto. Then he made a sick grimace. "Skin and flesh and grain . . . *caracoles!* That would be work, Bateau. My father, he told me before he died . . . 'Son, there are two real sins in this world, only two, and. . . .'"

"And they are working and fighting," mocked Bateau. "Working and fighting. If a man avoids both, he will surely go to heaven."

"Yo soy mi pichón azul," hummed the gross Mexican. "You are my blue pigeon. *Sí,* Bateau, that is right. My soul is sensitive, made only for eating and singing and being happy. Besides, I think you are foolish to set your trap lines outside our Vallejo Escondido. Remember, we are squatting right in the middle of Longbitland, *diablo* curse it. If you insist on staying here, at least you could be prudent."

Bateau didn't answer. He had raised his head suddenly. He wiped his Green River on greasy leggings and stuck it in its brass-studded scabbard. Jacinto began playing again.

"Arrima tu piquito," he murmured. "Nestle your little bill close to mine. . . ."

Bateau stood up. *"Basta!"*

Jacinto's fat hand hovered over his strings. *"¿Quién es?"*

"Listen."

The Mexican listened, mouth sagging with concentration. *"Pues, I hear nada."*

Bateau picked up his Jake Hawkins rifle, his shoulder belt.

"Of course, you hear nothing, *ami.* All the little animals have stopped making their noises in the bushes, all the birds have quit singing. Haven't you learned what that means yet?"

"Someone is coming," Jacinto said, beaming at his own perspicacity, then his grin faded, and he jumped to his feet with an alacrity foreign to such a ponderous bulk. *"¡Indios!"*

"Indians would circle around and come from above," said Bateau, drawing him into the bushes surrounding the clearing. "The birds stopped singing downslope first."

"Señor Longbit?"

Bateau shoved him on his fat hams in the chokecherry, then squatted down himself. "Maybe."

The hoof beats were muffled by the carpet of pine needles. They were not aware of the rider until the horse walked into the open from the dense shadows of the timber. Bateau had seen some ruined mounts in his life. This one made him draw a hissing breath between his teeth. There was absolutely no flesh left on it and the ribs looked ready to poke through the scarred, torn hide at its next step. It halted, quivering, nostrils frothed. The rider wasn't in much better condition, buckskins ripped and frayed, face pale and feverish beneath matted, cockle-burred hair. Bateau swore under his breath, dropping his rifle, rising to run across the clearing and catch Mira Phillips as she reeled out of her saddle.

"I've been hunting for you so long," she sobbed against his chest. "So long. . . ."

Jacinto had slung his *guittara* onto his back, and it thumped sonorously as he puffed up behind Bateau. They carried her to the fire, and wrapped her in a buffalo robe. Bateau got a flat wooden keg of Pass Brandy from one of his packs *supplémentaire,* forced some of it between her lips. She choked. Faint color came to her pale cheeks. Finally she opened her eyes, and spoke weakly.

"I wouldn't have found you except for your trap lines," she said. "All the Longbitmen use Hansel traps. When I stumbled across a Lecroix down where that creek comes out of this valley, I knew it was yours. You're a pig-headed fool, Bateau Severn. Any day Longbitmen are going to find your lines."

"First Longbitland . . . now Longbitmen!" he growled. "Listen, Mira, trapping is my living, and no man in this world can stop me from making my living in a free land."

"There are others who said that, too," she said. "Longbit stopped them. Have you seen anyone since you left the Portugee Houses?"

He shook his head. "My wound took a long time to heal. You're the first one from the outside who's come in here."

"Then you don't know how strong Longbit has become," she stated darkly. "He's stretched his paws all the way up the Powder, Bateau. He's established river stations as far north as Lake de Smet. Instead of making the long trek down to the Houses each month with their harvests, the Longbitmen just leave their plews at the nearest post on the river. From there, the French *voyageurs* pole the furs on down to the Houses in *bateaux*. Longbit has already organized two brigades. They're working the streams in pairs, and they cover the eastern slopes of the Big Horns from the Houses to the Sioux hunting grounds."

Bateau sat back on his heels, rubbing his golden-shot beard. "*Sacre bleu,* how could he take over so quick? Those men down at the Portugee Houses were only a small part of all the free trappers up here. I can understand how he took over there. He got the jump on us, and he had it all planned. But in the mountains . . . ?"

"He's squeezed the free men out, one way or another," she said bitterly. "Men like Cotton or Squawman Samuels, who didn't have the courage to buck Longbit, were quick enough to come down out of the hills and join his organization. Then there were others, like Douglas Fowler, who sincerely believed they would profit by working in brigades. That leaves very few who are actually fighting Longbit, Bateau. And those he is methodically eliminating. His brigades track them down like animals. Longbit said he would organize up here. He has."

Jacinto sat open-mouthed. He scratched his bulbous nose absently. Fat popped on the spitted meat. Bateau turned the bear steaks absently.

"A number of free trappers, too, have been misled into joining Longbit because of the influence my father's name has," said Mira finally. "You know what a reputation Portugee has up here. That's the only reason Longbit is keeping him alive, for his influence with the trappers, and the Indians."

"Has your father been . . . ?"

"No, he didn't have to torture Father. He has a better hold over him that that," said the girl through thin lips. "Me."

Bateau turned sharply to her. She shrugged, looking blankly into the fire.

"I've been unharmed," she murmured. "Longbit made it explicit what would happen to me if Father did anything out of order. And now, Longbit and Father are headed north, to the summer camp of the Oglala Sioux. Longbit wants the Indians to stop trading with the free trappers that are left. Then you'll have no source of supply within five hundred miles, no market for your furs north of Bridger's Fort. It will do more to get rid of you free men than all the murdering the Longbitmen can do."

Still trying desperately to grasp the full purport of the thing, Bateau frowned. "How does the yellow-hair expect the

Oglalas to consent to that? Just because he asks them?"

"Longbit won't ask them," she said. "Portugee Phillips will. They'll give their consent . . . to him."

"But with you escaped, Longbit won't have any hold over Portugee," grunted the French Canuck.

"I told you they went north. I escaped two days after they left," she explained. "I was at the Portugee Houses. They didn't take me along. Father doesn't know I'm free. I went to the other independent trappers, what few were left. I went to Farness up on No Wood, to Guidon up by Two Crows, to Kentucky. They wouldn't do it. They said it would be suicide."

"What would be suicide?"

She didn't answer directly. "When Longbit has gained the consent of the Oglalas not to trade with you any more, it will be his last step to a strangle-hold on the Big Horns. He will have complete control. He won't need Father's influence or his name any longer. Maybe he won't even bother to bring Father back from his trip. . . ."

"I see," growled Bateau, rubbing his beard. "How did you escape?"

"Does it matter?" she muttered indifferently. "A long time ago Father dug a fur cache under the main House, and from the cache a tunnel leads to the river. The trap door in the floor was hidden by a fur press. None of the Longbitmen knew of it. They kept me in that main room, and sometimes Gotch Ear was my guard, and he is a stupid animal. . . ."

"And you are such a clever girl." Bateau grinned. "Does he get drunk quick?"

She sat up. "You're evading me. Tell me, yes or no."

"You say they went north?" he asked.

She nodded. "The Oglalas are the strongest of the Sioux. Their consent would be the consent of all the Indians. You know where they've been pitching summer camp, up where the Shoshone meets the Big Horn. If Longbit wins their favor, there won't be a free trapper left in the Big Horns by next spring. And Portugee Phillips. . . ."

She broke off, biting her full underlip, the black pupils of her eyes growing big as she watched Bateau. He had stood, and his white teeth showed through his short, thick beard in a flat-lipped grin.

"Suicide." He chuckled. "Taking Portugee away from Benjamin Longbit. Suicide. Who said that?"

"Farness," she almost whispered. "Guidon. Kentucky."

"Like trying to take a cub from a mama grizzly," said Jacinto hopefully.

"*Oui*, like taking a cub from a grizzly." Bateau laughed.

Some of the hope left Jacinto's voice at that laugh, but he still tried. "You ain't going to do it, Bateau. I know you do some loco things. *Por supuesto*, not this, please not this. Not Longbit."

"Why not?" asked Bateau. "We'll get so fat sitting around up here Longbit can come and pot us like he was knocking a couple of *yalotis* off a spruce branch with a stick. Besides, Portugee Phillips has been my friend. You want yes or no, Mira? It's yes, by gar!"

Jacinto's eyes rolled upward, and he subsided back onto his fat hams, moaning sickly: "*Por Dios*, more fighting, more bloodshed. . . ."

"Perhaps you'd rather stay here?" Bateau grinned.

Jacinto gained his feet with that amazing agility. "Oh, no, Bateau, no, no. *Por supuesto*, it must be done, it must. Although it revolts me. I am already going to get my gun. See, I am going."

He waddled toward the stacked *aparejos*—the X-shaped pack saddles of leather padded with straw, used by the muleteers down Taos way. Mira looked after his bandy-legged figure, and her voice held a shadow.

"*Sí*, you had better get your gun," she said. "The minute you leave this valley, you'll be fair prey for every Longbitman from here to Prince Rupert's Land."

III

They headed north as soon as the girl had recovered. She had ridden her own mount to death. From his meager string of saddle stock, Bateau gave her a bay mare he had traded from a Santa Fé horse breeder. It was a single-foot, and Bateau watched for Mira to have trouble with the rare gait. It only took her a couple of good runs, however, to savvy the sideways turn to its gallop. Before they had left Hidden Valley, her seat was as easy as if she'd known the mare since it was foaled.

Bateau grinned to himself. *Sacre,* he thought, *w'at a woman!*

The gunsight notch, cut through the granite saddle by the creek, was so narrow they had to ride in the water itself. Finally the notch widened somewhat, and from ahead came the rumble of falls. The steep, rocky trail followed the waterfall down some two hundred feet, cutting sharply back and forth across the face of the cliff. At the bottom was a large pool, hung with misty foam from the tons of plunging water, and below the pool was the section of creek where Bateau had set his Lecroix. He gathered up his traps, stuffing what beaver had been caught into an *aparejo.* The pelts he had dressed filled one more pack. The rest of his mules were empty.

They hit the Big Horn and followed it north for two days, then cut back into the mountains, striking No Wood Creek. The girl cantered her little mare up beside Bateau.

111

"This is the way to Farness's camp. I told you he wouldn't help me."

"The least he can do is hold my outfit for me," said Bateau. "We won't make any speed with this whole pack train."

The beaver had been thick enough along No Wood for Farness to establish a permanent camp there the last three years. Bateau was first to ride into the clearing. The girl followed, and Jacinto trailed the mules, *guittara* thumping across his fat back with a hollow, twanging sound.

Farness was a big, lanky man with skin the texture of undressed buckskin. In place of a shirt he wore an unfolded Mexican serape, a hole punched in its center for his head, poncho style. He sat against a juniper on the opposite side of the clearing. It looked as if he had slid down the tree from a standing position, because some of the alligator bark had been scraped off and lay on his shoulders and in his lap. His mouth hung open; his eyes stared sightlessly at the riders as they came into the open.

"Voilà!" hissed Bateau.

He struck a moccasined foot into his buckskin's flank, skirting the smashed skinning frames, the scattered pile of empty *aparejos*. He slid from his saddle and squatted beside John Farness. Either of the bullets would have killed the man, the one through his neck or the one in his chest. They had seeped a lot of blood, the bullet holes, and Bateau didn't look very long.

The single-foot snorted behind him. The girl's voice shook a little. "I told you Longbitmen would be working over here soon enough. They must have come right after I left."

They buried Farness, and turned back into the main valley. It was four days north before they struck the next free trapper's camp. They came across Guidon's traps first, strung out along Two Crows Creek. There were some two dozen of them, big, heavy Lecroix traps, and each one had been carefully smashed so that it would never close on a beaver again.

Up on the slope, it was the same thing they had found at Farness's site. The skinning frames had been wrecked, the sod cabin stove in, the *aparejos* ripped and scattered and emptied of any plews they might have contained. Guidon was nowhere to be found.

Bateau left his pack animals there. Good browse grew in the coulées above the creek. He hoped the mules would stay in close enough so he could round them up when he got back—if he got back. . . .

It was a long, weary, heart-breaking ride from Guidon's desolate camp to where the Shoshone and the Big Horn met, up in the northern reaches of the great broad basin that lay between the Big Horn mountains on the east and the Shoshones on the west. When they finally came down out of the Big Horns and stopped there on a ridge that overlooked the Oglala encampment, the days behind them were a dim memory of riding from dawn to dark and of eating little and sleeping less.

Bateau swung off his jaded buckskin and led the girl and Jacinto up to the rim rock on their bellies. They lay there and looked down upon the meeting of the two great rivers, and on the summer campsite of the Oglala Sioux. Bateau's eyes under their shaggy brows had a feverish glow and there were hollows beneath his cheek bones. He pulled at his gold-shot beard, grown longer and matted now, and his glance swept the scattered skin lodges, the ant-like figures running back and forth through them, the knot of men gathered around a big campfire in the center of the teepees. Finally he pointed to a grove of aspens down by the Big Horn River, fluttering gold with coming summer.

"Longbit's there. See his horse lines under the tree."

Mira didn't say anything, but her breathing grew faster.

The ridge they were on formed a number of transverse ridges that ran down into the valley like the spreading fingers of a hand. Between each pair of ridges was a box cañon that gradually opened out into the main basin. In the mouths of one of these cañons the Sioux had planted their camp, and back farther they had herded their horses. Bateau nodded at the animals, spread out and grazing in the cañon below their ridge.

"An unfortunate place the Oglalas chose for that."

Jacinto was the only one who had lost no weight on the grueling ride. Other than the tight set that showed even beneath the layers of fat on his face, he revealed no sign of strain. "I don't see why," he said. "They make their camp like that a lot. The horses can't get out of the cañon because the teepees are in the way. It makes a natural corral."

"A lazy man's corral," said Bateau, "which is why you see merit in it. Suppose the herd stampeded? Think what it would do to that camp."

Jacinto pouted. "It would take a lot to stampede a loose-herded bunch of horses down the cañon. The Oglalas are not fools."

"They gather them in at night."

"And double the herders," countered Jacinto.

"Still," said Bateau, smiling thinly, "I think tonight will see a stampede of the first water. The Sioux have raided south far enough to have some Mexican horses, my Hyacinth. If you could cut out a Mexican stallion, its *manada* would follow you. The nighthawks gather their horses in after sundown. And if you stampeded your *manada* into the herd then. . . ."

"*¿Manada?*" said the girl.

114

"You haven't been south?" asked Jacinto.

"Not beyond the Platte," she said.

"The *dons* in New Mexico herd their horses in *manadas*," said Jacinto. "Each *manada* consists of a stallion and some twenty mares. After they have run together for some time, there is no separating them. Rope the stallion, and you have its *manada*. And like Bateau, he say, the Sioux have raided south."

Bateau motioned up the box cañon to where the benches of grazing animals thinned out. "The herd boys are below us now. You ought to be able to rope a stallion up there without letting them see you. There are plenty of draws where you can hide the *manada* so the nighthawks won't spot you when they come to draw the horses in. As soon as they have the herd gathered tight, stampede your bunch straight down the cañon and into them."

"And you?" asked the Mexican.

"I will be getting Portugee Phillips," said Bateau.

"Are you loco?" said Mira. "With the stampede going right through those teepees?"

"That's the idea," said Bateau. "Confusion . . . to put it mildly. Longbit and the Indians will be busy enough getting out from in front of those horses. I can't just walk in and ask him for your father, can I?"

"Then I'm going with you," said Mira.

He took an impatient breath. "There were about a dozen men with Longbit when he first came to the Portugee Houses. Would any of those same *hombres* be with him now?"

"Only Danny Gunn," she answered. "Gotch Ear is at the Houses. The others are on the trap lines."

"Then these men Longbit has with him here were imported from the river towns and arrived at the Houses after I left," said the French Canuck. "They've heard of me. They wouldn't know me by sight. But they would know you."

"He's my father, Batueau," she insisted. "I have as much right as you."

His voice raised a little. "One of Longbit's men would be sure to spot you. It would ruin everything."

"I'm going. . . ."

"*Sacre,*" he snarled suddenly, "I should know better than to argue with a squaw. Wait for me here until dawn, no longer. Jacinto, hold this wildcat till I'm gone."

He slid backward down the slope so he wouldn't be skylighted when he rose. He got to his feet and turned and swung off through the dusk, and behind him he could hear the girl struggling in Jacinto's grasp. The dusk had thickened by the time he reached the first lodges.

Fat squaws in dirty blankets waddled through the teepees, carrying greasy trade kettles of water from the river, bringing in wood. Naked papooses ran, squalling, underfoot. A pair of young hunters passed Bateau, one behind the other, a birch pole resting on the right shoulder of each Indian. Legs lashed to the pole so it hung upside down between them was a blacktail buck that had fallen to their arrows. Features were hardly distinguishable in the darkness, and, if they glanced at Bateau at all, it was with indifference. Patently they would take him for one of Longbit's imported *voyageurs*.

Down by Longbit's horse line a couple of tall Yankees were unhitching the string of pack mules, leading them one by one toward the center of camp. If Portugee Phillips's influence with the Indians needed any help, the whiskey and trade goods in those *aparejo* packs would be Longbit's bid.

A blocky figure materialized from behind a teepee, coming from the center of camp, and it wasn't any Indian. Bateau put his head down and kept going forward. The man was still walking when he spoke.

"What you doing up here? You know what Longbit told us about leaving the squaws be. Get down there with the others and start leading those mules in. . . ."

Bateau thought the man was going to walk on past him, but suddenly the chunky bulk of him stopped there. In the gloom, Bateau discerned the black hole of his opened mouth in the pale blur of his face. He spoke again thickly, and surprise was in his voice. He was looking past Bateau. "She's here," he said. "Mira Phillips!"

IV

Bateau didn't look around. He threw himself forward. But already the man had taken a step backward, clawing for the knife in his belt.

"She's here!" he was screaming. "She's here, Longbit! Mira Phillips . . . !"

Then Bateau's body hit him and they smashed into a teepee and rolled off onto the ground. Bellied down on the man, Bateau brought a hairy fist back to smash him in the face. He caught the metallic click of a cocked gun, and the coldest voice he had ever heard said: "That's all, Severn. Get up."

For the space of the breath Bateau took, his fist stayed poised like that. Then he rose. Danny Gunn stood there in the gloom. His six-shooter was pointed at Bateau. Bateau looked past him to the girl. He couldn't see the expression on her face. She made a small, helpless gesture with her hand.

"Bateau," she said, "I had to. . . ."

He was made for violent moods and his lips whitened with the raw anger that swept him. Then he shrugged. It had been his own fault really. Squaws were all right to dance with, and he had danced with every one west of St. Louis and should have left it at that.

"We'll go see Longbit," said Gunn. "He's in by the fire."

Bateau turned and walked past the man he had knocked down. He could hear Mira behind him, and Gunn. There was a big crowd around the main campfire. The outer circles were of women in red and black Navajo blankets. The smell of wood smoke and buffalo meat and sweat and bear grease that emanated from them almost gagged Bateau. Farther in were the younger bucks, black hair gleaming, eagle feathers nodding. The inner circles were made up of old men hunched cross-legged in their shaggy buffalo robes, smoking kinnikinnick in long pipes. Already some of the warriors were tipsy with the Taos Lightning and the Pass Brandy that Longbit had been giving them. The other sounds gave way to a single voice as Bateau shoved through. It was rolling and sonorous, orating in the long-winded manner so loved by the Indians.

"The free trappers have come into your hunting ground, harvesting the beaver that should be yours, hunting the game that is your rightful heritage, taking your squaws. . . ."

Benjamin Longbit towered over the others who stood around him, talking that way. Power sat well with him. His beak of a nose appeared even more rapacious, his strange, pale eyes more self-assured. He said something that made the Indians beat their feet against the ground and whoop. Smiling, he held up his hands to quiet them. Then he caught his first sight of Danny Gunn marching Mira and Bateau toward him. A slow, sardonic smile spread across Longbit's narrow, reddish-brown face, and he spoke with his hands still held up. "Well, it looks like we have one of those free trappers now. Come right in, Severn. Yes, come right in."

Beside Longbit sat Portugee Phillips, wrapped in a tattered Chimayo. There was a weary sag to his shoulders beneath the blanket. His dark eyes lacked the old fire. Most indicative of his utter defeat at Longbit's hands were the great gold earrings. They were dull and tarnished; they had not been polished for a long time.

Portugee rose when he saw his daughter, and the buffalo robe dropped from him, piling up at his feet. She ran to him and sagged against his chest and sobbed like a little girl. Bateau was suddenly sorry for any anger he had felt toward her. Longbit watched Portugee and his daughter with that cold smile, then he turned to Bateau.

"I gave you your warning down at the Houses, Severn. I told you what would happen if you didn't get out of Longbitland. Rumors have been coming in about your holding up in some hidden valley south of here. I didn't think you were quite that big a fool."

Suddenly Bateau felt himself stiffening. He had heard it. Beneath the buzzing talk of the braves and the grunts of the old men, beneath Longbit's words. No, not heard it, either. Felt it. Through his feet he had felt it. He grinned up at Longbit.

"Free trapper land, *m'sieu*. Not Longbitland," he said.

Longbit's smile faded. "I think I'll let the Indians have you. They possess a certain talent with things like that."

It was growing now. Not a sound yet, exactly, a certain trembling of the ground, an ominous shudder to the breeze. One or two of the old men in the crowd raised their heads. Mira Phillips quit crying. She shot a wide-eyed glance to Bateau. He pulled at his matted beard, nodding imperceptibly.

"Did you think you could come and take Portugee Phillips away, just like that?" Longbit asked.

"Did you think," said Bateau, "that you could keep me from it?"

"They told me you'd brag when the devil came to get you," said Longbit. "I didn't believe it until now."

More Indians were becoming aware of it. An old man stood in the inner circle, lifting his head to listen. The talk was stopping, and a heavy silence settled over the crowd.

Danny Gunn's face bore no expression, but his eyes shifted to Longbit for an instant. Bateau saw Longbit's thin smile disappear. The tall man tried to see over the heads of the crowd. Mira Phillips was flushing excitedly. Bateau turned his glance to Gunn finally. When it came, the cold-faced man would react somehow. That moment would be Bateau's only chance.

The two things happened about the same time. The trembling of the ground turned into a pulse beat of sound that rapidly became completely audible and completely recognizable to any man who had heard it before. And a brave pounded in through the lodges on a lathered horse, screaming in Sioux that the whole herd of horses was stampeding directly toward the village.

Gunn's reaction came then. Cold and indifferent though he was, he couldn't help that automatic, half-turning motion toward the Indian rider. Bateau had been waiting. He lunged forward sideways so his hip would strike across Gunn's belly, and he swiped viciously at the six-shooter with his left hand.

Gunn pulled the trigger before he had jerked all the way back toward Bateau. But the French Canuck's hand was already slapping the weapon aside, and the barrel jerked hot and hard against his palm. He felt the singe of lead across his side. Then his hip struck Gunn, and they went down.

Bateau got both hands on Gunn's right wrist, letting his momentum roll him on over the man. He bounced to his feet beyond Gunn's body with that arm held between his legs and twisted back over Gunn's head. The cold-faced man screamed, and the Paterson cap-and-ball dropped from his hand as he tried to wrench his twisted arm free. Bateau let go and fought through the milling, shouting crowd leaving Danny Gunn lying back there on the ground.

The girl was pulling her father toward where Bateau had

stood, and she bumped into the red-shirted French Canuck as he butted through a pair of running bucks. He screamed at them in order to be heard through the tumult.

"Longbit's horse lines! Over this way!"

Longbit came through the press of shifting bodies, elbowing, kicking, biting. He threw himself at Portugee, clawing his big Green River skinning knife out, sardonic mouth twisted with rage. Bateau was running behind Portugee and the girl. He caught a warrior by the arm, spinning him around and shoving him hard into Longbit. Both Oglala and white went down in a flailing mass of bare legs and buckskin leggings. Bateau caught Longbit's jarred curse as he hit the ground beneath the Indian.

Then Bateau was around in front of Portugee, plowing a way through the crazy mess for them. A big *voyageur* loomed up, a Longbitman. Bateau swept him aside with a backhand blow. A drunken brave stumbled into the way, and Bateau tripped him, and pulled Portugee over the fallen body.

The guard at the horse line was trying to fight off half a dozen frenzied Oglalas. Bateau jumped around him, knocked the reins of three horses free.

A red-bearded Yankee tried to mount one. Bateau ducked beneath the belly of his near mount and grabbed hold of the foot the man had thrust into the stirrup. He yanked the moccasin out and kicked the man in the stomach with one violent motion. The red-bearded Longbitman rolled away, bent double.

Mira helped boost her father into the saddle, then swung aboard herself. Bateau hit saddle leather without touching a stirrup, and the startled mount wheeled and reared before he was settled. Fighting to control the mare, he caught his first sight of the stampede.

Straight through the camp they thundered—pintos and

blacks and buckskins and grays, stallions and mares and geldings and colts, a roaring wave of tossing heads and rippling
manes and pounding hoofs, sweeping everything before
them, smashing teepees beneath them, scattering campfires,
running down Indians and Longbitmen alike. Along the
fringe of the stampede rode a madman shouting crazily in
Spanish, beating his huge sombrero against his buckskin leggings, shooting off his gun. Knocking constantly against the
eddying ranks of Indian ponies, he thundered down on Bateau. The French Canuck whacked the ends of his reins
across the rump of Portugee's horse, then he wheeled his own
mount and screamed at the man riding the stampede.

"Hyacinth! Over this way, you greasy old *paillard!*
Jacinto!"

The Mexican waved his huge hat at Bateau, then clapped
it to his black head and jammed his gun in leather, because it
would take both his hands and all his weight to veer his running horse. Bateau's slap had sent Portugee's horse bolting
through the lodges toward the Big Horn. With Mira just
ahead of him, and Jacinto following, Bateau whipped his animal into a headlong gallop.

He dodged through three teepees set in a triangle, jumped
a wailing papoose, barely missed the frantic squaw as she
came running for her baby. Jacinto caught up with him, re-
loading his gun, swaying in his gigantic California saddle.

"*¡Hola!*" he gasped, sweat streaming down his face. "I
haven't ridden a *caballo* like that since my *amorata's* father
had his men chase me out of Taos."

Shots slapped out behind them as they cut through toward
the grove of cottonwoods. Looking over his shoulder, Bateau
could see the pursuit. Somehow, Longbit had escaped the
stampede and had gathered half a dozen of his white-coated
voyageurs. His lanky, yellow-haired figure was plain beneath

the rising moon, rocking backward and forward to the gallop of a horse that looked ridiculously small beneath him.

Bateau jerked his mount aside before it could smash itself on the first tree, ducking a low-reaching branch. The moonlight came through the cottonwoods in a dappled pattern, flitting across them crazily as they thundered through the grove. Suddenly Bateau realized that Jacinto was no longer beside him. Behind him he heard more shots and the frenzied scream of a stricken horse. He jerked savagely on the cruel spade bit, rearing his animal up and around, careening back toward the sounds. The scream had come from Jacinto's mount. It lay on its side in an open patch of ground.

Peerless rider that he was, the Mexican must have jumped free as it went down beneath him, for he stood a few paces beyond the dead mount, his bandy legs spread wide. His fat fingers had never been made for skill with a trigger. He was a fanner.

He stood there with his incredible paunch stuck out proudly before him, knocking out a shot with every slap of his fat hand against the big single-action hammer. Already one Longbitman lay dead beneath his writhing horse on the fringe of the clearing.

"Y-a-a-h, you Longbit *malditos,* you pot-bellied *bastardos,* come out and get me!" yelled the gross Mexican. "You gobling *mujers.* Longbitmen . . . huh! *Castrados,* that's what you are, geldings . . . !"

Behind the Longbitman lying beneath his horse, a shadow flitted from one tree to another. Jacinto shouted, slapped his hammer. The Walker dragoon bellowed and bucked in his hand. There was a scream and the sound a heavy body makes pitching full length on the ground.

Then Bateau had wheeled his horse recklessly into the

clearing and up beside Jacinto. "Get on behind me, you loco Hyacinth."

Jacinto fanned his gun again. "Just one more, Bateau. Just let me get one more of those Longbit *borrachos.*"

A gun spoke out of the shadows. Jacinto grunted and bent over, but his hand slapped viciously at that hammer, and his gun roared again. Bateau threw himself from the frightened mount, grabbing Jacinto.

"One more, Bateau!" cried the Mexican, fighting him. "Just one more, please . . . !"

Even as Bateau lifted him onto the horse, Jacinto twisted around so he could knock out another shot. Then the French Canuck pushed the Mexican's wooden-heeled boot from the stirrup, jammed his own moccasin in, swung up behind the saddle. The mount leaped forward under his kick. They pounded out of the moonlit clearing with bullets slathering at the foliage above their heads.

The girl and her father sat their horses side-by-side in the shallows of the Big Horn. Bateau splashed his lathered mount into the water, holding the horse's head up so it wouldn't founder, turning to listen. But Jacinto's bellowing dragoon had stopped Longbit back there, and no pursuit was audible now.

"Longbit mentioned our valley to the south," said Bateau.

"He couldn't know where it is," Mira said. "Nobody knows but us here. Not even the free trappers. Longbit only heard the rumors, like I did from Guidon and Farness."

"Still, if he follows us, he'll expect us to go south," said Bateau. "I want to get back to Hidden Valley eventually. Right now we'll head north."

He turned his horse upriver, suddenly realizing how big and tall the animal really was. It towered above Mira's horse by three or four hands. The cantle of the saddle, too, must have climbed half a foot up Jacinto's fat hams, a California rig.

"Bateau," Mira said sharply, "you've got Longbit's mare!"

The singular thumping twang of Jacinto's *guittara* came mutedly across the campsite beside the spring in Vallejo Escondido, up where the red-tipped pine soughed in the warm breeze and the tame *yalotis* sat dumbly on the bowed spruce branch. The huge Mexican had attained his usual indolent position against a tree, and his desultory song had a touch of Taos in its lazy cadence.

Tu eres mi paloma blanca. . . .

Mira was spitting blacktail steak for the evening meal. Her father squatted by the fire. He never talked of what he had gone through at the Portugee Houses, but it was in the perceptibly deepened lines of his face, the lackluster of his eyes. There were things beside torture that could break a man. Portugee's whole life had been wrapped up in those log cabins down on the Powder, and his golden earrings still remained unpolished.

You are my white dove. . . .

"Is that the only song you know?" asked Mira.

"*Pues*"—Jacinto grinned—"why learn another when I can sing this one all the time?"

They had gone north from the Sioux camp for a day, then had circled into the Shoshones, returning through those mountains to Hidden Valley. Jacinto's wound hadn't been bad. He was almost beyond the grumbling stage. Spring was nearly over, the beaver were molting, and in a few weeks Bateau would have to gather in his traps until fall when the pelts became prime again. He sat by his skinning frames, graining a soft, dark plew.

Yo soy tu pichón azul. . . .

The line of horses suddenly began pulling at their tethers. One of them kicked and squealed excitedly. Bateau reached for his rifle without rising.

"If I was an Injun," said the man who had just stepped from the fringe of pine, "you'd all be corpses."

"Jacinto makes too much noise with his *guittara*." Bateau grinned. "But you did better than any Injun, Kentucky, finding this valley."

"I been hunting for it a couple of weeks," said Kentucky. "Just fool luck I spotted that gunsight notch where the creek comes in."

He moved wearily up toward them, his face bearing the haggard look of a man who had traveled fast and far. His buckskins were ripped and torn. There was a dark stain on his leggings, just above the knee, and he limped slightly. The sign for Bateau, however, was Kentucky's bullet mold, slung from his rawhide shoulder belt. Bateau saw that the iron plates were blackened with wood smoke, the rawhide wrapping on the wooden handles greasy and tattered and burned in places. Kentucky caught Bateau's eyes on the mold, and he glanced down at it, too, a wry grin twisting at his mouth.

"I ran enough balls in the last few days to supply Ashley's brigades all winter." He spat. "Longbitmen chased me clear down from Lake de Smet."

"You shuck of them now?"

Kentucky nodded. "I worked a fake trail over by Farness's

old camp. They'll be follering those tracks clear back to the lake before they realize their mistake."

"Sit down, then," said Bateau, "before you fall down."

Kentucky might have been thirty, or sixty. His face was seamed till it looked like old leather, but many young men got that way when they had been out in the sun and the wind long enough. He cuffed off his shaggy wolf-skin hat and threw it down beside him when he sat, and his hair was black and long and queued like a Pueblo Indian's.

"You said Longbitmen," muttered Bateau, hunkering down.

"That's right," said the trapper. "When you stole Portugee, Longbit couldn't make the Oglalas promise not to trade with us independent trappers. It didn't stop the yellow-haired varmint none. His brigades are over on this side of the Big Horns now, and right down into the basin. I reckon you come across what happened to Farness on your way north after Portugee. That's what happens to any free trapper those Longbitmen come across. There aren't many free men left, Bateau. But word's out among them that are still sticking to their Jake Hawkins guns."

Bateau looked at him from beneath heavy brows. "What you mean, word's out?"

"About you, Bateau," said Kentucky. "That's why I was hunting for you down here. I met a kyesh named Humprib up by the lake. Remember him?"

"I worked the streams with him years ago."

Kentucky nodded. " 'If the Longbitmen cut your trail,' this Humprib says to me, 'if the Longbitmen cut your trail, you hunt up Bateau Severn. He's down south somewhere, holed up in a hidden valley. He's the craziest, wildest, braggin'est coot in the Big Horns, but he's squatting right in the middle of Longbitland and thumbing his nose at the big, yellow-haired weasel bear, and it's the only place north of the Platte you'll be safe.' "

Bateau tugged uncomfortably at his sunburned beard. "Humprib told you that?"

"He did," said Kentucky, "and, like I said, there's still a small passel of free trappers left. Not many, but a few. They'll be coming in, Bateau, like I came."

The girl had straightened from her blacktail steaks, and her eyes shone in the firelight. Jacinto stopped thrumming his *guittara*. Bateau stood up, absently shoving a piece of wood farther into the fire with his worn Ute moccasin.

"Why should they come here?" he grunted. "I can't help them any. Longbit will find this valley sooner or later, just like you did. It isn't any safer here."

"It ain't the valley so much," said Kentucky. "It's you, Bateau. You were the only one to buck Longbit down at the Houses. Nobody would've even dreamed of trying to get Portugee away from Longbit and all those Oglalas. You did it."

Bateau jerked his head with an impatient grunt. "*Sacre bleu.* I still can't see why they come here. . . ."

"Oh, you fool," cried Mira suddenly, stepping around the fire and coming up to him. "One of the reasons Longbit has run all over the independent trappers is because they have no organization, no leader. Can't you see they're beginning to look toward you as that leader?"

"She's right," said Kentucky. "That's sort of the way I felt."

"*Parbleu,*" declared Bateau angrily. "I've trailed alone all my life. I'm no leader. What would I do with a whole possible sack full of trappers coming in here?"

"You wouldn't know what to do with them?" mocked the girl, putting her hands on her hips. "You'd have a whole army of free trappers, and you wouldn't know what to do with them? They were right when they said you were the craziest coot in the Big Horns. You'll get drunk and sneak your harvest of plews through a whole war party of Blackfeet like you did last year. You'll fight savate in your bare feet against a wildcat. You'll take Portugee Phillips right from under the noses of Longbit and all his *borrachos* with all the Oglalas thrown in for good measure. You'll do all those crazy things because you're crazy yourself and you like to do them, the way a bear enjoys honey. But when it comes to settling down to a steady fight and taking responsibility on your shoulders, that's different. You are Bateau! You've trailed alone all your life. You don't want to be saddled with a whole possible sack full of free trappers!"

"*Sacre bleu.* . . ."

"Shut up," she panted. "You couldn't have stopped Longbit, anyway. You're like a racehorse. You can go fast, but you haven't got any bottom. You're nothing but a crazy, wild trapper who spends all season gathering pelts and then throws away the money he gets for them in a week's drunk down at the Portugee Houses. That's what you are, and that's what you'll always be, and anybody who thinks different is as loco as you are. . . ."

She turned and stumbled toward the sod shack they had built, and the way her shoulders were hunched up and shaking Bateau knew she was crying. He held out his hands in a helpless gesture.

"*Sacre,* w'at a woman," he said. "I didn't know she hated me so much."

"Sometimes, when a woman gets that riled about a man," said Portugee Phillips, "it means she's in love."

V

Bateau Severn stood knee deep in the quiet pool below the falls that came out of the gunsight notch, and the morning shadows fell across him somberly. The beaver were thick in the creek here outside Vallejo Escondido. They built their lodges beneath spreading bowers of cottonwoods and formed their slides on the slick rises above the dark pools.

Two weeks had passed since Kentucky came to their camp. Bateau realized that it must have laid at the back of his mind ever since Longbit first came to the Portugee Houses, but it had taken the girl to bring it out into the open and show him what must be done—and now he no longer avoided the certain knowledge that the battle between him and Longbit had settled down into a steady, deliberate, terrible thing that would end in but one, inevitable way.

Morning sun came meagerly down through the browning cottonwoods, casting a few vagrant patterns of dappled light across the west bank. The cold gloom laying over the rest of the pool suddenly struck Bateau as ominous. He shrugged. They had been talking too much of Longbit, that was all. A woodpecker broke into a tattoo somewhere upstream. Bateau turned jerkily, checked himself halfway around. *Nom d'un chien!* Like an old woman.

The shadows on the east bank fell across him with a strange, dark portent as he bent to the trap. Slung on his shoulder belt was a horn full of beaver medicine made from

131

the bark stone of the male beaver, nutmeg, whiskey. It was supposed to attract the animals, and it had such a foul odor that a man who used it stank like a polecat from one end of the season to the other. Bateau pulled the stopper of the horn and smeared some of the medicine on a stake fastened to the Lecroix.

The beavers were strange, gregarious creatures. They lived in clans and built bridges and lodges together, and had a singular method of warning each other when danger was near. A man did well to heed the frantic slap of their broad tails against the water, just as he did well to recognize a warning in the sudden cessation of the bird's song when a human being approached. Bent over, corking up the horn of beaver medicine, the sudden, loud slapping of a beaver's flat tail from somewhere downstream ran through Bateau like a tocsin. He let go the horn and straightened and took one swift step shoreward. Then he stopped.

The man stood in the gloom beneath the cottonwoods on the east bank. His mouth was an enigmatic slash in a dark, impassive face. His unreadable eyes were motionless behind narrowed lids, yet Bateau sensed they had seen everything necessary. He stood with heavy shoulders thrust forward slightly so that his thick neck sunk into their slope and his voice was flat. It held no humor when he spoke.

"I'm Adam Weaver," he said. "I've come to kill you."

For a moment, Bateau was taken off guard. Finally he managed a thin smile. "Longbitman?"

"My own man," said Adam Weaver, then he glanced toward the tall mare ground-hitched beside a pack mule. "Taking that hoss didn't set well with Longbit. I wager he's as peeved about you getting his mare as he is about Portugee Phillips. He's got a price on your head, Bateau, five hundred dollars to any man who brings in your scalp. I told him I would."

"Why didn't you pick me off from above?" asked Bateau, trying to fathom the man.

"Any man that I can't kill with my bare hands," said Adam Weaver, leaning his long rifle against a tree, "ain't wu'th the killing."

Bateau laughed suddenly, began to wade ashore. "By gar, Adam Weaver, I've been trying to figure you out. But you don't need figuring. You came up to kill me, just like that. No guns, not even Green Rivers. Bare hands. You're a man after my own heart."

Weaver crossed his arms and pulled his buckskin jacket up over his head. It caught on the bulk of his chest for a moment. Then he stood naked to the belt and his waist was as broad and square as his chest, and there wasn't an ounce of fat on him.

Bateau unbuttoned his red shirt and took it off. He was lighter than the other man, more lithe about the belly, more slender in the hips and legs. Yet two of the things that had come to him poling *bateaux* up and down the Missouri hadn't left him. One was his name. The other was the singular strength and development a man got in the shoulders and upper back when he worked on the river. It was a hidden strength, a deceptive development.

He took a step and bent forward slightly, flexing his shoulders to loosen them. A surprising hump of muscle rolled up thickly on either side of his neck, rippling beneath the fine, white skin like an awakened snake, coursing down into his back, and finally subsiding as he relaxed.

There was a certain new respect in the way Adam Weaver moved in to meet him. Bateau licked his lips, drew them back flat against his teeth in that wolfish grin.

"All right, Adam Weaver," he yelled, "come and get my scalp if you can!"

They met with the slapping, fleshy sound that drew a grunt of expelled air from each of them. Sand spurted from beneath their churning feet. Bateau dug his elbow experimentally into Weaver's belly; it had the consistency of a pig of Galena lead. Weaver's ham-like fist smashed into his face in a wicked, driving hook. Mouth filled with blood, head roaring, Bateau slid down until his shoulder was digging into the other's square, hard groin. He braced his feet. That lump of muscle ridged up across the shoulders, and he shoved.

As Weaver fell over backward, he hit Bateau behind the neck in a vicious rabbit punch. Then the square-bellied man was on his back, and Bateau sprawled forward into the sand under the blow. They regained their feet like cats, and circled, and Bateau had a pretty good measure of the man who had come to kill him.

He spat blood, gasping: "*Sacre bleu*, I haven't had a fight like this since the river."

Weaver lowered his head and came in like a rutting bull. Bateau side-stepped and lifted a moccasined foot in a high, hard kick that caught the other man on the side of his head and bowled him over and over into the shadows of the creek.

"That's savate, Adam Weaver, that's the way they fight on the Missouri. Do you know savate?"

Weaver got up, dripping water, choking. "I know savate. Do you know the Flying Dutchman?"

He came out of the water in a pounding drive, launching himself in a sudden, headlong dive. Bateau tried to spin away, but his foot slipped in the mud, and Weaver's Flying Dutchman caught him dead center.

They went down together, rolling until they brought up against a tree. Weaver was on top. He got one thick forearm behind Bateau's neck, shoved the heel of his other hand into Bateau's bearded chin. When he put on the pressure, Bateau could feel his neck bending backward like a hickory bow, vertebræ grinding together. He drove a desperate jab into Weaver's belly, and he should have known better. He tried to arch the man off, and it was just as useless as the jab. A crackling pop echoed down his spine and spread out over his back in a flood of blinding pain. Straddling Bateau, Weaver set himself for the last pressure that would break the French Canuck's neck. Then Bateau got his arm levered against Weaver's chest, and his shoulders rippled and bulged, and, while he held Weaver locked for that moment, he drove upward with his bent knee.

Weaver didn't make any noise. He rolled away and lay flat on his back in the churned sand, incapacitated long enough for Bateau to grope blindly over to him. Feeling the man's body beneath him, Bateau reached for his long, greasy hair. He twisted his fingers through it and sat on Weaver's hard belly and began hitting him in the face with his free fist. Weaver jerked weakly to one side. Bateau jerked him back by his hair and slugged his face again.

Weaver got his thick hands up on Bateau's arm. Gasping, Bateau slugged again. Weaver grunted, and it was the first sound he'd made. Again, Weaver's hand slid down Bateau's arm. Again! Weaver lay still beneath Bateau.

It took a long moment for Bateau to gather the strength for rising. He tried to walk to the stream. He fell full length with his face in the water. It revived him, and, after washing the blood and sand off himself, he dragged the unconscious Weaver to the stream. He sat there, shaking and panting, waiting for the cold water to bring the man around. Finally Weaver sat up. He shook his head, choked, spat, regarded Bateau solemnly.

"Nom d'un chien," gasped Bateau. "If I wasn't the toughest *homme* north of Mexico City, Adam Weaver, you'd be."

The other wiped blood off his face with the back of his hand. "You're the first man who ever licked me, Bateau, guns or Green River blades or bare hands or otherwise. I think I'll stay here a while."

"But you came to kill me."

"And you showed me it couldn't be done," said Weaver. "Where I made my mistake was seeing Longbit before I saw you. That error's corrected now, and I think I'll stay here a while."

Still blowing and quivering like a wind-broken horse, Bateau got to his feet. "By gar, Adam Weaver, I think you and Jacinto will make a pair."

Stiff and sore and bloody, they climbed through the gunsight notch and followed the creek through Hidden Valley up toward the spring. Weaver forked a stud as solid and square-bellied as himself. Bateau rode Longbit's tremendous mare.

"You're a fool to set your lines outside this valley," said Weaver. "I spotted 'em first off and knew all I had to do was wait around for you to come."

Bateau's heavy brows drew together. "I don't know how to put it exactly, Weaver. There aren't any beaver inside the valley. One of Longbit's biggest aims up here is to drive the free trappers out. Whether he discovers my trap lines or not, he's bound to find Hidden Valley sooner or later. More and more men are getting to know about it. If I pulled my traps out because of him, it would be admitting he'd licked me."

Weaver swiped a gash on his bruised face. "I see what you mean, in a way. And I see what was wrong with both me and Longbit when we came to dealing with you. We did a powerful sight of underestimating."

The ring of axes came down through the spruce to them, and Weaver glanced upslope, and Bateau grinned.

"Bent built a fort down on the Arkansas," he said. "Bridger, on Black's Fork of the Green. And now, Bateau. . . ."

They broke into the clearing, and he raised his arm. The timber had been cut away on all sides of the rising fort. No approach was possible without utter exposure to guards on the half-finished wall of undressed white pine logs, set stockade-style, fifteen feet tall and sharpened at the top.

"Kentucky said they would be coming in, the free trappers," Bateau told Weaver, "and he was right. That long drink of water chopping the pine for the wall is Thomas Hunter. He was an axe man in Tennessee before he turned trapper. That bald-headed *homme* came last Monday. He was a blacksmith once, and he's going to make us a pair of iron-bound gates that will stand against a herd of buffalo. . . ."

He cut off suddenly. In the temporary camp above the fort a string of pack horses was drawn up, and a crowd was gathered around the rider at their head, a rider who wore a long eagle feather in his roached hair. Bateau kicked the mare into a trot, muttering: "*Mon Dieu,* an Oglala."

Portugee Phillips was in the crowd, and Kentucky, and Mira. There were many trappers among the Indians. They had formed a big part of Portugee's business, selling their plews for trade goods he shipped in from St. Louis.

"W'at is it?" Bateau asked. "A Sioux, here."

The Indian turned. His face had a hawk-like cast to its sharp features; his black eyes glittered with a hard intelligence. He wore a gaudy Navajo blanket and his bare legs forked his scrawny nag loosely, the muscles in them standing out like drawn bowstrings.

"We always brought our pelts to Portugee down at the

Houses," he said in Spanish. "Now we learn he is here. There will be others behind me."

Bateau glanced involuntarily at Kentucky. *There will be others behind me . . .* the old trapper had said the same thing. And now the Indians.

"*Parbleu,*" said Bateau, "we have no trade goods. We haven't even got any money. We can't let you have guns or powder. You know that."

"Portugee Phillips is here?" asked the Oglala bluntly.

Bateau nodded. "Of course. You see him."

"You are here?"

"But, yes. . . ."

"It is enough," said the Sioux. "I'll leave my pelts with you. When Benjamin Longbit is driven out, you'll be able to get trade goods again. You can pay me then."

He dismounted and began to unlash his *aparejos,* tossing the square bales of peltries to the ground. Bateau kneed his horse forward, opening his mouth to protest. Portugee Phillips grabbed at his stirrup leathers.

"Wait a minute, Bateau," said the old man. "Don't you see, it's like the Portugee Houses all over again. First the free trappers coming in, now the Indians. What you know, I think I'll go polish my earrings."

The old man trotted off down the slope, cackling.

Bateau swung down, aware that Mira was watching him intently. He put a hand self-consciously to the purplish bruise on his cheek.

"What happened to you?" she asked.

"You said I was crazy enough to fight savate barefoot with a wildcat." He grinned. "I was."

Adam Weaver still forked his stud where he had stopped it behind Bateau's mare. His face was even more cut up than Bateau's. There were slashes where the French Canuck's knuckles had split the flesh across his cheek bones, his lips were swollen and puffy, one eye was closing and turning blue.

"This is Adam Weaver," said Bateau.

There was a light to the girl's eyes. "Did you tangle with a wildcat, too?"

"No," said Weaver solemnly, "a grizzly. Which a wildcat is no match for. And which yellow-haired polecats are no match for, either."

"I never saw a polecat with yellow hair."

"There's one down at the Portugee Houses right now," said Weaver.

Bateau told Weaver to feed his horse and himself, and he left Kentucky to count the Sioux's peltries. He slipped the reins over his mare's head and turned to lead her toward the fort. The girl followed him, slipping her hand into his free arm. Her black hair shimmered and gleamed like a wet beaver plew, swinging with her stride. There was a strange, sweet scent to it that thickened the blood in Bateau's throat. *Sacre, w'at a woman could do to a man.* He was realizing more and more how much he wanted her. Yet, whenever she came close like this, he had to think of Squawman Samuels and all the other squawmen he had known. Never Squawman Bateau. Never!

"Was it a good fight?" she asked him.

"Weaver," he said, "will be a valuable addition."

"Still the same crazy, wild Bateau." She laughed. "Always ready to fight or get drunk or do something loco. Yet different in a way. There's something new in you. Maybe it's the responsibility, or the fort."

He grinned—he liked to talk about the fort. "Dutchie Peters was a journeyman carpenter before he took up the traps. He's building the cabins inside the fort out of dressed pine logs, dovetailed like the Portugee Houses, with shake roofs and even barn sash windows. He says they'll be so tight a heel fly won't be able to find a way in. We're sinking a room in the northwest corner for the powder, too."

"It will be a good fort," she said. "In a way, I'm almost glad Benjamin Longbit tried to take over the Big Horns. In the old days, I saw you once a month at best, sometimes no more than once a year. Think how much we can be together this way."

He tried to disengage her hand suddenly, but she only slipped it in farther. He swallowed the choked-up lump in his throat, humping his shoulders uncomfortably, muttering in his short beard: "*Sacre*, never Squawman Bateau . . . never!"

"What did you say?" she asked.

"*Rien,*" he mumbled. "Nothing."

The days passed like a herd of blacktail deer flitting through the dark forest on their run from a harrying timber wolf. The cottonwoods down in the bottom of the valley had been turned sere and brown by summer, and now they were dropping their foliage, and the beaver had quit molting and were growing their pelts thick and glossy again in nature's preparation for the coming winter. The free trappers were still coming into Hidden Valley and, with them, word of Longbit. The yellow-haired man's lobo brigades had the whole area under their control now.

The wind that came down off the ridges had a chill touch of early fall, and Bateau sat in the dim light of the cabin Jacinto had named the Beaver Room. The walls were piled high with bales of pelts and there was a heavy, musty smell in Bateau's nostrils as he sat cross-legged on the floor, fleshing a plew. Before him was a smooth birch log about three feet long, two pegs raising one end, the other end resting on the puncheon floor. The plew laid spread out on the log, fur side down. Meticulously Bateau scraped all the fat from the stiff hide. Then he reached into a wooden bowl by his side for the beaver brains used to make the pelts pliable. He was working the brains patiently into the fleshed skin when he heard the hard pound of horse's hoofs from outside, the hubbub of excited voices. He wiped his hands on greasy leggings and went to the door.

Jacinto's blowing horse stood in the open space left for the guns. He saw Bateau and he kneed the animal through the men who had gathered around him.

"They've come, Bateau, they've come," he panted. "I was riding guard above timberline. I could see the whole valley. They didn't come through the notch. From over the mountains behind me, right down through the talus. A dozen of them. Fifty. I don' know, maybe a hundred."

"W'at are you talking about?" Bateau asked him, but he already knew.

"Longbitmen," said the Mexican, wiping his sweating face. "And Benjamin Longbit himself!"

For the first few moments after that there was confusion. Mira and her father came running from the two-story building set against the back wall of the fort. Sneed, the baldheaded blacksmith, wanted to set his gates up before Longbit came. He tried to get half a dozen trappers to help him. There would be no time for that, and Bateau had to argue him out of it. Then the French Canuck sent a runner into the timber for Thomas Hunter and his axe men, cutting the logs to fill the last gap in the wall. Things settled down after that.

There were over a dozen men in the fort now, and Bateau placed them as best he could. He put Sneed and three others to building a barricade across the open gate. When Hunter came in, he put the tall, skinny Tennessee woodcutter and his crew on the catwalk that ran around the four sides of the fort behind the wall. Portugee went with Sneed to load the rifles. Bateau took Weaver and Jacinto and Kentucky to the hole remaining in the wall, on the north side of the main building. There were piles of débris for cover, and Weaver hunkered down behind one, turning to Bateau.

"Most of the Longbitmen are scattered from the Houses to Lake de Smet, still trapping," he grunted. "Longbit was going to wait till winter set in before he hunted you out. That way he could use all his men without losing any furs. I don't think this is the real business."

Bateau began loading his Jake Hawkins. "Maybe he was hunting streams with his brigade in those mountains to the east and just happened to climb into this valley. How many men does he have to a brigade?"

"Don't know exactly," said Weaver. "Ashley ran a hundred men in his, but I don't figure Longbit has more'n fifteen or twenty to a bunch."

Jacinto took out his Walker dragoon and checked the loads with a grimace. "*Caracoles,* all this work building the fort has been hard enough on my delicate sensibilities. Now we have to fight. More bloodshed, more pain. And I was born a man of peace, made only to sing and eat and laugh. Not to work and fight. I can't bear much more of this."

The tip of a deer horn formed Bateau's charge cup, suspended from the bottom of his powder horn by a buckskin thong. He unstopped the powder horn with his teeth, filling the charge cup level with fine black grains of Dupont, pouring the powder carefully down his rifle barrel.

"*Oui.*" He grinned. "You hate to fight. It pains you. It was pure agony for you to shoot those Longbitmen when we got Portugee."

Jacinto's face twisted sickly, and he covered his eyes with a fat hand. "Do you have to remind me of my past sin? The memory clabbers my blood. All those poor *hombres* on the Big Horn, all those poor *hombres*."

On the right side of the Jake Hawkins oak stock was a hinged plate of brass, covering the trap that contained grease and linen patches. Opening the brass cover, Bateau took out a patch, greasing it.

"*Oui,* those poor *hombres*." He grinned, then he mimicked the Mexican. " 'One more, Bateau, just one more. Longbitmen . . . hah! *Castrados*, that's what you are, geldings. Just one more, please let me get just one more.' "

"Bateau, stop!" moaned the Mexican, eyes rolling upward. "I didn't say that. Please, tell me I didn't. Fighting is one of the two greatest sins in the world. That I should revel in it like a drunk is unthinkable."

Laughing, Bateau took a half-ounce ball of Galena lead from his cat-tail shot pouch. He rested it on the greased patch and slipped it into the muzzle, ramming it home hard enough to touch the powder and yet not crush the grains. "I wouldn't want to hurt your delicate sensibilities," he said with a long face. "Maybe you'd better go into the main building and find a possible sack to stick your head in till it's all over."

"Oh, no," said Jacinto hurriedly. "No, no . . . after all, where a thing is necessary, it is necessary. I wouldn't want you to think me a coward. Just sensitive, Bateau, a gentle soul thrust haplessly into a cruel world where all men do is work and fight. Oh, a cruel. . . ."

The girl slid in behind them. "Everything is ready."

Bateau nodded, then pointed to the fringe of timber upslope. "They're coming from the ridge. The first *homme* to show himself will wish he hadn't."

Kentucky absently scratched at the lice in his greasy hair.

"That's too far, Bateau. They'll see the fort afore they come into the open. They'll break from that timber a-running and a-shooting. It would be impossible to hit a still target at that distance, much less a moving one."

"*Sí,*" said Jacinto. "Nobody could hit a man that far away, not even Benjamin Longbit himself."

"What?"

"Not even you, Bateau," hastened the Mexican. "Not even the great Bateau himself."

"That's better," growled Bateau. "I thought for a minute you believed Longbit's lie. Just because he says he's the best shot in the world doesn't make him so. He couldn't be, anyway, because I am. And I don't have to brag about it. Everybody knows I am matchless on a Jake Hawkins."

Grinning, he squatted down and pressed the set trigger into position; now the rear trigger would go off at a touch. He checked the screws on his flint, tightening them with the blade of his knife. *Bien.*

"You watch now, and I'll show you who can make this shot and who can't," he said, shoving his gun out over a pile of débris.

He sprawled onto his belly, putting his cheek gently against the dark oaken stock of the gun. He wet his finger and held it up to the wind. From the north and the west. *Bien.* He squinted down the four-foot barrel until both sights were clear. He lifted his shoulder against the butt plate, tilting the gun down a trifle. Just so. *Bien.*

It became very still. The girl's breathing was audible. Weaver settled back against the logs, unreadable eyes going from Bateau to timberline. Jacinto still muttered.

"*Caracoles,* an impossible shot."

"Shut up," said Bateau.

Then Weaver leaned forward and the sound of the girl's

144

breathing stopped. They must have seen it about the same time Bateau did, that slight movement among the trees so far across the clearing. Bateau's left hand slid forward along the stocked barrel of his Jake Hawkins; his right moved up until his index finger was curled around the set trigger. He wet his lips.

There was more shadowy movement among the trees, then a long wait while Longbit was apparently getting the lay of the land. The free trappers hadn't yet dug out the series of huge boulders strung across the cleared space between fort and timberline and their bulk formed the only cover in that open stretch of ground.

The Longbitmen broke into the open as Kentucky had said they would, running hard toward those rocks, shooting as they came. There were a dozen strapping *voyageurs* in their dirty white blanket coats, London Fusils blazing, and a handful of renegade trappers. The first of them to appear out of the spruce trees was Bateau's target, an incredibly tall man with yellow hair that streamed out behind him and an exceedingly long Jake Hawkins gun bucking at his hip. Benjamin Longbit.

Bateau sighted low, leading the loping figure. His finger pressed the trigger. The mainspring jumped with an even, velvety click beneath the sure pressure; the Hawkins bellowed. With the echoes slapping dully up the slope, Bateau raised his head slightly, peering through the curl of gray smoke. He heard Mira expel her breath with a hissing sound. Disappointment rode Jacinto's Spanish curse. Benjamin Longbit's loping stride hadn't broken a fraction, and he took a last long step and dove into the corner of the first boulder.

For a moment Bateau's face was blank. He rose to his knees, eyes still turned in an unbelieving way upslope. His heavy brows drew down suddenly, and he whirled to the

Mexican. Jacinto snuffled, wiped his nose, refused to meet Bateau's gaze. Bateau turned to Weaver. The enigmatic man's eyes were watching the timberline. Finally Bateau looked at the girl, and she was the only one who would meet his eyes, and her look held a strange sort of compassion.

"All right," he said harshly, and took a breath. "So I missed."

He settled down to load his gun again. Neither Kentucky nor Weaver had fired, because the shot was a long one, and Longbit and his men were all safely into the cover of the boulders. More of Bateau's men came to the rear wall now that they knew the direction of the attack.

Weaver spoke finally, uncomfortably, still not looking at Bateau. "I still don't think Longbit'll force it. He didn't bring enough men, and he ain't the kind to play unless the odds are stacked his way."

He was right. Longbit and his men worked through the rocks carefully, coming a little nearer. The firing was desultory. Sneed got a ball through the shoulder. Kentucky caught a big French *voyageur* who exposed too much of himself from behind a boulder. Dusk fell softly, and Bateau was the first to see Longbit's retreat, mere shadows flitting through the semidarkness back into the forest.

Jacinto rose excitedly from behind the barricade. "They're running, Bateau!" he shouted, jumping across the pile of logs. "We've got them running. Look at the *pendejos!* Y-a-a-h, Longbitmen, come back and fight!"

Bateau tried to grab him but he was already outside the fort, waddling uphill in his bandy-legged stride, slapping at his Walker dragoon, emptying the gun at the shadows melting into timberline. Bateau leaped out after him.

"Hyacinth!" he shouted. "Come back, you fat fool!"

Bateau was only a few paces out from the fort when the last

Longbitman disappeared into the timber. Jacinto wasn't much farther beyond. It was a long shot from the trees to the Mexican, practically as long as the one Bateau had tried, and missed. When Bateau saw that flitting, unreal movement beneath the spruce, a sudden fear turned him sick. He hardly recognized his own voice.

"Hyacinth!"

Bateau didn't hear the shot until after he saw the Mexican jerk suddenly and bend over forward. Then the sharp detonation came to him, wafted downslope by the wind. Jacinto was still staggering uphill, desperately trying to remain upright. With each jerky step, his prodigious torso sagged farther forward. Like a top-heavy doll he finally went onto his face, right foot kicking out from beneath him, then left foot.

Bateau reached him, rolled him over. The bullet had punctured Jacinto's *charro* vest directly over the braided left breast pocket. Adam Weaver came out and stood there in the lowering night, looking down at the dead Hyacinth, then the girl, and the others. If the Longbitmen were still in the timber, it was too dark now for them to hit anyone else. Finally Kentucky spoke.

"Powerful long shot from the trees. I wouldn't believe it if I hadn't seen it with my own eyes."

"I still can't believe it," choked the girl.

Bateau's face was bleak and empty, his voice hollow. "Benjamin Longbit always did claim he could shoot a Jake Hawkins gun better than any man in the world."

VI

The fort was finished now, and there were more than twenty free trappers sleeping within its walls regularly, besides the Sioux who passed through bringing their pelts. The beaver were taking to their lodges, and the wind whining down off the ridge held winter in its knifing chill. The day came when Bateau realized how thick the carpet of autumn leaves had grown beneath his feet down on the creekbanks below the falls and how naked the aspens and the cottonwoods appeared against the slate-colored sky. It was time to put his Lecroix away in their buckskin trap sacks and to wash the stench of beaver medicine off him for good. There was no reluctance in him at this. He was ready for winter, and Longbit. The cabins were as tight as Dutchie Peters had promised, and the iron-bound gates of the blacksmith, Sneed, would stand against all the buffalo bulls in the Big Horns.

The first snow came a week after Bateau had taken in his trap lines, sweeping down from the north ridges and hunting out the coulées and draws, filling them deeply and banking up in soft, white drifts against the base of the stockade. And with it came Squawman Samuels.

He appeared one morning at the gate, a pitiful figure staggering out of the white-snowed spruce and across the clearing. They let him in and crowded around him by the big fur press in the middle of the courtyard. He had tied a tattered Chimayo blanket around his gaunt torso in place of a shirt and had walked his Paiute moccasins through; his foot-steps leading from the gate to the press had a stain on them, dark, significant. He hung onto Bateau's shaggy buffalo coat, hands shaking.

"Bateau," he babbled, "you've got to take me in, got to. Longbit just as soon kill me as fast as not if he found me. Bateau, you've got to. . . ."

Bateau supported him reluctantly, the contempt in his dark eyes giving way to a certain pity. "You wouldn't come with me that first time, Samuels. What changed your mind?"

Samuels's haggard face twisted, lower lip trembling. "Most of those damn' Longbitmen are scum up from Saint Looey town and Saint Joe and the other river places. Not one in ten is a real trapper. Up here, not seeing a white woman year in and year out, you know how they get. I shouldn't have stayed at the Portugee Houses, I guess, but Longbit made me. He kept his men in hand for a while. Then one night a bunch of *voyageurs* came in with a month's harvest of plews. They threw a drunk, and my woman. . . ." He broke off, sobbing, cursing bitterly.

Bateau's mouth thinned; he looked around the circle of men. Mira broke through and put her arm around Samuels.

"We'll take him in, Bateau. We've got to."

Bateau's heavy brows drew together. "He's been in Longbit's camp a long time. We're in no position to take a chance."

"You let the others in without question," she flared. "You let Adam Weaver in, and he came here to kill you."

Bateau glanced from Weaver to Samuels, and his comparison of the two men was plain in his face. Mira tossed her dark head, ordering a pair of trappers to take Samuels into the main hall and feed him. When they were gone, she turned back to the French Canuck.

"I didn't want to say it in front of him, but what harm can a poor squawman do? He hasn't enough life left in him to spit, much less harm us."

"An old, spavined, flea-bit gelding can cause a stampede if you put him in the middle of a herd," he said thinly.

But he let Samuels stay, because there was nothing else to do. Patently the man would die out in the woods. The main hall was a square, two-storied structure backed up against the rear wall, its porch stretching across the front and facing the inner courtyard. Every morning Samuels hunkered down there in the new Navajo blanket Mira had given him, lifeless eyes staring blankly at the activity around the fur press. Bateau tried to put him to work, for everyone had a job. But it was useless, and he gave up in disgust. He was preoccupied with the powder room, anyway. They had sunk it at the northwest corner of the fort, flanking the main building, and were lining its walls with rocks. Already there were many kegs of Dupont stored there, some brought in by the Indians, some by a wandering trader up from Taos.

The night before they were going to roof the sunken chamber, Bateau climbed to the catwalk that ran around the four walls, leaving enough of the white pine logs above its level to form a breastworks the height of a man's head, with loopholes at every third foot. A wind howled through the snow-heavy forest outside, peopling its empty corridors for a time with sibilant voices. Then it stopped, and silence lay over the valley as thick as the blanket of snow covering the cleared space around the stockade. Weaver was captain of the guard. He and Bateau stood side-by-side for a time. The French Canuck hunched down into his buffalo coat.

"So quiet, by gar. I don't like it."

Weaver cocked an ear toward the corral built behind the fort with its entrance through the rear wall. "Animals seem all right. They'd give the first sign. We're snug here, Bateau. Ain't all the Longbitmen in the world can take us now. Longbit knows that. He found it out the last time he was here."

"That's just it," said Bateau. "The next time he comes, he'll know what he's up against. It won't be any single brigade out hunting new streams and stumbling on the valley by accident. It's winter now, Adam, and all his men are in off the trap lines."

Weaver shrugged. "We've doubled the guard, and I put Hunter to watch on the powder room. All we can do now is wait."

Bateau nodded soberly, took a last look out into the white desolation, turned to climb down the ladder. The rawhide-lashed spruce creaked mournfully beneath his weight. The snow in the courtyard gave his footsteps a soft, muffled sound. The wind started up again, and somewhere on the roof of the Beaver House a loose shake clattered. . . .

Bateau got into his bunk fully dressed, putting his hands behind his head, staring at the rough boards of the bunk above him. Benjamin Longbit, by gar. Well, let him come. He'd find out what it was to tangle with a grizzly bear. A grin split Bateau's beard, the golden streaks in it fading now that the summer was gone. He was still grinning when the explosion came.

It rocked through his consciousness with a deafening, earthshaking roar, bringing him to his feet in the middle of the bunkroom without knowing how he got there. He grabbed his rifle and shoulder belt automatically, elbowing through the milling, shouting men.

It had been the powder room. Most of the north wall was blown away, and the side of the main building nearest the sunken chamber was smashed and blackened. The corral had been wrecked, and the horses and pack animals were screaming and snorting and stampeding out into the clearing behind the fort. Thomas Hunter was dragging himself out of the smoke toward the Beaver House. Bateau ran to him.

"Squawman Samuels," gasped the axe man. "Came up behind me. Knifed my gizzard. Already had his fuse. Flint and steel. All that Dupont in the powder room . . . couldn't stop him. . . ."

Whether it was the explosion or the knife wound that ended it for Hunter, Bateau would never know. The man put his face in the snow, and the breath quit pulsing through him and he was dead. Bateau whirled toward the main building, bumping into Weaver.

"I was hunting for you," said Weaver in the same tone he would have used to discuss the weather. "Longbit's outside, all around. The fire's on the catwalk and I can't keep the men up there to do any shooting."

"Gather as many as you can and meet me in front of the main building!" shouted Bateau.

Weaver turned away. Portugee Phillips showed for an instant in the lighted doorway of the big hall, a gold-mounted Spanish pistol in each gnarled fist. Behind him was Mira, Jacinto's Walker strapped around her waist.

The explosion had started a fire that was already blazing on the south wall and along the catwalk. The first Longbitman raged through the gap blown in the wall, a yelling, running shadow in the flickering red light cast by the flames. The shot sounded thin above the other noise. The man didn't make any sound that Bateau could hear; he pitched onto his face amid the smoking rubble. At the corner of a smashed bunkroom, Kentucky loaded his Jake Hawkins again.

Then Portugee and Mira were beside Bateau, and Weaver was coming up with the baldpated blacksmith and the heavy-set Dutchie Peters and a dozen others. A section of the burning wall collapsed, showering them with sparks and chunks of flaming white pine. The wind shifted and black smoke swept over the little group.

Choking and coughing, Bateau yelled: "No use burning to death in here! Make for the gap blown in the wall! Maybe we can get through those Longbitmen!"

The burning wood was a hot spur beneath his feet as he reached the section of wall that had fallen in and ran on past the blaze toward the hole just north of the powder room. Other Longbitmen were in that gap now, shooting, yelling. Bateau met the first one with his rifle thrust out before him like a spear.

The big, white-coated *voyageur* grunted sickly as the iron butt plate of the Hawkins smashed into his body. He bent double and fell over sideways. Shots blared around Bateau; gun flame was bright and blinding. A renegade trapper loomed up in front of him with a six-gun in either hand, shouting, face twisted. Bateau swung his rifle in an arc, and that face disappeared from before him.

Squawman Samuels must have been running to get out of the fort when the Longbitmen came in, their press stopping him. Bateau stumbled over a figure, cowering beneath one of the great white pine logs that had smashed down against the side of the main building, leaving a space under it. The French Canuck reached out a sooty fist and bunched the Navajo blanket up under Squawman Samuels's chin, holding him that way while he dropped his Hawkins and snaked his Green River knife out.

"No, Bateau," slobbered Samuels. "No! Longbit made me. He said he'd do me in like he did my squaw if I didn't blow your fort. We decided on the day. He was waiting out in the timber. Bateau, don't, please. . . ."

He collapsed against Bateau's arm, bawling like a baby, screaming, struggling weakly against that iron grip holding him up. All around them the fight raged. Somebody fell heavily against Bateau's leg, slid to the ground, groaning. Suddenly Bateau spat disgustedly. He put his knife away and shoved Samuels back under the log.

"Squawman," he snarled, "you aren't worth killing."

He grabbed up his rifle and moved forward again, finding Weaver and Kentucky and the others hunched up against the last of the Longbitmen on this side. It was hazy and unreal to him after that. He didn't know how many men he struck with his heavy rifle. The faces would loom up twisted and screaming and blackened in front of him, and he would swing, screaming back like a wild animal, and suddenly they would be gone. The roaring crackle of the fire was dim in his ears. He couldn't seem to pull enough air into his laboring lungs. His buffalo coat got torn off him somewhere, and his red shirt clung wetly to his sweating torso.

Suddenly they were through, and ahead of them lay the open stretch. He glanced behind him to see that Mira was still there, face smudged, a savage light in her eyes, Jacinto's gun smoking in her small brown hand. He grabbed her and shoved her ahead of him, bending low and cutting for the timber with his lips drawn flatly against his teeth. He threw himself, panting, into the cold, black shadows beneath the spruce trees. Weaver came in behind him. Kentucky cast himself down in the snow and lay there, taking great gulps of air. Portugee Phillips collapsed against the bole of a tree, clutching his pistols, both empty. Half a dozen others came in on the run, limping, gasping.

Bateau squatted beside Weaver, still breathing hard,

pointing back to the fort. "Longbit made his mistake in rushing the fort. If he'd just stayed out here on the edge of the timber, the fire would have smoked us out, and he could have nailed every one of us before we made it across the clearing."

"The whole idea in blowing that powder room was to make a hole in the wall so's he could get in," grunted Weaver. "I guess he never figgered on a fire, what with the timber still green, and the snow."

Longbit's men had converged on the walls from all four sides. Those at the front and on the north side were unaware that the free trappers had broken through their net into the forest. But Longbit had seen Bateau's rush, and already he was running down his line of men, shouting, his tall, yellow-haired figure lit weirdly by the fire.

"Were there any left in the fort?" Bateau asked Weaver.

"None but the dead ones. Six or eight in that bunkhouse built to one side of the powder room. The explosion took care of them. Longbit picked three or four of my men off the cat-walk. We lost some in the gap, and running across the clearing," said Weaver, pointing to the three dark sprawls strung over the open space from fort to timber.

"A dozen of us left, then," muttered Bateau. "How many Longbitmen you figure?"

"He had to leave some to hold the river stations, and the Portugee Houses," said Weaver. "I reckon he could've mustered three or four brigades . . . maybe fifty, sixty men."

"Not that many now," said Bateau, looking toward the gap in the stockade where they had fought so intensely for those few moments.

"They're coming," said Kentucky.

Longbitmen were spreading out across the clearing in a skirmish line, rifles held across their bellies, heads turning nervously this way and that toward the timber. Patently they didn't know Bateau's exact position. Smoke and flickering light from the flames made their swiftly moving figures poor targets. Bateau tried to make out Longbit, but silhouetted against the light that way one black outline looked like the next.

"We can't let them get any closer," he said. "Give them your ball. Then we'll pull out."

He picked his man. The trigger jumped smoothly beneath his finger. The man went down. Shots made their deafening crash around him. Then he rose and tallied the free trappers one by one as they went by him single file into the forest. The volley had stopped the Longbitmen and they were wavering indecisively. The last thing Bateau heard was Longbit's voice rising above the crackle of the fire and ordering his men on forward, and Bateau knew they would be coming again.

The snow was deep and the drifts met the running trappers, soft and maddening. Stumbling, panting, cursing, they ran down the slope toward the creek at the bottom of the valley, but their age began to tell on the two older men, Sneed and Portugee, and the girl was ready to drop, and finally they all had to stop and rest.

They squatted around in a circle, looking at each other. Bateau's face was blackened and bloody; his red shirt was ripped down the front, and his hairy chest heaved up and down with the breath passing through him. He was tired running, somehow. There wasn't much point in it, any more. They had no food, no horses. They wouldn't stand much chance out in the forest with winter already setting in. Maybe it would have been better to die back at the fort, where all their hopes and their dreams had died.

Bateau looked at Weaver, and in the man's glance he saw his own thought reflected. He looked at Sneed. The blacksmith was a small, uninspired man nearer sixty than fifty, and the last mad hour had brought out the age in his lined face. But there was something else besides the age. He had been chased by Longbitmen all the way down from above Lake de Smet. Maybe he was tired of running, too.

Mira caught the silent glances passing between the men. Her eyes narrowed. She looked sharply at Bateau, then at Weaver. She stood up. "You're running because of me," she said. "If I wasn't here, you'd stand and go down fighting. That's true, isn't it, Bateau?"

He didn't answer. She would know if he lied.

"It *is* true," she said. "Well, we're through running now. When you built that fort, I thought you said it was going to be a fight to the finish. This is the finish. You don't have to run any farther because of me. I'd rather die than see the Big Horns called Longbitland for good. Let's stop here."

Bateau glanced around the circle. Sneed shifted uneasily. Weaver grunted, shook his head. "I wouldn't feel right," he said.

"You big mule," she spat at him, "can't you forget I'm a woman just once?"

Bateau rose. "We'd better go."

The others got up, one by one.

"I'm staying here!" she cried. "I don't care if the rest of you run. I'm staying."

Bateau took the step to her and picked her up by the waist and slung her over his shoulder. The others began to move forward again. Holding the kicking, squealing girl with one hand, he picked up his rifle and broke into a jog trot behind Weaver.

The first shot cracked the emptiness of the forest behind them, and a free trapper went over with a neat, round hole in his back, and there was no use stopping for a dead man.

After that, the Longbitmen were behind them and on their

flanks like a pack of wolves harrying a blacktail buck. Weaver turned and took a snap shot on the run; someone howled away behind them.

"Cut to the left," gasped Bateau. "That draw on our left."

They turned into the dense timber, single file, Bateau last, and ran head on into a party of Longbitmen who had flanked them. Bateau saw Weaver suddenly stop ahead of him. Danny Gunn had quartered through the spruce beyond Weaver, and stood there for that hung second, as surprised as the free trappers were. Then more Longbitmen came through the trees behind the first, and Gunn's Paterson cap-and-ball leaped from his holster, and its roar was the first shot.

Weaver took the slug in his belly with a hollow grunt. He dropped his Hawkins and took a step forward, eyes on Gunn.

The cold-faced man shot again.

Weaver jerked to the slug, but he didn't go down. His arms went out, and he staggered on toward Gunn.

Danny Gunn took a pace backward then, and his Paterson bucked in his hand for the third time.

Weaver bent over a little, in a sick, spasmodic way, but still he didn't go down. His eyes fixed on Gunn with a terrible concentration, he went on forward, stumbling like a great, square-bellied bear. Gunn's cold mask disappeared suddenly as if it had been wiped off; fear and surprise slid across his face. With a high-pitched, broken cry, he shot once more.

Weaver twitched, took yet another step. He struck Gunn going down, and he got those arms around the man, and they went into the snow together.

The other Longbitmen opened fire then. Bateau set Mira on her feet, and was already lunging forward, empty rifle clubbed. Shots whining about him, he struck savagely at the first Longbitman.

To his right, Dutchie Peters sank to the earth with a machete buried hilt-deep in his thick chest. Sneed choked, clutching at the black-handled Bowie that had thumped into him. Bateau saw Gotch Ear then. The man who liked to juggle knives had his third blade behind his head for the throw.

Bateau dropped his rifle and leaped. The knife came big and bright in his sight. He felt the thin cold pain of it jarring into his ribs. Then he hit the man and they rolled hard to the ground. Even as he went down beneath Bateau, Gotch Ear jerked a fourth blade from his belt of wampum. He thrust up, expelling his breath with the force of it. Bateau struck hard at the upcoming wrist with the edge of his stiffened palm. Gotch Ear cried out, and the blade slipped from his paralyzed fist.

Bateau rose on bent knees and jumped with both feet fully on the man's ugly face. Gotch Ear's body collapsed and the snow sifted whitely across his pockmarked head as he sank into the drift. . . .

Adam Weaver was crouching on hands and knees over the man he had killed with his bare fists. Coughing up blood, he reached weakly for Danny Gunn's Paterson. Slowly, painfully, he began jacking out the four used caps. Without looking at Bateau, he spoke.

"Get up the draw ahead. This iron has six loads. I'll give you that chance."

Kentucky came across the snow, dragging his rifle. Blood matted his queued hair, leaked down the side of his seamed face. The girl staggered through the trees, holding Jacinto's gun in one hand, helping her father along with the other.

"Please," said Mira, "let's stop here. With Adam. We can't run any more."

Weaver shoved the last fresh slug out of a loop in Gunn's belt and punched it into an empty chamber. He spun the cylinder, coughed weakly. "Get the gal out of here, Bateau. Prop me up against a tree, and get out."

"Please, Bateau, don't run because of me. Not any more. . . ."

Without looking at Mira, Bateau dragged Weaver over to a spruce, using the thick, snow-covered branches to brace him up. For a moment he squatted there beside the enigmatic man, and their glances met. Neither of them spoke. Finally Weaver waved the gun slightly.

"They're coming."

From down the white corridor behind them came the pad of running feet, the soft call of a French-flavored voice. Bateau turned and got the girl by the elbow; she was past struggling. He picked up his rifle, and his face was bleak and harsh when he shoved her forward and began to take up the run again. They hadn't gone far when Adam Weaver began shooting.

VII

The sun was up by the time Bateau and the other three had come far enough up this draw to see its dead end. Bateau was last in line, slogging through the heavy drifts, chest heaving with the hard run. He heard the shot crack out on their back trail. He went down with the ball searing into his leg, and he felt no surprise.

The girl turned and came back to him, and there was a dull triumph in her eyes. "I'm glad they shot you, hear, I'm glad! Now you can't run any more because of me. You have to stop and fight. We're the last ones, and we're through running, and I'm glad they shot you!"

"*Sacre,*" he gasped, "w'at a woman."

Kentucky and Portugee helped him to a gully that ran up the side of the draw. It was fair cover with a few scraggly serviceberry bushes thrusting up out of the snow and forming a screen. Bateau tried to get them to take the girl on, but she refused to go, and Kentucky and Portugee were in no condition to carry her as Bateau had done.

The French Canuck began loading his shot. Then he shoved the long barrel through the serviceberries.

The timber was all around them, and the first Longbitman came plunging into the open, intent on their trail in the snow. It was an easy shot.

"Bateau Severn, by gar," muttered the red-shirted man sprawled in the gully, "and you'll be sorry you ever heard of him before it's through here."

A crazy smile flitted across Mira's face and her eyes shone. This was the way she had wanted it all along. With the body lying out in the snow, the Longbitmen must have known who squatted up there with his fabulous Jake Hawkins rifle. They couldn't find the heart to follow that first man out. They spread through the trees and began pecking at Bateau. One tried to work upward through the timber and get above the gully. Kentucky waited for him to expose himself. He didn't get above the gully.

Then Mira called huskily and pointed across the bottom of the draw toward the opposite slope. While the Longbitmen in the timber kept up a covering fire, one of their number was working up the other side of the draw. Bateau saw the rustle of chokecherry. Farther up, the snow was duffled by a man's foot as he snaked from the bushes to a boulder thrusting out of the snow.

"Is he crazy?" Bateau muttered. "Does he think he can hit us from there?"

Kentucky scratched absently at the lice in his hair. "I recall when Jacinto was killed. If you'd asked the trappers in the fort, nine out of ten would have said that shot from timber was just plain impossible. I figger the kyesh who nailed Jacinto would pull a stunt like this."

"Yes," said Bateau, "I figure he would, too."

He filled his charge cup level and poured it down the long, wooden-stocked barrel, then filled it again, and poured. It would take all of that double load to reach Benjamin Longbit, there, across the draw. The bear grease in his trap was congealed with the chill air. Bateau had to hold a gob in his hand and warm it before he could grease his patch.

"Loaded up, Severn?"

Longbit's mocking voice was born clearly across the draw

in the still cold air, and it brought Bateau's head up. His lips peeled back from his teeth.

"I'm loaded, by gar!" he shouted. "Watch your right eye when you shoot, Longbit. That's the one I'm going to knock out."

"Don't you know when to quit, Severn?" said Longbit. "Won't you stop bragging even now? You can't hit me at this distance and you know it. There was another time you tried. You didn't do any knocking out then."

Bateau poked his Jake Hawkins through the bramble. He squinted down the barrel till both sights were clear. *Bien.* He shifted the gun upward till the boulder across the cañon covered them squarely. Longbit was behind that boulder. *Bien.* Then he began to wait, and that was hardest of all. He couldn't help remembering Jacinto, and the shot that had killed him. As Kentucky had said, nine out of ten men wouldn't have believed it possible, hitting a target at that distance. Yet it had been a clean shot, a deliberate one, no lucky chance.

Bateau's brows drew down because along with the memory of the shot that had killed Jacinto was memory of another—the one Bateau had bragged about, and had missed. A bitter self-blame had grown in him since that day. If he had stopped Longbit, Jacinto wouldn't be dead now, and all those others between this draw and the fort wouldn't be dead.

He hunched his shoulders suddenly. *W'at the hell?* So he had missed it. All right. He wasn't going to miss this one. It was a longer shot still, and the pain of his leg was beginning to distract him, but he wasn't going to miss. He stretched out and wiped his sweaty palm on greasy leggings. He shoved his shoulder snugly against the butt plate. He settled his cheek into the stock.

The Longbitmen down in the timber had stopped

shooting now, perhaps sensing that this last was between Bateau and Longbit. The breathless hush that had fallen seeped through Bateau's consciousness slowly. It didn't help. It told him they were waiting. The Longbitmen, down there. And Kentucky and Portugee, and Mira—they were waiting, too, and they were depending on him this time. He wouldn't miss. By gar, he couldn't miss. . . .

The flash of yellow hair behind that boulder, and the momentary glimpse of an elbow formed his target suddenly. His finger closed on the trigger. The mainspring jumped like velvet. The gun roared and bucked up against his cheek. Even with the oak butt slamming into his face, he jerked to the sudden sledgehammer blow on his right elbow. The force of it, and the terrific stabbing pain, threw him over to one side, and he couldn't stop himself from rolling down the steep side of the gully, and the girl's sharp gasp echoed in his ears.

"Oh, Bateau . . . !"

He lay there in the bottom of the gully, knowing his elbow was shattered, and knowing he had missed.

Mira slid down through the snow to him, trying to help him sit up. He shook off her hands and began crawling back to the top. She called after him tightly.

"Bateau, you can't make the shot with your elbow like that. Show yourself again and he'll kill you."

He didn't answer her. His head was hurting curiously. He clamped his teeth shut so he wouldn't scream with the agony in his arm. Kentucky and Portugee crouched there, watching him, knowing they couldn't do anything to help him.

He had trouble loading. He dropped two patches in the snow, lost a ball in the drift piled up against the bushes. Finally he shoved the Hawkins out again. He knew this was his last chance. The boulder blurred before his eyes, and his rear sight refused to stand still. The pain had flooded his body now. He couldn't have said where it was most intense. When he breathed, it was a series of small, choking sounds. His right arm wouldn't move to his will. He pressed that shoulder against the butt plate and slipped the index finger of his left hand around the trigger.

Now, Longbit, now!

It was that flash of yellow hair, that bit of elbow. They were clear and distinct for an instant. The contraction of his finger was automatic reaction.

Following the thunderous sound of his own shot, something whined over his head like a haunted banshee. Looking down his rifle barrel and through the smoke curling from its muzzle, he realized what that whine had been. Longbit had risen slightly from his boulder. He was bent forward from the hips, and both his hands were clapped up to his face, and his Hawkins gun was canted toward the sky.

Bateau's slug had reached Longbit the instant he had shot, jarring his gun upward, causing the bullet to go over Bateau's head. Slowly the rifle slipped over the boulder and down into the snowdrift in front. Then Longbit sagged down against the opposite side and disappeared behind the big rock.

"Bateau," whispered the girl in an awed voice, "you did it."

He rolled over on his back and took a shuddering breath. "Why not? I can shoot a Jake Hawkins gun better than any man in the world."

The Longbitmen had quit the timber and were working up the opposite slope. They went cautiously, hesitantly, until they saw that Bateau wasn't going to open fire on them. Then they gathered around the dead man behind the boulder.

"You knocked his right eye out sure enough," said Kentucky, "and I reckon those men know they're looking at the end of Longbitland right there. We sort of depleted their ranks as it is. Without Longbit they won't hold together a week. The Frenchies will drift back to the river towns, the trappers who were afraid to buck Longbit or who thought they could make more money in his breegades won't want to be staying around and meeting us free men."

Mira knelt beside Bateau, fishing for his Green River. She started to cut his red wool sleeve off the bloody elbow, and automatically he pulled away.

Her face colored. "Why do you always do that? Are you afraid of me?"

"I'm not afraid of anything," he grumbled.

"Then why do you always pull away like that?" she asked. "Don't you like me?"

"Too much," he said. "That's just the trouble. I danced with every squaw this side of Saint Looey, and none of them ever bothered me. I haven't danced with you yet. But when you get close like that, I begin to lose control. Squawman Samuels let that woman of his get too close. Not Squawman Bateau. Never Squawman Bateau!"

"You fool!" she flamed, sudden understanding dawning in her eyes. "Do you think I'd let you get like Samuels? Do you think I'd want a man like that, sitting around the fort all day and letting his wife do all the work, and getting soft and weak? If you ever stop being the craziest, wildest, braggin'est coot in the Big Horns, I'll take a horsewhip to you all the way from here to Yellowstone. *Now*, pull away!"

She bent over his arm again, panting, and her hands had that disturbing softness working to cut his sleeve from the wound. He didn't pull away. He grinned suddenly.

"*Sacre*," he said, "w'at a woman!"

The Beast in Cañada Diablo

When Les Savage, Jr., completed the short novel he titled "The Beast in Cañada Diablo", he sent the manuscript to his agent, August Lenniger, in the summer of 1945. The novelette was accepted by Fiction House on September 10, 1945. The brasada region of Texas where this story is set was named after the Spanish word *brazada,* meaning a region densely covered with thickets and underbrush, and was an area that particularly intrigued the author. "The Beast in Cañada Diablo" was first published under the title "The Ghost of Gun-Runners' Rancho" in *Lariat Story Magazine* (5/46). For its appearance here, the author's original title and text have been restored.

I

It was the first apprehension Eddie Cardigan had felt since this started. His saddle emitted a mournful squeak as he turned to stare behind him. There was nothing but the gaunt pattern of brush the border Mexicans called *brazada* and the dim shapes of running, bawling cattle, half hidden in a curtain of acrid, yellow dust. Navasato came back wiping his sweating, brown face, a burly man in buckskin *chivarras* and vest, bare shoulders and arms patterned by brush scars, fresh and old.

"Why did you stop them here?" Cardigan asked.

"We come to Cañada Diablo."

"All right," said Cardigan, shifting his long body irritably. "All right, so we come to Cañada Diablo. You just gonna sit here and let them catch up to us?"

"We got to go back till we hit the Comanche Trail," said Navasato. "I didn't realize we'd crossed it. We can't go through Cañada Diablo."

Cardigan leaned toward Navasato, his dark eyes narrowing. There was a lean intensity to his face that might have indicated a certain violence in him, and deep grooves from his prominent, aquiline nose to his thin mouth that might have indicated a rigid control of his natural tendencies. The wool vest he wore over his red, checked flannel shirt had not been designed for brush country, and it was ripped in several places, and covered with burrs and dirt.

"You know we'd walk right into them if we turned around now. Why can't we go through here?"

"Nobody ever goes through this part of the *monte.*"

"*¿Nagualismo?*" asked Cardigan.

"The *nagual,* the *nagual,*" said Navasato, waving a square, callused hand half impatiently, half fearfully. "*La onza.*"

Pinto Parker had milled the cattle from the point by now, stopping them, and came trotting his spotted bronc' back through the settling dust, sitting his seat with the same broad swagger that marked his walk, white Stetson shoved back on blond hair that took on a tight curl when it got wet with sweat this way. "What's our tallow-packing pard babbling about now?" he said.

"*Nagualismo,* or something," said Cardigan.

"*Sí, sí,*" muttered Navasato. "*La onza, la onza.*"

Pinto Parker threw back his head to laugh, and Cardigan wiped his hand irritably on his shirt. "What is it?"

"Some crazy Mex story." Pinto grinned, his teeth flashing a white line against his sun-darkened face. "You get it all the time down here. Started with the Indians farther south, I think. Has to do with their religion or something. It spread up here and got the *brazaderos* in a big lather."

Cardigan pulled his reins in and felt the jaded dun draw a weary breath and stiffen to go. "Forget your ghost stories, Navasato. We're going through."

"No, Cardigan, no. *En el nombre de Dios. . . .*" With an abrupt decision, Navasato pulled his big Choppo horse around. "I ain't going."

The dun was ready for reaction when Cardigan put his reins against the neck, and it stepped broadside of Navasato's Choppo, putting Cardigan face to face with the man, their animals standing rump to head. "They'll get you if you go back, Navasato," he said through his teeth. "You ever see a bunch of rustlers hanging from a tree? That's what you'll get, Navasato. No less."

The Mexican turned pale but tried to urge his Choppo on past Cardigan's dun. "I don't care. Let me go, Cardigan. You can find your way to the border from here if you want. Not me. I won't go through Cañada Diablo."

Cardigan realized what a primitive fear must hold the man if he would risk hanging rather than go on, and he understood there was only one thing now, and he did it. "You're coming with us. Go up and help Pinto on the point."

Navasato stared at the big .46 in Cardigan's hand. The little muscles around his mouth twitched. His eyes met Cardigan's for a moment, and Cardigan didn't know whether the fear there was for him, or something else. With a small, strangled sound, Navasato jerked on his reins. The Choppo jumped with the big Spanish bit biting his mouth, turning sharply after the cattle Pinto had started up again. Once the Mexican turned back to look at Cardigan, then he disappeared in the haze of rising dust.

There were maybe a hundred head of the animals, and it would not have been a big job for three men in the open, but through this brush it was hell. Cardigan had ridden brushland before, but nothing like this. The brasada was really a dry jungle, and for hours he had fought it as he fought no other country, the black chaparral clubbing at him constantly with a human malignancy, the *granjeno* clawing his bare hands and face, alkali settling in each fresh cut to sting and burn. Yet, this was the first time they had stopped since running into it that morning, and the utter primal force of the land had not clutched at Cardigan till he had pulled his dun to a stop there a few minutes ago and stared back. Well, they had told him how it would be, hadn't they? Or had tried to tell him. No man could describe in words the sensation that came when he stopped like that, for the first time, with the dust settling back into the stark ground from which it had risen, and the dull, cattle sounds dying out in the emptiness of the brush, and the inimical *mogotes* of chaparral closing in on all sides, black with a hostility that was almost human, suffocating, waiting.

"Hyah!" shouted Cardigan, trying to dissipate the oppression in him by yelling at a thirst-crazed *orejano* that had tried to break into the thickets away from the main herd. "Get on back, you bug-eyed cousin to a. . . ."

It was the sound that cut him off. At first he thought it was a woman screaming. It rose to a shrill, haunting crescendo, somewhere out in the brush, and, stiffened in his saddle by the utter terror of it, Cardigan sensed more felinity in the cry than humanity. It ended abruptly, and the silence following beat at Cardigan's eardrums. As if snapping out of a trance, he put spurs into his dun with a jerk, leaping it ahead to meet Pinto Parker as the man appeared in the dust ahead.

"Did you hear it?" shouted Pinto.

"Sounded like a cat," said Cardigan.

"I never heard no bobcat squall like that," said Pinto. "Where's Navasato?"

"I think he was riding point."

"Cardigan!" It was the Mexican, his voice carrying a cracked horror in its tone, coming from the brush somewhere ahead. "Cardigan, I told you, *la onza, la onza.* Come and help me. *Dios,* Cardigan, *madre de Dios,* come and get me . . . !"

The crash of brush around him drowned the cries as Cardigan raced through a prickly pear thicket. His own animal whinnied with the pain of tearing by the thorned plants, and Cardigan's sleeve was ripped off as he threw his arm across his face to shield his eyes. He pulled the horse up and swung down, hauling the reins over its head and whipping them around a branch. As he whirled to dive through the thicket on foot, he saw Pinto erupt from the prickly pear behind. Then Cardigan was struggling through the beating madness of black chaparral, tearing at the branches with one hand, his gun in the other. He could hear no sound but his own labored breathing as he finally ran into the next clearing, and saw Navasato. He stood there a moment, staring at the spectacle. Pinto crashed through behind Cardigan. Cardigan was the first to move over toward Navasato.

"Dead?" asked Pinto in a hollow voice.

Cardigan nodded, squatting down beside the mutilated body. "No brush clawed him up like that."

Parker was stooped over, looking at something on the ground, beyond Navasato. "What did he say about the *onza?*" he asked.

"Perhaps you had better ask Florida that, *compadres,*" said a man's voice from behind them, and Cardigan started to raise his Remington as he turned, and then let it drop again.

The man standing there possessed a strange affinity with the brush. His face was lean and saturnine, and dark secrets stirred smokily in his strange, oblique eyes. He had thick, buckskin gloves on his hands, holding a gun in a casual, indifferent way, as if he wouldn't have needed it anyhow.

Pinto Parker's equanimity had never ceased to amaze Cardigan. Parker spoke to the man now without apparent surprise, a grin crossing his face easily. "You Florida?"

"No, Lieutenant Dixon," said the man. "I am not Florida. I am Comal Garza."

"Lieutenant Dixon?" asked Pinto.

"Yes." Garza's murky eyes passed over the animal lying beyond Navasato's torn, bloody body. "I see you brought the Krags. Where are the rest of them?"

At first, Cardigan had thought it was Navasato's Choppo horse, the dead animal over there, but now he saw it was a mule with an Army pack saddle on its back. Its throat had been ripped and steaming tripe was rolling out of a great, gaping hole torn in its belly, and Cardigan did not look long. Pinto had taken his rifle from the saddle scabbard on his horse, and he glanced at it involuntarily.

"Yeah, I got a Krag. What cows does that rope?"

Garza allowed a faint puzzlement to cross his face, studying Pinto. "I refer to the Krags on the mule. Where are the other mules? Stampeded?"

"This is the only mule I seen," said Parker.

Garza's gun had raised enough to cover them again. "What are you trying to do, Lieutenant Dixon? It is unfortunate your guide had to die this way, of course, but you certainly can't blame me. It's rather obvious what caused it. We all knew you were coming today, but we didn't expect you to appear driving a herd of cattle. Did you have to use the beef as a blind?"

"The beef is all we had," said Pinto. "You must have us mixed up with someone else."

"No one else would have come this far south of the Comanche Trail, *señor*," said Garza sibilantly, and he drew himself up perceptibly as if reaching a decision. "I did not expect you to act this way, Lieutenant. But of course, if you would betray others, it's not inconceivable that you wouldn't be honest with us. Did you think we weren't prepared for that contingency?"

"You're riding an awful muddy crick," said Pinto.

"I will make it clearer. I will ask you to relieve yourself of the implements."

Garza inclined his head toward the Krag .30 Parker had. Pinto grinned, dropping the rifle, fishing his Colt out and letting it go. Cardigan did the same.

"Kamaska!" called Garza.

Cardigan could not help growing taut with surprise at the man's appearance. He made no sound coming from the thicket behind Garza. He was short and stubby and walked like an ape with his thick shoulders thrusting forward from side to side with each step. Kamaska's broad black belt was pulled in so tight it would have dug deeply into a normal man with a belly as big as that, yet it made no visible impression on his enormous, square paunch. His eyes passed over Pinto and Cardigan with opaque indifference in a wooden face, and Cardigan was expecting him to grunt when he bent over to pick up the guns, and was disappointed. Pinto Parker looked at Navasato in an automatic way, and Garza's voice came with a nebulous, hissing intonation.

"We'll leave him there."

"*¿Nagualismo?*" said Cardigan.

Garza's head raised, and a thin smile caught at his flat lips. "Perhaps, *señor*. Perhaps. And now?"

His thin, black head was inclined toward the prickly pear, and he let them precede him. Pinto swaggered ahead of Cardigan, grinning back at him once, not caring much what this was about or trying to figure it out, because he was that kind. There were two other saddle animals with their horses. There was no room between Kamaska's belly and that belt, cinched up as it was, for the revolvers, so he dropped them in a fiber *morral* hung on the saddle horn of the hairy, black mule he had, and swung aboard with surprising alacrity for such a bulk, still holding the Krag in one hand.

Garza did not mount till Cardigan and Parker were in their saddles. Kamaska led through the brush, moving so steadily and surely that Cardigan finally realized they were following some sort of trail. Mystery was in Garza's vague smile and his eyes were smoky and secretive.

"We will be there presently."

"I don't suppose it would do to ask you who you are?"

"I am Comal Garza."

Up ahead, Pinto laughed. Kamaska turned for an instant, staring opaquely at Parker as he would stare at an animal he did not understand.

Cardigan had no measure of the distance they rode through that weird brushland before they reached the house. It was hidden by chaparral until they were almost there, then the clearing thrust itself upon them, with several ocotillo corrals on the near side and an adobe structure across the intervening flat that might have been a bunkhouse. Some two hundred yards past that was the main building. It was typical of the dwellings in the Southwest, although larger, its rafters formed by *viga* poles thrusting out the top of the wall a foot or so to cast a shadowed pattern across the yellow mud, shutters closed against the heat of the summer sun. A man rose from where he had been hunkered against one of the uprights forming the *portales* that supported the porch roof running the length of the front. He wore the usual *chivarras* and a tattered red Chimayo blanket, poncho style, its four corners dangling to his knees. His eyes were small and bucolic and his mouth was thick-lipped and brutal. Garza tossed his reins to the man.

"Did Florida get back, Innocencio?"

"No," said the man. Garza pointed toward the house, and Cardigan took it they were to go in. The living room was dim and musty.

"All right, Lieutenant Dixon," Garza told Pinto.

Parker's mouth opened slightly. "Lieutenant Dixon?"

"You were the one with the Krag," said Garza.

"Krag? It's my rifle."

"I'm glad you admit it," said Garza. "Now, if you'll tell us where you've got the other Krags . . . ?"

"Oh, the Krags," said Parker, as if something had dawned on him abruptly. Grinning, he turned to Cardigan. "Now just where *did* we put those Krags, Cuhnel Cahdigan?"

There were times when Parker's irresponsible sense of humor galled Cardigan. "Shut up, Pinto," he said. "Can't you see they mean business?"

"Yes, Lieutenant Dixon," said Garza. "We mean business."

"Now, Cuhnel Cahdigan, suh," said Parker with mock gravity, "you-all know Ah'm serious as all hell. Ah jes' can't seem to recall where we put those Krags. By Gad, my name ain't Lieutenant Dixon if I can. . . ."

Garza had taken his forward step before Cardigan realized what he meant to do, moving without perceptible effort, and his hand made a dull, slapping sound across Parker's face. Garza had put no apparent force in the blow, yet it sent Pinto reeling back against the wall so hard a hand-carved *santo* fell from its niche. Pinto stood there with his hand up to his face. Finally he grinned again, without mirth.

"You shouldn't have done that, Garza."

"I don't appreciate your broad humor, Lieutenant. Or were you being humorous? When Zamora came from contacting you in Brownsville, he said we might have some trouble. If you think of holding out for a higher price, don't. We already made the arrangements, and you are here. Now, tell us where the Krags are and you'll get your money."

"You made a mistake," said Cardigan. "This isn't Lieutenant Dixon. It's Pinto Parker. We were just running some cattle through."

"Your cattle, I take it."

A trace of Pinto's humor had returned. "Now, you don't

suppose we'd be herding somebody else's beef, do you?"

"You have a bill of sale for a hundred Big Skillet steers?" said Garza.

"Is that what they were?" Pinto asked.

A thin impatience entered Garza's voice. "Let's quit this sparring. If you chose to use a bunch of rustled Big Skillet cattle as a blind, it is no concern of mine. You know what I'm interested in."

"Oh, is there a woman in the brasada?" said Pinto.

Garza drew a sharp breath, then he inclined his head toward a hand-carved Mendoza chair that sat in high-backed austerity against the wall. "We'll put him in there, Kamaska."

"Wait a minute."

"I would advise you to keep quiet, *señor*," said Garza, turning the gun on Cardigan. "Innocencio will be watching you, and his characteristics are hardly those his name would imply."

Innocencio had taken a singularly evil-looking *belduque* from beneath his Chimayo blanket, and he moved toward Cardigan, running a thick, callused finger down the bright blade. Garza was forced to snap the rifle's bolt before he could persuade Pinto into the chair. Cardigan stood by the wall, bent forward tensely, his breath fluttering white nostrils in a hoarse audibility. Kamaska got a rawhide dally from a wooden stob in the wall. Parker started to jump from the chair as he realized what it meant, then sat back down slowly for the cocked rifle was aimed at his belly. Kamaska pulled the rope so tightly it dug into Pinto through his fancy-stitched shirt. Garza shoved Pinto's white Stetson off and it rolled to the floor.

"Now, Lieutenant Dixon, are you going to tell us where the Krags are? You have one more chance."

Cardigan never ceased to marvel at Pinto's reckless nonchalance. Even now the man's grin held nothing forced. "You got us wrong. Parker's my name. We're just a couple of 'punchers."

"Very well," said Garza softly. Kamaska had gotten an ancient Spanish nutcracker of beaten silver from the oak table. Pinto's arms were lashed along the arms of the chair with his fingers protruding over the edge. Garza watched Kamaska slip Pinto's right index finger into the jaws of the nutcracker. "It was made to crack Brazil nuts, Lieutenant. It executes a remarkable pressure."

Pinto could not help the gasp, and his grin turned to a grimace of spasmodic pain. His eyes remained closed while Kamaska opened the nutcracker from his finger. The beaded sweat stood out on his face. Finally he opened his eyes and looked at the mashed nail.

"Hell," he said, and grinned.

"Muy bien," said Garza. "Very well."

Kamaska slipped the nutcracker on Pinto's middle finger. Cardigan knew his first anger; it had only been irritation before. He had not comprehended fully what it was all about, and it had only been irritation, and a remnant of the revulsion at what had happened to Navasato, but now it was anger. He had seen how Pinto's first gasp drew Innocencio's attention for that moment, and he watched Kamaska begin to squeeze the nutcracker. Innocencio stood facing Cardigan with that *belduque* in his thick fingers. Pinto's face contorted again, and once more he could not stifle a deep moan. This time Innocencio's reaction was less marked. Cardigan barely caught the flicker of his eyes toward the sound, and moved when he did.

Innocencio tried to jump backward and throw the knife at the same time, but Cardigan's foot lashed up and caught his hand before the blade had left it. The knife flew upward to strike the low roof with the impetus of Innocencio's toss.

"I told you to watch him!" shouted Garza, whirling with

the rifle. Cardigan's jump had carried him to Innocencio, and he caught the man about the waist, whirling him toward Garza before the man could fire. Innocencio struck Garza like a sack of sand, carrying him back across Pinto and knocking chair and all over onto the floor. Cardigan heard Parker shout with the pain of their weight smashing down onto him. Cardigan had tried to set himself, but his legs would not hold the terrible force of Kamaska's charge. He felt himself stumbling backward across the hard, earthen floor, and the wall struck his head and sent a roar of pain through his whole body like a cannon going off.

He tried to roll over and drive an elbow between them as a wedge to keep Kamaska from grabbing him, but the man caught his elbow and jammed it aside, and then one of those thick arms was about Cardigan's neck, and he thought he had never felt such incredible strength in a human being before. He heard the snap of bones and his own scream of pain. Then Kamaska's fist exploded in his face, and the room spun, and then he couldn't even see the room. Somewhere, far away, he felt his own body make a feeble effort at struggling, and one of his arms moved dimly. Then Kamaska's fetid, sweating bulk shifted against him, and he knew that fist was coming again and he knew that would finish it.

"Kamaska!"

At first Cardigan thought he had said it. Then he realized it had come from across the room. Kamaska's arm slipped from around Cardigan's neck, and the man stood up, breathing heavily. Cardigan had trouble focusing his eyes. At first all he could see was the Burgess-Colt repeater held in the small, brown hands of a dim figure across the room, light from the open door glinting on the rifle's silver-plated receiver. Then he heard Pinto's voice.

"I guess I wasn't joking. There *is* a woman in the brasada!"

II

His name was Esperanza, and he shuffled around the bunkshack like a ringy, old mossyhorn, growling through drooping, white *mustachios* so long their tips were dirty from brushing against the chest of his white cotton shirt. After the fight in the house, Innocencio had brought Cardigan and Parker out here to the bunkhouse, a structure even more ancient and odorous than the main building, its roof so low Pinto had to remove his Stetson before entering. Cardigan sat at one end of the long, plank table, still too sick from Kamaska's brutal blows to eat anything of what was before him. Innocencio stood by the door, glowering at Cardigan and nursing his hand.

"*El mano,*" he kept repeating.

"You must have broken his hand with that boot of yours," said Pinto, the pain of his mashed fingers having little effect on his appetite. He forked up a huge mouthful from the tin plate, grimacing as he spoke around it. "This is the foulest concoction of hog tripe I ever wrapped my lips around."

The deafening crash of guns drowned him out, and he jumped up, knocking over his chair and spewing the food all over the table. Cardigan was bent forward, both hands gripping the planks, staring at Esperanza. The old man held a smoking, stag-butted .45 in each hand, his red jowls quivering.

"You don't like my food!" he shouted apoplectically.

"Don't get me wrong, *amigo*." Pinto laughed shakily, staring at the smoking guns with the surprise still on his face. "Your *alimento* is marvelous. I wouldn't eat anywhere else. It's just an old Texas custom. Like throwing salt over your left shoulder. You say it out loud, see? You say this is the foulest concoction of hog tripe I ever ate, and then . . . *diablo*, he don't come up to get it. An old Texas custom."

"*¿El diablo?*" said the old man, squinting at Parker, still suspicious. They were literal-minded in many respects, these *brazaderos*, with the superstition of peasantry to whom the devil was as real as the coma trees in front of their *jacales*.

"All right," growled Esperanza finally, waving one of his .45s. "Sit down and eat it, then. I make the best *chiles rellenos* in all *Méjico*. Why do you think they call them the children's dream, ah? I take the greenest of peppers and stuff them with the tenderest of chicken and the yellowest of cheese and dip them in a batter *El Dios* Himself would be proud to be dipped in, and I cook them in the purest of hog fat till they come out as golden brown as my very own skin. For twenty years I cook them for General Díaz. Porfirio Díaz Santa Anna Esteban Esperanza. That's me. Why do you think they call me that, ah?"

"Esperanza," said Florida Zamora from the door, "haven't our guests already been shown enough bad hospitality?"

The grin that spread Pinto's face as he looked toward her held an infinite appreciation. "It's about time you come out." He chuckled. "I wasn't going to wait much longer."

Cardigan had seen women in Brownsville react to Pinto's animal magnetism. Florida took in his great height, and the breadth of his muscular shoulders beneath his fancy-stitched shirt, and his blond hair, and her smile answered his. It drew a resentment from Cardigan he could not understand, and, angered at himself for feeling it, he did not smile when the woman's eyes passed to him. He met her gaze almost sullenly, and her smile faded. Her rich underlip dropped faintly, as if she were about to speak, then she closed it again, and moved to the table. There was nothing masculine about the way her buckskin *chivarras* fitted across the hips, or about what she did to the white silk shirt just beneath its soft collar. Pinto was taking that all in as she placed the Krag she had brought on the table, and then pulled their revolvers from her waistband and put them down.

"You must forgive us, gentlemen," she said. "Esperanza is an irascible old reprobate. I'm sure you'll overlook his peculiarities. As for Garza, he made a very grave mistake. We were expecting someone else. He mistook you for them."

Cardigan tried to keep his eyes off her, and could not. There was something Gypsy in the way she wore a red *bandeau* drawn tightly about her head, hair with the sheen of a blue roan falling soft and black from beneath that to caress the shoulders of her white shirt. There was undeniable aristocracy to the arch of her thin, black brows, the proud line of her nose.

"I'm glad to see Esperanza fixed up your fingers," she said, and Cardigan sensed her mind was not on the words.

Pinto glanced at his bandaged fingers. "I never knew prickly pear poultice. . . ."

"Will cure anything from *dolor de las tripas* to a fifty-caliber hole through your head." Florida smiled faintly. "Or almost."

Pinto let his eyes cross her features. "You've got some white blood?"

"My father was Mexican," she said. "He married an American woman from Brownsville. This is Hacienda del Diablo. It's not really as forbidding as Estate of the Devil would suggest. The country south of the Comanche Trail has always been known as Cañada Diablo. I could never see why."

"*¿Nagualismo?*" said Cardigan.

Her turn toward him was sharp, as if she had forgotten he was there. "The land was named long ago," she said finally.

"And this *nagualismo* only started lately?" asked Cardigan.

"You seem to know," she said.

"Garza seemed to think you were the one to know," said Cardigan. "Just what is *nagualismo?*"

She hesitated, her eyes dropping from his face, then she spoke abruptly. "*Nagualismo* really originates farther south, in the Mexican peninsula. It's a belief among the Indian tribes down there. The Caribs subscribe to it, I think. In Yucatán, a *nagual* is an Indian dedicated at birth to some animal by his parents. The rapport between child and animal finally becomes so strong the *nagual* can change himself at will into the animal."

"A cat, maybe?" asked Pinto.

She nodded. "They have jaguars down there."

Cardigan remembered, then, how Pinto had been bent over beside Navasato, looking at something on the ground, when Garza came. "That's what you found?" he said.

"By Navasato?" asked Pinto, and nodded. "Big ones. Just like cat tracks. Only they couldn't have been cat tracks. Cats don't grow that big in Texas. Or anywhere."

There was something frightened in the silence that fell. Florida stared at Pinto for a moment, then gave a rueful little laugh.

"We're letting our imaginations carry us away. Why even dignify such an absurd superstition by considering it in that light? I've lived in the brasada all my life and admit having seen some strange things. I've never seen any evidence of a man having the capacity to change himself into an animal at will, however. If Garza came on you right after you found your dead friend, you undoubtedly did not get a chance to study the tracks closely. We have large bobcats around here, and a few jaguars come up from Mexico. Even a mountain lion or two from the Sierras. I'm sure you'd find one big enough to account for the tracks."

"I've seen the biggest mountain lions they got," said Pinto. "I never seen one with feet that big. And the way it took Navasato. He didn't even have his gun out."

She sat tapping the table with a long finger, finally shrugged it off. "Garza said you were running a cut of Big Skillet steers. Have you got a bill of sale?"

The abruptness of it took Cardigan off guard, but Parker's grin was easy. "Garza picked us up so fast we didn't have a chance to bring our duffel along. The bill was in my sougan."

"I thought so," said Florida.

Parker's look of growing indignation was almost genuine enough to convince Cardigan. "You don't mean to insinuate . . . ?"

Florida Zamora stopped him with an upraised hand. "Never mind. Whether those cattle were wet or dry doesn't concern me. I just wanted to know. Men who run wet cattle wouldn't be as particular about the kind of jobs they do as men who run dry cattle, shall we say?"

"Their discrimination between the legal and illegal aspects of an occupation might not be as keen as a man who never ran wet cattle, true," said Pinto.

"Would you like a job here?"

Pinto picked up his Colt, spun the cylinder. "What's going on?"

"Nothing particularly. We just run *mestenos*," said Florida.

"You just run mustangs," mused Pinto, slipping his gun back into its holster, "yet you'd rather hire a man who might overlook a legal technicality than one who wouldn't."

"If these weren't your cattle," said Florida, "you couldn't get to the north without running into a posse. Sheriff Sid Masset's a hard man to shake if he happens to be riding your trail. On the other hand, no lawman has come into Cañada Diablo in a long time."

"¿*Nagualismo?*" said Cardigan.

The woman turned sharply toward him again, a faint flush of anger rising into her cheeks. With an audible, indrawn breath, she turned back to Pinto. He had begun to eat again, and spoke around a mouthful of beans.

"The advantages of your little *estancia* sound pleasing. Tell me more."

"The financial arrangements might interest you. For a hundred steers on the wet market you couldn't get more than three pesos a head. I could see that you draw down more than that in a month here."

"A man would have to work pretty hard for that kind of chips."

"It all depends on what you do," she said. At Pinto's inquiring look, she smiled, tapping his Krag. "You're not unknown down here. We've heard what you can do with an iron."

Pinto nodded, forking in more *frijoles*. "Then you're not hiring us to run mustangs."

"I'm hiring you to run mustangs," she said. "But if something comes up that necessitates the use of that hardware you pack, I hope I'm right in thinking a man who runs wet cattle would be less reluctant about using it than a man who runs dry cattle, and more skillfully."

Pinto wiped the gravy out of the plate with the last piece of tortilla, leaned back, smacking his lips. "Doesn't sound bad to me."

Florida turned to Cardigan. "How about you?"

"What if we don't take the job?" asked Cardigan.

She hesitated a moment, then spoke with a certain control tightening her voice. "It seems to me you would be better off accepting it."

"You say no lawman has been here for a long time," said Cardigan. "Maybe this *nagualismo* business has scared everybody else out, too. Maybe we're the first outsiders you've entertained in quite a spell. Maybe you'd rather not have us reach the outside again, knowing you were expecting a Lieutenant Dixon."

"You take an unfortunate attitude." Anger was slipping through that control in her voice.

"I just wanted things clear," he said. "Does Garza still think Pinto is Lieutenant Dixon?"

"I don't," she said.

"Does Garza?"

She pulled in her lips impatiently, then shrugged. "All right, so he does. What difference does that make?"

"It might make a big difference."

"What does it matter, Card?" said Pinto. "She's right about us not being able to get out of the brasada by the north now. This is as good a place to camp as any till the Big Skillet ruckus blows over, and we get paid to boot."

"I'm glad you will stay," she said, moving toward the door. She took a last glance at Cardigan, then spoke as she turned away. "We're riding this afternoon. You might like to come along."

Pinto got up and went to the door to watch her walk across the sunlit compound toward the house, making various appreciative noises. He leaned against the door, tucking his good hand into his gun belt, turning to grin at Cardigan. "She really must have wanted hands bad."

"Why?"

Pinto laughed softly. "She didn't even ask us if we knew how to run mustangs."

III

The wind whispered through mesquite with a haunted sibilance and the black chaparral was so thickly matted and so low in some places that a man trained in the brush could see a buck's antlers rising above it half a mile away, and so tall in other places a horsebacker could ride for miles without ever seeing more than twenty feet ahead or behind. Riding through it, behind Florida Zamora, Cardigan was filled with a nebulous oppression he could not shake off. They had left Hacienda del Diablo earlier that afternoon, riding past the huge, cedar-post corrals filled with half-tamed mustangs. They went at a fast trot that kept Cardigan dodging post-oak limbs and ducking outstretched branches of chaparral, his face and hands continually clawed by mesquite. He marveled at the ease with which Florida seemed to drift through the brush, her movements to avoid the growth hardly perceptible. Finally they crossed a clearing, and she allowed her pony to drop back, smiling faintly at Cardigan as he dabbed irritably at a scratch on his face.

"Riding the brush is a little different than open country, isn't it? You don't learn it in a day, Cardigan. I've been running the brasada most of my life, and I still get knocked off now and then."

"Garza seems adept enough," said Cardigan. "I got the impression somehow that he wasn't native to the brush."

"He's only been with me about six months," she said. "He

came from Yucatán, I think."

"Funny he would give me the idea you were the authority on this *nagualismo*," Cardigan told her. "If it originated in the Mexican peninsula, I should think a man from Yucatán would know more about it."

"Maybe he does," she said. "How about you, Cardigan? Where are you from?"

"I've been a lot of places," he answered.

"How long have you been with Pinto?" she asked him.

"I met him in Brownsville."

"You're so specific." Then she was looking at his hands. "They don't look like Pinto's."

"They've got ten fingers."

She drew her lips with irritation. "The rope burns on them are fresh."

"We were working cattle when you found us."

"But all the rope burns on your hands are fresh. Pinto's got some old ones."

"Maybe I got tired being a bank clerk," said Cardigan.

"You don't get legs like horse collars sitting on a stool."

"Maybe I used to tuck my feet in the rungs."

"Then you admit you haven't been in the wet-cattle business long?"

"How long have you been in the mustang business?" he asked.

"That's irrelevant," she said hotly. Then she quieted, something pensive entering her eyes. "Who are you, Cardigan?"

"I'm the hand you hired to run mustangs," he said, and saw the impatient anger this drew from her before he had to swoop beneath a hackberry limb. He rose in the saddle again. "I never heard of an outfit this size spending all its time chasing mustangs. What happened to your cattle?"

"Mustanging is a profitable business," she said evasively. "We're coming to the watering hole for a herd we've been after for some time now. We haven't staked out here for a week or so now, and our scent should be gone, and the wind's toward us, so they shouldn't smell us. Tighten the noseband on your animal. When they show, try to keep the *manada* from breaking into thick brush."

"¿*Manada?*"

She glanced at him. "They run in *manadas,* herds of twenty or thirty mares with a stallion. Get the stallion, and the mares are all disorganized."

"¡*Caballos!*"

It was Kamaska's voice, and it settled an immediate silence over all of them. Garza stood beside his *pelicano,* a stiff, arrogant figure in the gloom. Parker was beside him, taller, his broad shoulders carried in a sway-backed stance. Parker felt his dun's throat swell with a nicker, and he caught at the noseband. Then he saw them, drifting into the open as silently as a file of thunderheads climbing from behind a peak. The leader was a huge, white stallion, prodigiously muscled for a brush horse, his chest and shoulders moving with the striated sinuosity of thick snakes beneath his pale, silken hide. He was wildness incarnate, moving with a delicate, ferine prance that barely touched his sharp, clean hoofs to the ground, the proud arch of his neck never still as he moved his head ceaselessly from side to side. Rather than marring his appearance, the brush scars patterning his body only lent it a bizarre beauty. Cardigan watched, fascinated, his breath catching in him as he saw the animal stop and raise its head, and thought it had scented them. Then it went on, switching its long, white tail, and the mares followed. When they were almost by, Cardigan saw Garza turn and lift his foot into the stirrup and knew it was the sign. Without a word, all of them

191

mounted, the faint stir of movement they made rising above the small night sounds and then breaking into a shocking, thundering noise, as Garza laid the gut hooks into his *pelicano* and jumped it through the brush with a pounding crash into the open. Cardigan lost his hat, bursting through that first *mogote*, and after that all he could see was the white stallion.

It was reared up at the brink of the water hole, noble head twisted toward them. With a piercing scream, it whirled, plunging directly into the mucky water and floundering across. Cardigan drove his horse directly after Garza, hearing someone's wild shouting and not realizing it was his till he was in the water himself.

The spray shooting around him was sticky with mud. He came out on the other bank, pawing at his eyes and cursing. He saw Kamaska make a throw at a mare and forefoot her, and the ground shook as she went down. Then Florida passed Cardigan, bent over her pony. She hit the first growth hard on Garza's tail, and passed through its massed brush with a swift ease. Then Cardigan met it. He saw a branch of chaparral dead ahead and dropped off to one side to go under, and put his face right into a growth of prickly pear. Howling with the pain of torn flesh, he tore his head upward to escape that and was caught by the branch he had tried to dodge in the first place. The blow on his head knocked him backward, and he barely caught himself from going over the dun's rump. Blinded, cursing, he was still in that position when some mesquite caught one of his outflung feet, tearing it from the stirrup, and he slid over the other side of his horse.

He managed to catch the fall on his other heel, bouncing it off on his buttocks and rolling over to smash into a low spread of mesquite. He got to his hands and knees, shaking his head, spitting out grama grass and dirt. Finally he got to his feet and looked after his horse. It had disappeared in the brush, along with Florida and Garza. Then the thud of hoofs from the other direction turned him that way, and he saw Kamaska riding in from the sink on his black mule.

"It takes a lifetime to ride the brasada with such skill as the *señorita* possesses," he said enigmatically.

"Hell with the brasada," snarled Cardigan, wiping dirt and blood off his cheek. "I thought you were taking care of the mares."

"I have two tied to mesquite trees," said Kamaska. "The *señorita* told me to keep an eye on you."

"I thought, maybe," said Cardigan. "And who keeps an eye on Parker?"

"He knows the brasada," said Kamaska.

"That isn't why she wanted you to watch me," said Cardigan.

Then his head raised slightly. He had never seen Kamaska evince any emotion before. Perhaps it was the man's eyes. The opacity had left them and they were filled with a luminous, startled light that changed in a moment to the animal fear Cardigan had seen in a dog's eyes when it sensed something beyond the pale of human perception. Kamaska's dark hands tightened around the reins of his mule till the knuckles shone white, and his voice shook on the word.

"*Nagual,*" he said hoarsely, and gave a jerk on the reins that pulled the mule completely around, sending it crashing into the brush, Kamaska's voice echoing back as he said it again in what was almost a cry, this time: "*¡Nagual!*"

The wind had ceased, and, after the sound of Kamaska's passing had died, the utter silence pressed in on Cardigan with a physical, suffocating weight. The ashen *cenizo* across the clearing was still trembling from the passage of the man who had appeared through it an instant before, only accentuating the complete quiescence of the man himself, as he stood there and of his two shaggy hounds, motionless, on either side of him. A pair of greasy *chivarras* were his only covering. His black torso was bare, a scabrous covering of fresh scars and scar tissue peeling from old scars giving him a leprous, revolting appearance. His black head was covered with hair like a thick mat of curly grama grass. The whites of his eyes gleamed in his dark face as he spoke and his voice held a hollow, bell-like intonation.

"I am Africano," he said.

"Cardigan's mine."

It was almost as startling as watching a statue come to life when the man named Africano moved, coming toward Cardigan with a smooth, flowing, soundless walk. "You came to help *Señorita* Zamora?"

"I didn't know she needed help," said Cardigan, stifling with some effort the desire to put his hand on his gun.

"You must know," said Africano. "You came to help her."

"There are a lot of things I don't know," said Cardigan.

"But would like to."

"I would," said Cardigan. "And a lot of other folks, too."

"But you especially," murmured the man, his eyes white and shining on Cardigan.

Cardigan studied the negroid features, trying to reconcile the luminous intelligence in those eyes with the primal brutality of the low, heavy brow, the coarse line of lips and nose. "What do you mean, me . . . especially?"

"Comal Garza thought your *compadre* was Lieutenant Dixon."

"Are we going through that again?" asked Cardigan wearily.

"Comal Garza did not consider you." Cardigan could not help the way the lines deepened about his mouth. It was the only sign, but he realized Africano had noted it. The man took something from inside his *chivarras*. It was a flat leather case about a foot long and five inches wide. The moon had risen, and Cardigan could make out the lettering on the case. *Tío* Balacar. This time Cardigan tried to keep it from showing, but something must have passed through his face, for there was a satisfaction in Africano's hollow voice. "I thought it might mean something to you."

"He's here, then," said Cardigan through set teeth.

"What else?" said Africano. "I found it down near Mogotes Oros. Camp had been made there."

"Anything else?"

"Rumors," said Africano.

"Why show this to me?"

"There was a man named George Weaver," said Africano.

Cardigan's brows raised as his head rose, wrinkling his forehead when he finally stared into Africano's eyes. "What's happened to him?"

"About a month ago." Africano waved a repulsive hand. "Also down near Mogotes Oros."

"What happened to George?" The grim insistence in Cardigan's voice drew Africano up.

"*La onza.*"

"Don't give me that!" Cardigan dropped the case in a sudden burst of anger, grabbing the man by his thick shoulders, voice rising to a hoarse shout. "Everybody I asked says it that way. I'm damn' tired of it. *Nagualismo. La onza. Nagual.* Give it to me straight, damn you. What happened to Weaver? The same thing that happened to Navasato? You know! What the hell made tracks that big around Navasato? And Kamaska. He called you *nagual*? I never thought I'd see him scared like that at anything. Tell me, damn you!"

It was the sound that stopped Cardigan, before the actual pain. Africano had stood motionless in his grasp, and Cardigan did not realize why until the guttural eruption from his feet. Then he gasped, releasing his hold on Africano, jumping backward to lash out with his leg. Both dogs were at him now, the one which had bitten his leg leaping away, and then darting back in savagely to catch at his swinging arm. Cardigan had been reaching instinctively for his gun, but the slashing pain of teeth ripping his hand caused him to pull it up again with a howl. His backward momentum carried him off balance, and he went down beneath them, kicking violently with his legs and throwing his arms over his face.

"Tuahantapec!"—called Africano without much vehemence—"Bautista!"—and then it was gone. One instant Cardigan had been the center of a whirling, snarling mass of fangs and fur and claws, the next he was lying there on an empty clearing, the hoarse rasping of his own breath the only sound. He sat up, nursing the slashed hand, blood soaking down his Levi's from the long rip there. Perhaps it was the riders that had frightened Africano away. They came into the open with a crackling of brush, and Pinto Parker was the first to dismount from his steaming horse. Getting to his feet, Cardigan could see Kamaska behind Garza, his eyes still wide and luminous with that fear.

"I told you," Kamaska said. "Look at him, look at him. *Nagual. La onza.*"

Garza swung down, a strange, baffled look in his eyes as he stared at the slashes on Cardigan's hand. "What was it?"

"A *negro* and a couple of big dogs," said Cardigan sullenly.

Cardigan saw relief cross Garza's face, and the man let his breath out and seemed to force a small laugh. "You must mean Africano. He's not *negro*. He's *mestizo*. Part Aztec, he claims."

Parker had picked up the brown case from the ground, staring at the gilt letters on its flap with a frown that held more than puzzlement. "Who's *Tio* Balacar?" he said.

IV

They were called Mogotes Oros, which meant the Gold Thickets, because of the huisache that grew through them in such profusion and turned yellow in the spring. Almost every Saturday the *vaqueros* held a bull-tailing there, providing almost their only form of entertainment, gathering to eat and drink and gamble. It was two days after the dogs had attacked Cardigan, but he was still feeling mean, his hand swollen and painful as he swung down off the dun and stood there a moment looking at the group of *jacales* to one side of the clearing, the inevitable house of brush and adobe in which the *brazaderos* and their families lived.

A pair of squat, ugly women in shapeless skirts of tattered wool and dirty white camisas for blouses had begun building the fire and driving cottonwood stakes into the ground for the spit. Behind a *jacal* was a large corral containing a dozen ringy bulls, the nervous lather about their jaws and their raucous bawls and incessant stamping showing how recently they had been brought in from the brush. Beyond the corral was the somber brasada, its depths stirring restlessly when a faint breeze fanned the summer heat momentarily. A saddle creaked beside Cardigan, and Comal Garza's voice was soft in his ear, mocking somehow.

"It is a strange land to a newcomer, no? Perhaps you are beginning to realize how impossible it would be for you to find your way out alone. Many men have been lost here, *señor.*

The brasada is more deadly than the desert . . . to those who do not know it intimately."

A mirthless smile crossing his dark face, he moved toward the group of *vaqueros* lounging in the shade of a coma tree.

Pinto had dismounted now, hitching the reins of his spotted pony to the mesquite, a narrow speculation in his eyes as he studied Cardigan. "What's going on?"

"I thought it didn't bother you."

Pinto made an impatient gesture with his hand. "First the girl. Then this Garza *hombre*. What's between you and them? The way Florida watches you."

"Getting jealous?"

"More than that," said Pinto, easing his girth more onto one leg. "I wouldn't mind if it was your native charm attracting the girl. But it's something more." He studied Cardigan's intense face. "I really don't know much about you, do I?"

Cardigan shrugged. "I don't know much about you, either. We've got along that way."

"You know what I am, Cardigan."

"You know what I am, Pinto."

"I thought I did," said Parker. "Who is Lieutenant Dixon?"

Cardigan met Parker's eyes. "I don't know any more than you do, Pinto. Evidently this Dixon was bringing a bunch of Krags to Garza, and they expected him the same day we passed through, the same spot."

"Why should Garza want a load of guns?"

"Maybe he has other interests besides mustangs."

"Gunrunning? Who to?"

"How should I know?" Impatience had leaked into Cardigan's tone. "The revolutionists in Coahilla. The *federales*. There's always a market down there."

Pinto shook his head, not satisfied. "More than that, Cardigan. Just a simple little smuggling wouldn't upset the whole brasada like this. I can feel it. See it. This *nagualismo* business is mixed up in it, too, somehow."

He trailed off as the sound of a fiddle rose from across the clearing. A blind *brazadero* was sawing on his ancient instrument and tapping a foot against the hard ground, and one of the younger Mexican girls had already glided into the varsoviana, the high heels of her red shoes tapping the hard-packed earth like the click of castanets. Cardigan drifted that way, and Pinto cut out in front of him with a laugh.

"Not this time, *compadre*. I'm claiming this first dance with the prettiest gal here."

Florida had been talking to one of the women at the fire, and Pinto caught Florida up with a whoop, swung her out toward the others. Innocencio had brought his guitar, and, as his playing joined in with the fiddle's, the excitement caught at Florida. Cardigan could see the flush climb up her neck into her cheeks and her eyes widen and flash. She was laughing as Pinto whirled her into the cradle dance they called a *cuna,* and more couples wheeled out until all Cardigan could see was Florida's shining black hair spinning through the brown faces and whirling bodies. He knew a twinge of envy at Pinto Parker's facility with women, and then smiled at himself for that. Garza was drinking pulque from a big Guadalajara jar with Kamaska and three other *vaqueros,* and Cardigan felt them glancing toward him once. Then he saw Parker and the girl had stopped dancing and were coming through the crowd toward him, a puzzled frown on Parker's face. Kamaska left the group of *vaqueros* and moved over toward the horses in his shuffling, anthropoid walk.

"I can't figure what you got on this gal," said Parker as he came up to Cardigan.

"What do you mean?"

Parker wiped his sweating face with a fancy bandanna, and his grin looked forced. "She wants to dance with you."

"I don't dance," said Cardigan.

"Then it's time to learn," Florida told him, and the soft touch of her hand against his back caused him to stiffen. She felt it, and looked into his eyes, and then laughed. It angered him, and he swung her out almost roughly. Why should he let her touch do that to him? Enough other women had touched him. She was still laughing as she tried to teach him the steps. As they swung in the *cuna*, she let herself come up against him with a bold smile, and he thought she was coquetting and his lips spread back from his teeth in a disgusted way. Then he realized it wasn't for that she'd come near. Her breath was hot against the side of his face as she spoke.

"It's the only chance I'll get to tell you. They're up to something. Watch yourself and don't go off alone. I don't know what it is, but they're up to something."

The desperate intensity of her voice caught at him. "Who's up to something?"

"*Señores y señoritas,*" called Garza from where the fiddler stood, "if you have had enough dancing, we shall turn out the first *toro* so we can get started with the feasting!"

A cheer went up from the *vaqueros* around Cardigan, and they left their partners on the spot, running across the compound toward their horses. With excited squeals, the women scattered toward the *jacales*. Innocencio and another man had driven a bull from the corral. He was a wild-looking bay with brown points, switching its rump from side to side and pawing at the ground.

"*¡Muy valiente!*" shouted Kamaska, leaping on his hairy mule, and the others mounted to follow him at a gallop into the open after the bull.

Garza led his *pelicano* from under the comas. "You have

tailed the bull, *Señor* Cardigan?"

"I've tailed a few," said Cardigan.

"It is a practice more common near the border," said Garza. "If you watch, you will see how we do it down here."

Cardigan couldn't help letting it goad him, although he knew that was Garza's intent. He stood by his dun, watching the riders haze down the bull. Kamaska was in the lead, and, as the bull broke for the brush, Kamaska ran his mule off to one side of the running animal and came in from there, leaning far out of the saddle to catch at the switching tail. The riders behind were whooping wildly and slapping at their *chivarras* with quirts, and the dust boiled up around the whole group as Kamaska caught the bull's tail and dallied the end around his saddle horn as he would a rope. With his free hand he jerked the reins against the mule's neck, and the mule veered sharply away. Cardigan saw the bull's tail stretch taut, swinging the animal's hind feet from beneath it. At that moment, Kamaska released the tail and galloped free, and the bull shook the ground with its falling.

"A good man can break a bull's neck that way," Garza told Cardigan. "Perhaps you would like to ride the next one. Whoever throws him gets the honor of eating his brains."

Kamaska must have broken the bull's neck, for he lay inert as a *vaquero* roped his horns with a rawhide dally and hauled him off toward the fire. Innocencio was goading another bull out of the corral, a big *sabina* beast, hide mottled with red and white speckles, one of his horns growing in a broken, twisted way down across his eye. The heavy, scarred head was tossing wickedly from side to side as he danced from the corral.

"Ah"—there was a certain satisfaction in Garza's tone—"this one I will ride myself. It is Gotch, *señor*. It will take a real man."

Cardigan swung an angry leg over his dun, knowing the

men had little respect for him after the sorry spectacle he had made in the ride after the mustangs. Maybe he didn't know the brasada, he thought, but if he couldn't tail a bull, he might as well sack his saddle right here. As he trotted the dun out after Garza, he thought he heard someone call from behind him.

"Cardigan, not that one, not Gotch. . . ."

It was lost in the whoops that rose from the riders as they wheeled out their horses in the rising dust. Innocencio gave the bull a last jab with his prod pole. The *sabina* bellowed in rage, evil little eyes darting from side to side as he shied around the fire. Then he spotted the free brush ahead and the scarred head lowered, and he made his first rush.

"*Viva*, Gotch!" yelled Kamaska, his quirt popping against his *chivarras* like a gunshot, and Garza jabbed his *pelicano* with silver-plated spurs the size of cartwheels, and the animal leaped forward with a shrill whinny. A bitter satisfaction swept Cardigan as he jumped his own horse into a run and saw how quickly it closed the space between him and Garza's prized *pelicano*. Then the excitement of reckless speed and wild sounds beat at him, and he didn't know whether the drumming beat inside him was the blood pounding through his ears or the thud of hoofs beneath him.

The yells of the *vaqueros* came to Cardigan through a din of galloping horses and the dust rose up yellow and choking and blotted out the brush around him and the screaming women by the *jacales*, and all he could see was a glimpse here and there of a rider through the haze, and the snorting, running bull in front of him. His big dun was long-coupled and set low to the ground the way a good roper should be, and Cardigan could feel the steady, vicious pump of its driving hocks behind his saddle. He passed Kamaska, and the main group dropped behind him, and then Garza was on his flank, beating his *pelicano* desperately with a plaited quirt. Give him a little slack on those ribbons and he might go faster was Cardigan's momentary thought, and then his long dun had stretched past Garza. In that last instant, his face was turned toward the coma trees where they had hitched their horses, and, through a hole in the choking dust, he caught a glimpse of Florida and Pinto Parker. The girl had hold of Parker's shirt, shouting something at him. Parker's broad face turned toward Cardigan, then he whirled toward his pinto. As the dust dropped back between them, Cardigan saw Florida leaping on her own horse.

Then the bull imposed his heaving, running silhouette between them and Cardigan, and Cardigan was leaning from the saddle to grab that switching tail. He caught the hairy end and yanked upward, snubbing it around his horn. There was just enough room between his running horse and the bull to stretch the long tail tightly, and, as Cardigan saw it go taut, he laid his reins hard against the inside of the dun's thick neck. The horse responded with all the incredible alacrity of a roper, turning aside the very instant the reins made contact.

Cardigan saw the bull's hind legs slide from beneath the animal, and heard the shriek of his rigging as the weight was thrown against it. He let go his hold on the tail, instinctively stiffening for the sudden release of weight as the tail snapped loose from around the horn, throwing the bull. There was a loud pop, and the saddle jerked beneath him, and in that last instant he saw that the tail was still dallied onto the horn and had time to wonder what had happened, and then to know, before the empty air beneath him turned to the hardest ground he had ever hit. His saddle had left the dun completely, and he hit still astride the rig, kicking free of the stirrups as his boots struck the earth. He rolled backward out of the saddle, his head striking the ground with a stunning impact, the bull's tail still snubbed on the horn, dragging the saddle across the ground behind him.

Through a haze of pain, Cardigan felt himself roll to a stop. He lay there a moment with noise droning around him. Then the sounds began separating themselves into something discernible.

"Don't turn him that way," someone was shouting, "you'll drive him right back at Cardigan! That saddle's got him crazy and he'll go right back. Let him go, let him go. . . ."

It was Florida's voice. Sight reeled back to Cardigan. He saw the *vaqueros* had cut the bull off from the open brush. The *sabina* had reversed.

"Let him stop, you fools." That was Pinto's voice, from somewhere behind Cardigan. "Give him a chance to slow down and his tail will slack up and let go that saddle. It's the saddle driving him loco."

It *was* the saddle. Crazed by the bobbing, rattling rig which followed his every movement no matter which way he turned, the gotched bull had reached the point of frenzy where he quit seeking escape and wanted only to reach his tormentors and vent his wild rage. He whirled toward Florida as she came in from the quarter, tossing her rope at his frothed muzzle. The bull made a wily jump aside, and the dally spun on past and dropped on the ground. The *sabina* lunged at Florida's horse, and she missed getting gored by inches as she jabbed her can openers into her animal, jumping it past the running bull. With his head down, the *sabina* thundered on past the rump of Florida's horse, his momentum carrying the beast straight toward Cardigan. He had been trying to move, in a feeble, stunned way, and it must have been this that caught the bull's attention.

The shaking ground beneath Cardigan told him how close

the bull was before he looked. Then his gaze swung up and caught that frothed muzzle and those wicked little eyes and that great pair of speckled shoulders.

There was no time for fear in that last instant. Only a shocking comprehension of how it stood. He made one last effort to rise, and failed, and knew it would not have helped anyway. Then, from somewhere back of the running bull, he heard a wild shout. Dust rose in a great cloud about the animal, hiding movement for an instant, sweeping across Cardigan where he was crouching. The steady shake of the ground to the running hoofs of the bull changed to a great, roaring shudder beneath Cardigan. A dim shape pounded through the dust to his right. He thought it was the bull, and wondered why the beast had swerved. Then the dust began to settle, and he saw it had not been the bull.

The *sabina* lay in a heap not two feet from Cardigan's hand, the hot, fetid odor of his great body sweeping nauseatingly across Cardigan, his hind legs twitching in a last, spasmodic way before he lay completely still. The shape that had passed Cardigan was coming back now. Pinto Parker swung off his spotted horse and caught Cardigan's arm, sweat streaking the dust on his face, the inevitable grin revealing his white teeth.

"Guess that will show them how we tail a bull north of the Nueces," he said cheerfully. "You're all right, now, aren't you?"

Cardigan was staring stupidly at the *sabina,* and the full realization of how close death had come to him was bringing its reaction. He got to his feet as quickly as possible, pulling his arm free of Pinto's grasp, not wanting the man to feel him trembling.

"Yeah. Yeah. All right." Then Cardigan turned to meet Pinto's gaze. "Thanks, Pinto," he said simply and saw the understanding in Pinto's eyes, and knew he needed to say no more.

Florida had brought her horse up, swinging off, with a wide relief in her big, dark eyes, and Garza pranced his *pelicano* in, glancing at the bull first. "I haven't seen a bull tailed like that in years, *Señor* Parker. You should have been born a *Mejicano*."

"Where are you going?" Florida asked.

Cardigan did not bother to answer. He stumbled in a grim deliberateness to where his saddle lay behind the *sabina*. The bull's tail was still snubbed tightly about the slick roping horn, and he had to jerk it off and unwind the rigging from around it before he could turn the saddle over. He had to lift the skirt up off the front girth before he could find it, and now he understood why Garza had held his reins in so tightly when he was quirting his horse, and why the dun had passed the *pelicano* so easily, and the others.

"That where the cinch broke?" asked Pinto, leading his pinto over.

"No," said Cardigan. "That's where it was cut."

V

Evening fell across the brasada insidiously, darkening the lanes through the outer thickets first, then creeping into the clearing of Mogotes Oros till the firelight blazed redly in the velvet gloom. New sounds came with the night. A coyote began its dismal howl somewhere far out in the brush. A hoot owl mourned closer in. Standing there at the edge of the clearing, Cardigan found it ineffably sinister. It was an hour after Pinto had saved his life. The *vaqueros* and their women were beginning to eat the meat of the dead bulls. Parker came across the clearing from the fire.

"Got your rig fixed?"

"I cut off a piece of my latigo and tied it to the cinch ring," said Cardigan. "It'll last till we get back."

"I still think you're loco, not having it out with them. If they cut your cinch."

"How would that improve our position?" said Cardigan. "It wouldn't bring us any closer to finding out which one of them cut it, or why. It would only antagonize the whole bunch of them. We're hardly in a spot to do that right now. At least we keep them wondering this way. They don't know for sure I found the cut in the cinch."

Parker was studying him. "Why do you want to stay here?"

Cardigan's eyes opened a little. "How do you mean?"

"When a man finds out somebody's after his guts this way,

his natural reaction should be wanting to get away."

"Should it?"

Parker studied him a moment longer, then a slow grin crossed his broad face. "No," he said, and chuckled. "No. I guess not. Not a man like you, Card. You'd want to stay and find out. You'd want to stay and nail the buzzard who tried to spill your guts on a gotch's horn that way."

"Wouldn't you?" said Cardigan.

"Let's go over and get some of that meat," said Parker. "I'm plumb ravenous."

Esperanza had come in a *carreta* drawn by a yoke of longhorn oxen, and he was officiating at the spit. "Ah, *señores*," he called, looking at Cardigan and Parker approaching, "you are just in time to see us unearth the head. We have a handful of oregano stuffed in the mouth for flavor, *sí?* All wrapped up in grass and tied with the leaves of the Spanish dagger, lightly roasted in ashes to make the fiber pliable. You have never tasted such a delicacy. And to you, *Señor* Parker, for tailing this *toro* goes the honor of the brains. Would you like the eggs, *Señor* Cardigan?"

"Eggs?" asked Cardigan.

"Eyes," Parker muttered, beside him. "Take them. They're ribbing you."

Cardigan let his glance circle the men. He saw the speculation in Kamaska's face, and thought: *Yes, you big ape, I know my cinch was sliced, do you?* The others were watching him, too. Garza had mockery in his smile.

"Sure," said Cardigan. "Back home I always get the eggs." Then he realized they were not watching him any more. Garza's glance was turned past Cardigan, and the mockery had been replaced by surprise. Kamaska made a sudden, abortive shift, across the fire, and then stopped. Parker turned around before Eddie Cardigan did.

There were at least a score of men, and they must have come in on foot so as not to make any noise. Cardigan had seen enough posses before to recognize one. The noise about the fire had dropped so low that Cardigan heard Garza's hissing, indrawn breath before the man spoke.

"Sheriff Masset," said Garza.

Sheriff Sid Masset moved with a graceful ease, surprising in such a prodigiously paunched man.

"Don't anybody do anything foolish," he said, and the lack of vehemence in his tone only lent to its potency. He moved on forward, the .45-90 he held across his hip swinging slightly with the side-to-side motion of his walk. "I'm taking you in this time, Garza. I've caught you outside your damn' Cañada Diablo and I'm taking you in and you better not object the slightest because I've got twenty boys here just itching to push that fresh-roasted beef out the back of your belly with some law-abiding lead."

"I don't understand," said Garza. "You have no charge."

"I've got two or three charges. A hundred Big Skillet steers was run off their home range a week back, and we got a pretty good description of the operators, two of which I see among you now. It's the last bunch of cattle you'll take into that Cañada Diablo, Garza."

"They aren't my. . . ."

"Then we got a number of dead men to account for," said Masset, his boots making their last, sibilant creak as he stopped in a bunch of short grass. "Deputy Smithers was found dead last month just this side of the Comanche Trail, all clawed up. There was a government marshal named George Weaver found the same way near these *mogotes*. It wasn't no ordinary cat done that, Garza. In fact, there's some think it wasn't no cat at all. The Mexicans say this is some of that *nagualismo* bunk. Whatever it is, your crowd is mixed up in it. Now, I want you to step out in front of me here, one by one, and drop all your hardware."

The irony of it was what struck Cardigan first—to be taken in for those cattle, to have the whole thing spoiled like this for a mangy bunch of Big Skillet stuff, when it wasn't that at all. The fire made its soft crackle behind him, and he had already thought of it. They were standing in a bunch of short grass turned sere by the summer heat. There was a general shift through the crowd of *vaqueros* as Garza moved sullenly forward, and it gave Cardigan a chance to step back without being noticed.

Cardigan toed a coal from the edge of the fire. The heat of it had penetrated the leather of the boot before he had it shoved into the grass. Pinto Parker was unbuckling his Colt when Masset's head rose.

"Stamp it out," he yelled abruptly. "Behind you. Stamp it out!"

Cardigan jumped aside with the heat of the flame searing the back of his leg. The coal had caught in the brown grass, and the fire was leaping forward toward the posse beneath the fan of the wind. Yelling wildly, Cardigan began stamping at the ground on his side of the growing fire. Pinto Parker turned with an immediate understanding, stooping to grab a handful of grass at his feet and pull it up by the roots.

"Throw dirt on it," he yelled.

"Don't be a fool!" shouted Masset. "You're just throwing more grass. You'll have the whole brasada afire."

"*Sí,*" shouted Garza, taking that chance for movement and jumping toward the fire, which brought him nearer the spot where his six-gun lay on the ground. "Stamp it out. You want all of the Mogotes Oros to burn up?"

The whole crowd of *vaqueros* was yelling and shifting now, and Cardigan saw Florida kicking more of the coals into the grass. Indecision spread through the milling crowd of possemen, some of them jumping forward toward the blaze, the ones in front of them backing up. The coals Florida had kicked out were catching, and the flames were rapidly forming a blazing wall between the posse and the *vaqueros*. Already Kamaska was turning toward the *vaqueros'* horses, hitched behind the coma trees. Cardigan was still kicking wildly at the fire and shouting, when the full realization struck Masset.

"I'll shoot the first man that moves!" he bellowed.

"It's blowing right into us," yelled one of the possemen.

"Do what I say!" shouted Masset. "Can't you see they did this on purpose? I'll shoot the first one that moves. Garza. . . ."

Masset's rifle drowned him out, but Garza had already dived through a hole in the blaze, and the roaring flames made his running body a deceptive target. While Masset was still turned, pulling down his lever to put in another shell, Cardigan caught Pinto by the back of his shirt, yanking him straight into the blaze. They ran through the flames, choking, gasping. Cardigan heard another gunshot from behind them, and his flat-topped Stetson was jerked off. Then they were on the other side of the fire. Parker's shirt was ablaze, and Cardigan threw himself on the man, beating at the smoking flannel till it was out. He realized someone else was also beating at him, and, when Pinto pushed him away, he saw Florida had a saddle blanket half wrapped around him.

"Let's go!" shouted Parker, laughing recklessly.

The *vaqueros* were running back and forth all about them now. Garza galloped past on his *pelicano*, followed by Kamaska. The second man wheeled his hairy, black mule toward Florida, jerking his foot from the stirrup. "*Señorita*," he shouted, "climb on with me!"

Florida cast a wild glance at Cardigan. "Go on, Kamaska.

Everyone for himself now. I'll get my own horse. We'll be safe as soon as we get into Cañada Diablo."

The fire had swept into the possemen, scattering them, and was rapidly filling the grassed-over section of the clearing and breaking into the thickets surrounding it. A great *mogote* of huisache went up in crackling glory, and, beyond that, a growth of chaparral began to blaze, lighting the thickets about it weirdly. Three possemen who had run around one end of the blaze burst from the thickets near the *jacales* and began to fire. With a wild yell, Pinto turned on them and threw down with his Colt. Cardigan saw one of the men drop. Then he had reached the horses, tearing loose the reins of his frenzied dun, and the girl's rearing black. The bulls, maddened by the fire, had burst loose of the shaky ocotillo corral and were running wildly through the clearing. Cardigan had all he could do to get on his frightened dun.

Parker was the first to break into the brush, the girl after him, a wild, swaying shape, her long hair flying, and again Cardigan knew amazement at her incredible ability at riding the thickets. She drove her animal straight at a growth of black chaparral covered thickly with huisache. There must have been a hole, although Cardigan could not see it, for she crashed through the chaparral, trailing the huisache from her head and shoulders, leaving a big aperture for him to follow through. He leaped a low spread of *granjeno* and, while his eyes were fixed on an upflung spear of Spanish dagger and he was dodging aside to miss being impaled, a post-oak branch appeared out of nowhere. Shutting his eyes instinctively, he ducked abruptly.

He felt the mesquite rake across his arm and he knew he had avoided it, and, just as he opened his eyes, another outreaching oak branch caught his head. Pain made a great roar in back of his eyes, and blackness swept him, and that was the way he hit the ground, no comprehension in between the striking branch and the hard blow of the earth. He lay there, spinning in a sick wave of nausea, trying to rise, and was dimly aware of a rattling crash somewhere above him. It was Florida, coming back. She drew her horse up onto its hocks and swung down.

"You've got to keep your eyes open!" she called to him. "No matter what happens, you've got to keep your eyes open. You'll never be able to ride the brush unless you do that."

"Go on," he tried to wave her away, blood dribbling into his eyes as he shook his head. "If the fire don't catch up with you, Masset will. I'm not worth waiting for. I'll never make a brush rider. I don't want to. The hell with it."

Frenzied by the fire, Florida's horse was plunging and rearing against her hold on the reins. "Don't be a fool, Cardigan. Get on, will you? I can't hold him much longer. Cardigan . . . Cardigan, get on . . . !"

Cardigan was still too dazed to do more than make a wild, vague grab at the flying reins as the horse plunged forward, taking Florida off balance and tearing loose from her grasp. The hoofs made their shuddering pound past him, and the brush crashed, and then the animal was gone. Florida stood there, above Cardigan, her face flushed, her bosom heaving. She looked down at him, and her lips peeled flatly away from her teeth in whatever she was going to say, before, with a disgusted exhalation, she bent to help him up. He was on his feet before they both heard the crackle of brush from the direction of the clearing. For a moment, hope shone in Florida's face.

"No," said Cardigan. "That isn't a horse. I told you, if the fire didn't catch up with us, Masset would."

VI

The thickets rose in sinister desolation on every side, standing in impenetrable mystery beneath the pale light of the moon that cast the shadow of each twisted bush across the ground in a weird, tortured pattern. This pattern slid constantly across the back of Florida's white silk shirt like some live thing, as she moved beneath the brush ahead of Cardigan. They had traveled on foot southward. The fire and its sounds were lost behind them, and nothing but the haunted silence of the night reached their ears, broken infrequently by the dim howl of a coyote, or the lonely call of an owl.

"We're in now," she whispered. "Masset won't follow us here."

"He doesn't look like the kind of man who'd be scared out by some Indian superstition."

"Masset's brave enough," she said. "So are a lot of other men. You don't see them in here, do you? You don't see any sheriffs or any marshals or any Texas Rangers, do you? The whole brasada's always been a hotbed of border hoppers and rustlers and killers, and a lawman was taking his life in his hands to enter any part of it after a man, and Cañada Diablo is the worst spot of all. Even so, there were always men who'd pack a badge in here. They knew what was waiting for them, and they knew how to fight it. Until this last year, that is. They can't fight this, Cardigan. It's always the same. They send their men in, and a few weeks, or a few months later, some *brazadero* finds them in the brush. You heard Masset. That marshal, George Weaver. Deputy Smithers. They're only two, and they were the last ones, and that was months ago. And so they've stopped coming. There's no use just sending a man to his death. Especially when there aren't any men left who'll come in. Would you? If you were a Ranger, or a deputy, would you come in, knowing what fate all the others had met? Even when they have something definite to follow, like those cattle?"

"You didn't talk that way back in the bunkshack," he said. "You weren't going to dignify any Indian ghost story."

She looked up at him in a strained, pale way, then turned her face to the side. "I don't know, Cardigan, I don't know. I've tried to tell myself such a thing couldn't be. All along, I've tried. But it's all around. Just waiting out there."

"And yet you live right in the middle of Cañada Diablo as safe as a kitten up a tree," said Cardigan, and it brought her eyes around to him again. "If someone were doing something in Cañada Diablo, it would be very convenient for them to have this *nagualismo* business keeping the law away, wouldn't it?"

"What do you mean . . . doing something?"

"It still seems strange to me that a spread the size of yours would devote its whole time to running mustangs . . . or gathering Krags."

She started to answer him, but her mouth remained open without any words coming out, and her eyes were staring blankly into the thicket. It came to him finally, and he let his hand drop to the butt of his gun.

"Masset?" he whispered.

"I told you he wouldn't come in here after. . . ."

It was the only way to stop her quickly enough. Cardigan felt her whole body stiffen against him as his arm snaked around her neck, and her lips mashed damply beneath his sweaty palm. The man rustled through the last chaparral and came into the open with his rifle held down at the hip, and Cardigan had met enough men that way to know what the expression on his face meant when he saw them, and to know what had to be done. He already had his Remington out of leather, and he threw his weight against Florida as he fired. Masset's .45-90 echoed Cardigan's gun, and the slug clattered through brush about the height of Cardigan's chest, if he had remained erect. Masset was already spinning around with the force of Cardigan's slug in him. It turned him in a half circle, and, by the time he took the stumbling step to keep from falling, it was carrying him in the opposite direction. He was bent almost double when he stopped, still on his feet, trying grimly to retain the rifle and snap its lever down again. From where he had thrown himself, lying half across the girl, Cardigan called to Masset.

"Don't, Masset. I don't want to kill you."

Still bent forward, Masset turned his head. His eyes, squinted with pain, took in the five-shot held at Cardigan's hip. Reluctantly he dropped the rifle.

Cardigan got to his feet, lips drawn back against his teeth. "Go on back now," he said. "You were a fool to come this far."

Masset had one beefy hand gripped across his shoulder where the bullet had hit. His words came out gustily. "I'm tired of fooling around, Florida. I'm going to clean you out of here if it takes an army. . . ."

"I told you to get out, damn you, before it's too late," snarled Cardigan. "You don't know what this is, Masset. You came in here just for a bunch of steers? You don't know what you're getting into. Now, get out!"

He almost shouted the last, in an anger he could not name

himself, and Masset drew himself up, grunting a little with the pain movement caused him, his eyes narrowing even more. "What are you talking about, pard?"

"Just what I said," Cardigan told him.

"*Tío* Balacar?" said Masset.

"What about *Tío* Balacar?" Cardigan's voice held an edge.

"We heard he's been seen in here."

Cardigan was surprised to hear Florida's voice behind him. "Heard from whom?"

"That nigger. Africano. How do you think I knew you'd be outside Cañada Diablo tonight?" Masset was looking at Florida now. "What's going on, girl? What's Balacar doing in the brush?"

"Masset, if you don't get out. . . ."

"Sure, I'll get out." Masset swung toward Cardigan. "But I'm coming back, and, when I do, it'll be for good!"

He turned heavily and crashed off into the thicket like a ringy, old bull. Cardigan was just starting to get Masset's rifle when the sound came. It seemed far away, at first, and yet close up, somehow, filling Cardigan with a vague awe. He turned toward Florida. Her mouth was open, and her eyes, staring at him, were blank with listening. The noise had died before her glance took focus with a perceptible jerk.

"What was it?" he said.

"Cat," she said in a hollow voice. "Sounded like a cat."

"I never heard no bobcat squall like that," he said.

"Jaguar. Mexican ones. They come down out of the mountains." She seemed to twitch then, and something like shame came into her face, and her voice lost its hollow tone abruptly, coming out quick and hard. "Are we going?"

He had not moved yet when the scream rang through the brush, so akin to another scream that his own shout followed it instinctively. "Navasato!" he yelled, and then realized the significance of his reaction and jumped toward the *mogote* into which Masset had disappeared.

"Cardigan," gasped the girl from behind him, "Cardigan, don't go in there. Please!"

But he was already bursting through the thicket of chaparral, Masset's unintelligible cries driving him. He crashed into a small clearing on the other side of the first thicket, face scratched and bleeding, and the screams had stopped. Masset lay beneath a bunch of ripped, trampled mesquite on the other side of the open space, his face mangled beyond recognition, his shirt torn from his fat, bloody back. There was a rattling out in the brush, and then that ceased. Cardigan stood there, staring at Masset, hardly aware of Florida as she came out of the thicket behind him and made a low, strangled sound of horror.

"I sent him into that," said Cardigan, a deep bitterness entering his voice. "I sent him into that."

"No, Cardigan." Florida's grasp at his arm pulled it down. "How could you know? It might have caught him anywhere. It wasn't your fault."

He didn't have to go down beside Masset to see if the man were dead, that was patent enough, but there was something else he wanted to see. Pinto Parker had said they were larger than any cat tracks he had seen. Cardigan struck a match for light, and bent down. Parker was right. It gave Cardigan a strange, suffocated sensation to stare at the prints of the huge, padded claws. Florida was staring at them, too, and then she was catching at his arm again as he rose, a swift, breathless desperation in her voice, as the flame guttered out.

"You know what this means, Cardigan? Masset was right. I've sensed it all along, but now I know it. This *nagualismo* isn't just a rumor. It's too deliberate. We can't let it go any further, Cardigan. I can't go any longer trying to feel you out, and waiting for you to make your move. I've got to trust you, and you've got to trust me."

He sensed that what had just happened was bringing it out of her like this. "What do you mean?"

She had him by both elbows, staring into his eyes with a driven intensity. "You think I'm one of them, don't you? You think I'm just rodding a bunch of rustlers and smugglers?"

"It did look like you were top screw in the corral."

"You know that's not true." Her eyes were pleading with him.

"Do I?" he said warily.

"I told you that's got to stop." Florida's voice was rising. "We've got to trust each other, Cardigan. Why do you think I kept them from killing you that first time?"

"I really don't know."

"You *do* know!" she almost shouted. "Will you quit evading me like this? There isn't any more time to play that game." She glanced at Masset, revulsion twisting her mouth. "You might be next, I might be next, Pinto might." Suddenly the warmth of her body was against him and her face was pressed into his sweaty, burnt shirt front, and he could see the fight she was making to keep from crying. "Cardigan," she mumbled against him, "please, please, I'm at the end of my dally, and you don't know how long I've been doing this alone, in the brush, all alone, against all of it, and, when you came and I thought . . . I thought. . . ." She twisted her face the other way against him, the hair drawn, taut and lustrous, across the top of her head. "Oh, Cardigan, please. . . ."

Holding her like this filled him with a strange weakness he had never known before, and all his wary, suspicious control left him, and he spoke in a harsh, guttural acquiescence. "What do you want?"

There was a triumph in the way she lifted her face to him.

"Who you are. I've got to know that, Cardigan. I've got to know where I stand now, whether there's anybody at all, or whether I'm still alone. I'm not, am I, Cardigan? Tell me I'm not. Tell me I was right about you."

The movement of her head away from his chest might have been what caused it. Suspicion returned in a swift inundation as he saw the triumph in her eyes. It might have been innocent triumph. He searched her face for guile, and found none. Yet he eased away from her, almost trembling with the realization of how close he had come. She saw what had happened, within him, and jumped backward like a cat in rage.

"You still won't trust me. You think they put me up to this? I guess I should have let them have you in the first place. You don't care. You know what *Tío* Balacar is up to, but you don't care. You'll just let him go ahead and do this. People think the brasada's a dangerous place now? Wait till Balacar comes. What's gone on before will just be a Sunday school picnic compared with what it will be after he gets through. You told Masset he didn't know how big this thing is? I don't think you know how big it is. I don't think you want to know. . . ."

"Florida. . . ."

"Shut up," she spat. "I was a fool to think you were any different than Parker. You're just a couple of tinhorn rustlers looking for a place to hole up till it blows over about those Big Skillet cattle. You were right. You'll never make a brush hand. You'll never make anything. You. . . ."

Perhaps it was the expression on Cardigan's face that stopped her. He had heard the sound before she did, because she was so deep in her rage. Now she heard it, and the angry flush seeped out of her face, leaving it pale in the moonlight. Cardigan's hand tightened around the butt of his Remington, and he raised the gun without being conscious he did it.

"Cardigan," breathed Florida, and took a step toward him, fear turning her eyes dark.

It came again, like the scream of a woman in mortal pain, weird and unearthly and terrifying. Then it ceased, and all Cardigan could hear was his own breathing. His burned, smudged face was greasy with sweat and he could feel it dripping down his sleeves, from beneath his armpits. The first impulse to move seeped through him vaguely, and he was about to answer it when the brush clattered. Both of them whirled, and the hammer of Cardigan's Remington made a sharp, metallic click under his thumb.

"*Buenas noches,*" said Africano, from where he stood beneath the chaparral with his two dogs. Cardigan stared at him blankly, unable to speak for that moment, and the girl stood with her underlip dropped slightly, making no sound. Africano's face bore no expression. "You heard *la onza?*"

"Yeah," said Cardigan finally. "We heard something." His voice took on a patient deliberateness. "What is it, Africano? What is *la onza?*"

Africano's eyes shone white as they dropped to Masset, then they rose again, meeting Cardigan's, and they held something he could not read. "*La onza* is a hybrid, *señor.* A cross between a bull tiger and a she-lion. There is nothing more deadly. There is nothing more terrible."

Cardigan jerked his gun to bear on one of the dogs as Africano started to move forward. "I'll kill those dogs if you bring them any closer, I swear it."

"They will not harm you unless you threaten me, *señor,*" said Africano softly.

"How do you fit in with this *onza?*" asked Cardigan harshly. "Maybe Kamaska isn't as dumb as we think."

"If you refer to his belief in *nagualismo,* there is nothing stupid about that," said Africano.

Cardigan couldn't help bending forward sharply. "Then you know. You. . . ."

"I know you had better get back to Hacienda del Diablo as soon as possible and never again get separated from your friend Parker as long as you stay in the brush."

"What are you talking about?" It was the first time Florida had spoken.

"*Tio* Balacar has come," said Africano.

VII

The black chaparral surrounded the compound of Hacienda del Diablo in endless undulations of skeletal malignancy, and the buildings huddled fearfully beneath a risen moon. One of the horses, standing hipshot before the long porch, snorted dismally. It was the only sound.

A yellow crack of light seeped from beneath the door and drew a rectangle around each of the two shuttered windows on the north side. Weary from the long hike through the brush, Cardigan stood by the ghostly pattern of a cedar-post corral, watching the house.

"Any way we can get in without being seen?" he asked.

The quick shift of Florida's head to glance at him caused moonlight to ripple across the glossy toss of her long, black hair. "They might not have locked the shutters on my bedroom," she said finally. "There's no reason for any of them to have gone in there."

They skirted the fringe of brush till they were opposite the north side of the house, then cut directly across the moonlit compound. Cardigan was tense with waiting for some reaction from Florida, and it puzzled him, in a way, that she had made no objection to coming in this way or had not tried to warn them. The heavy, oak shutters on her bedroom window opened with a loud creak, and Cardigan lifted a long leg over the low, battered sill. The bare, earthen floor of her room was as hard as cement, covered meagerly by a pair of hooked rugs he made out dimly in the soft light from outside. He passed her bed, a ponderous, hand-carved four-poster of Spanish origin, and reached the thick, wooden-pegged door. The handle of hammered silver felt cold to his touch, and it moved with less noise than the window. He cast one glance back at Florida before pulling the portal toward him. There was a tense, waiting line to the rigidity of her body. Then he turned his head, looking through the crack and down the short hall that led directly into the living room from this wing of the house.

He saw a broad-framed, thick-thewed man with the flat hams and skinny, bowed legs of the inveterate horseman, his jackboots black and polished, a fancy, gilt-edged sash about his heavy girth. His eyes were small and black and brilliant in the dissipated pouches formed by his puckered, veined, wind-wrinkled lids and his thick lips moved with sensual mobility. His hands were surprisingly delicate and slender, and he kept moving them expressively while he spoke, as if the words were spawned and shaped and caressed by his supple, ceaseless fingers, rather than coming from his mouth. With his first sight of the man, Cardigan knew who he was.

"I understand your . . . ah . . . reluctance to commit yourself, *amigo*," he was saying, and he moved across the living room in a pompous, stiff-legged walk as he talked. "I have myself, at times, endeavored to enhance my financial position by just such means. We will dispense with the moral grounds for our objection to what you are doing, though you will admit there are those who would call your attitude far from honest. We will be merely expedient. Expediency is so much more logical a basis than morality. And you can see the obvious expediency here. You have tried to improve your monetary standing in this way, and have failed. Why don't you just admit your failure and we can all be good *compadres* again and forget about it and take another drink together, and you will tell us where the Krags are."

Pinto Parker was seated at one end of the long table with a big jug of mescal before him, and he grinned thickly. "Don' know where any Krags are. I tol' you that."

Comal Garza had been standing a little farther down the table, and his pewter mug made a dull clank as he set it down on the furrowed boards. "I told you we were wasting time, *Tio*. We tried being polite before and it failed. We would have gotten it out of him the other way if Florida hadn't interfered."

"No, no," said *Tio* Balacar, his smile placating and sly at the same time. "We want Lieutenant Dixon to work with us. We want him for our *amigo*. There are things about those Krags we shall have to know before using them. Don't you see what a priceless asset an Army officer would be to us, Garza? We will never get any of that by antagonizing him. I'm sure if we could just make it clear to him . . ."—he pulled a chair from beneath the table with a flourish, and put one foot up on it, leaning forward with his elbow on the knee of his white pants—"now Lieutenant Dixon, if you will only tell us what it is you want, perhaps we can come to an agreement. We agreed on a price in Brownsville, of course, but if you want more, say so, and maybe. . . ."

"You got the wrong *hombre*." Parker grinned foolishly, taking another drink. "Wait'll Card gets here. He'll tell you."

"Perhaps Cardigan will not be getting here," said Garza.

"Sure he will," slurred Parker confidently. "Nothing can stop Card. Just a couple of cattle operators, see, *Tio*. Just running a bunch of cattle through. Let's have another drink. I haven't wet my whistle like this in weeks. Man needs to get drunk once in a while."

"You are already drunk, Lieutenant," said *Tio* Balacar,

and Cardigan could see the brilliant pinpoints of light catch in his small, black eyes. He took his foot from the chair and paced about the table, rubbing his hands together, frowning. Then he turned back, speaking to no one in particular. "It seems we have failed to make the necessary impression on the lieutenant. We offer him logic, and he says he is just a simple *hombre* trying to get along. We fill him with liquor, and his tongue does not become any looser in the direction we wish. There is very little left."

"That's what I say," Garza said.

Parker blinked owlishly at Balacar, patently not understanding the man's implication. Balacar moved around to the chair again, putting his boot up on it and leaning forward on his knee once more to peer intently at Parker. Carefully he took the glass away from him, then he put a hand on Parker's shoulder.

"Don't make us do this, *amigo*."

"Do what?" said Parker, reaching for the bottle.

Garza slid in and moved the bottle away. "No, *amigo*, don't make us."

"I don' getcha," said Parker, lurching toward the glass.

Balacar moved the glass daintily out of Parker's reach, then picked up the hand that Kamaska had used the nutcracker on, separating the swollen fingers from the rest. "It caused you some pain, eh?"

"Hurt like hell," said Parker.

"We would not want to cause you any more pain," said Balacar.

"I want another drink," said Parker. "Come on, Garza, let's toast to old Texas."

Balacar dropped the hand abruptly, swinging his foot off the chair to walk away from the table in those stiff strides. He stopped, facing the window. He slapped his hands together.

"All right," he said, without looking at Garza. "Go ahead."

"No," said Cardigan, stepping into the hall, "don't go ahead. Just stay right where you are."

He had never seen Garza display so much emotion. The man's jaw dropped and his oblique eyes were wide and blank. Cardigan's boots made a hollow tap into the room, and his lips were drawn back from his teeth in that mirthless grin. "Did you think maybe the *onza* got me, Garza?" he said.

Tío Balacar had swung around, and, after the first surprise, his glance crossed Garza's. "Cardigan?" he said.

"Cardigan," said Garza.

Cardigan moved across the floor without lost motion, his .46 swinging to cover what was necessary, and grabbed Parker by the arm. "Come on, Pinto, we're trailing out now."

"Card." Parker laughed. "I told them you'd be back. They didn't think so, but I told them. Have a drink."

"Get up. I said we're going."

The cold, flat sound of Cardigan's voice sobered Parker momentarily, and he blinked upward in that owlish way. "I thought you wanted to stay."

"Yes." Garza had recovered his composure now. "Yes, Cardigan, you aren't going to leave us now, are you? *Tío* even brought some more men to help us with the *mestenos*. Meet Aragonza. He is the best *jinete* north of Mexico City, and they say a horse doesn't live he can't fork, and he's reported to be just as skillful with his gun."

Cardigan had already taken in Aragonza, standing, slim and fancy, in a long Durango serape and glazed sombrero by the window, and he knew why Garza had done it. "I can see how many men you've got in the room without you pointing them out to me, Garza."

That pawky smile slid across Balacar's thick lips again, and he spread his hands out, palms up. "*Señor,* you misinterpret my *amigo*'s meaning entirely. We would not try to detain you forcibly if your desires lead you elsewhere."

Kamaska's restless shift across the front of the fireplace belied Balacar's words, and Cardigan hauled at Parker with a growing sense of urgency, knowing his one gun wouldn't hold them much longer. "Will you come on, Pinto."

"*Pues,* you are so insistent, *señor,*" said Balacar. "Is our hospitality that bad? Is it?"

"I don't think you have Florida to intercede on your behalf this time, Cardigan," said Garza.

"Watch it, Innocencio," snapped Cardigan, twitching his gun toward the man as he saw his hand slide toward his neck. "Pinto, will you get up? Damn you, will you come on?"

"Whatsamatter, Card," said Parker, rising halfway, then falling back. "I don' wanna go. Look at all the pulque they got left."

"Don't you see what they're trying to do?" Cardigan almost shouted, and coming out with it openly like that must have been what set it off, because everybody started to move at once, and Cardigan slipped his arm clear around behind Parker and yanked him upright, giving him a push that sent him toward the door.

"Cardigan!" shouted Garza, and Cardigan turned toward him with the gun. Garza stood by the table, unarmed, and, even as he realized his mistake, Cardigan had to admire the man's nerve, taking that chance. Cardigan's thumb was tight against the hammer, but he couldn't throw down, somehow, and he saw the triumph in Garza's face as he turned back the other way. It was too late. It had given them their chance, and Cardigan was not around far enough to recognize who it was when the weight was thrown against his arm. He shouted with the pain of two vise-like hands twisting his wrist back on itself, felt the Remington drop. Then he saw it was *Tio*

Balacar's sweating, sensuous face jammed into his shoulders and knew time to be surprised that the man's slender hands could hold so much strength. The man's position only allowed leverage on Cardigan's wrist from one direction, and, when Cardigan whirled the other way, he felt his arm jerk loose. As he whirled, he let his knee come upward. Balacar's sick grunt was reward for the pain of that wrist.

Garza had been on the opposite side of the table from Cardigan, and he was not yet around it as Balacar reeled back into a chair with both slender hands gripping his groin. Cardigan made a loud, grunting sound, heaving that heavy table over on Garza. Kamaska and Innocencio had jumped Parker, and he was on his knees beneath their combined weight, head bobbing down due to a blow from Kamaska's fist. It must have taken just about that long for comprehension to get through Parker's drink-fogged brain, because his reckless shout rang out as Garza went down beneath the long table.

"Well, damn you!" shouted Parker, and the floor might as well have heaved up from beneath Kamaska and Innocencio for all the good their mad struggle did to keep Parker down. He burst from between them like a raging bull, smashing Kamaska in the face with a bony elbow and knocking him back onto the overturned table, butting Innocencio in the belly, swaying up onto spread legs with that wild grin. "It looks like the boys want to fight, Card. That'll finish the evening just right."

"Get out, Pinto, get out!" yelled Cardigan, realizing this was their last chance, grabbing at Parker and trying to whirl him toward the door. Then he saw Aragonza over at the end of the room with a gun in each hand, and the first shot drowned all other sound, before the echoes died, someone else was shouting.

". . . at them, you *necio,* don't shoot at them. We want Dixon alive!"

It was Balacar who had yelled, and he hoisted himself up out of the chair with one hand still at his groin and a sick, greenish hue to his twisted face, and Cardigan tried to shove Parker out of the way. But Balacar crashed into Parker, tearing him loose from Cardigan's grip and carrying him on over into the upturned bottom of the table. Before Cardigan could reach them, a heavy body struck him from behind, and he went to his knees beneath Innocencio. Down like that, he saw Parker bring his knees up between himself and Balacar and lash out with them. It shoved Balacar off Parker, and the upswing of Parker's feet brought them past the heavy man's body, and Balacar screamed as both Parker's sharp-roweled spurs hooked him in the face.

Cardigan knew of that *belduque* and, with Innocencio on top of him, jerked aside as he heard the man grunt. Innocencio's thrust went past Cardigan's shoulder, the long knife sinking deeply into the hard-packed earthen floor. Cardigan caught the man's arm and used it for a lever to pull Innocencio over him onto the floor. Innocencio jerked the *belduque* free to jab again, and Cardigan had to sprawl bodily across the man to block it. From that position he caught another glimpse of Pinto Parker. *Tío* Balacar was holding his bloody face in both hands now and blindly trying to rise from where he had been thrown across the upturned table. Free of the man, Parker had gained his feet, whirling to jump feet first at Balacar again. This time the spurs crunched into Balacar's hands, and rolled down his forearms, tearing the sleeves of his silk shirt from cuffs to the elbows, dragging deep, red furrows through muscle and flesh.

"That's Texas fighting for you, *Tío,*" roared Pinto Parker, still filled with liquor, laughing crazily, and launched a final kick at Balacar that struck the man's head and rolled him down the table bottom till he crashed into an end leg hard enough to crack it off.

Cardigan was still sprawled across Innocencio and had just about realized it was Innocencio holding him down, rather than him keeping the man on the floor, when a great, crushing weight landed on him from behind and his head was driven into Innocencio's chest by a rabbit punch behind his neck. He had seen a man hit that way before and, through the fog of stunning pain, knew instantly who was on top of him.

"Kamaska," he gasped involuntarily, and then his blind struggle for the *belduque* was rewarded.

He had both hands on Innocencio's knife wrist and had finally gotten it twisted around beneath his own chest, when Innocencio shouted with the pain of it, and the long blade was free. Sensing above him the stiffening of Kamaska's body for another blow, Cardigan grasped the knife's hammered silver hilt and lunged back over his shoulder, blindly.

"*¡Sacramento!*"

It came from Kamaska and was so full of animal pain that Cardigan knew he had struck. The blade was held in a solid, fleshy way for a moment, and then jerked a little, and was free in his hand again. Kamaska's weight was slack enough on top of him for Cardigan to thrust himself from beneath it, slashing at Innocencio as the man sought to hold him. Innocencio jerked back to keep from having his face ripped, and Cardigan was free. As he got to his hands and knees, he could see Pinto Parker again.

Garza had finally crawled from beneath the table, and his leap must have taken him into Parker and carried both of them past Cardigan and Innocencio into the wall, because the two of them were up against the wall now. Whatever Parker did to Garza left him lying inert on the floor against the adobe *banco* that ran around the room to form a bench against the wall. But Aragonza jumped in from the other end of the room and had Pinto Parker on his hands and knees above Garza and was beating at his head with both those guns. No telling how many times Balacar's man had struck Parker before this. Parker's blond head was red with blood, and he was dripping it all over Garza's face beneath him, and he was sobbing as he tried to make what was evidently his last attempt at rising. Aragonza grunted as he slugged again with the barrel of his right hand gun, and it knocked Pinto Parker flat across Garza.

Aragonza must have seen Cardigan roll from between Innocencio and Kamaska with that knife, for Cardigan was still on his hands and knees, just stiffening to rise, when Aragonza turned from Parker and Cardigan saw his intent plainly in his face. Maybe they wanted Pinto Parker alive. He was the only one. Aragonza was an old-style gunslinger, pulling his gun hand up as high as his head so that when he let the weapon drop back, the weight of the gun itself would carry the hammer back beneath his thumb, and it would be cocked as the revolver came down. But as soon as he saw Aragonza's hand begin to rise, Cardigan knew what it meant, and his reaction was without thought. He tossed the knife while still on his hands and knees, throwing all his weight over onto one palm to free the other hand. It caught Aragonza just as his hand reached the level of his head and started to drop down again. The hammer must have already started to cock from the weight of the dropping gun, because the knife driving into Aragonza's forearm hit it so hard the gun exploded at the roof. The weight of the big knife and the force of the throw carried Aragonza back against the wall the way a blow would have, pinning his arm against the mud, the *belduque* sunk hilt deep through his wrist and into the adobe.

Even as Aragonza went into the wall, Cardigan was whirling toward a sound from behind him. Kamaska was getting to his feet, his hand clutched across one shoulder, blood seeping between the fingers. Innocencio had started to rise, but he seemed suspended there with his knees bent, staring at Aragonza in a stunned surprise, as if he found something hard to believe. Cardigan flung himself at Innocencio, his weight carrying both of them crashing into the overturned table where Balacar had broken a leg off. Cardigan came up on top of Innocencio, clutching at the smashed leg. There was a good length to it, and the wood came free when he yanked it.

"No!" yelled Innocencio, "no," and then gasped wretchedly with the twelve inches of solid oak smashing him across the forehead. Cardigan still had the leg as he jumped to his feet, because he knew what was behind him. Kamaska was already coming at him. He didn't move fast this time, or slow. He came with both hands outstretched, in a lurching, deliberate walk, each step a little longer than the preceding one, each one a little quicker. Cardigan jumped out to meet him, knocking aside one arm with the table leg. Kamaska cried out with the pain, but did not stop. Cardigan had knocked his arm aside to come in against him, and this time his blow was across the top of Kamaska's head with all the weight and force he could bring into it. He heard the crack of wood, and Kamaska dropped a full six inches. He stood there a moment against Cardigan, his knees bent, his one arm still outstretched.

Cardigan raised the leg, brought it down again. Once more the cracking sound. Kamaska dropped another six inches, his face buried against Cardigan's belly, that one arm clutched around Cardigan's hips. Cardigan brought it up for the third time. Then he held it that way, staring stupidly up at the short stub of wood in his hand. The leg had broken in two.

He stood there a moment longer, dropping his head to look at Kamaska. Then he stepped back. Kamaska went to his hands and knees. Then he slid quietly onto his belly.

Cardigan swayed there, trembling, panting, his shirt ripped from his lean torso and hanging from his belt. *Tio* Balacar was sitting over on the *banco*, bent forward, with his elbows on his knees and his bleeding face in his hands.

"I can't see," he said stupidly, "I can't see. Where are you, Aragonza? I can't see."

Aragonza was crying like a baby as he twisted one way and the other, still pinned against the wall, desperately trying to pull the knife free. At his feet, Comal Garza was stirring feebly beneath an inert Pinto Parker. Finally Cardigan's dim perception reached the hallway. Florida stood there, holding Garza's gun.

Cardigan spat out a tooth. "Well," he gasped. "What are you going to do?"

VIII

A fog had swept in from the Gulf Coast to shroud the brasada in a gray oppression, the morning after the fight. Gaunt mesquite reached out of the viscid mist like helpless, skeleton hands supplicating the unseen sky. The *cenizo* sprawling about the bunkhouse door blended its dead, ashen growth with the shreds of turgid vapor seeping into the room. Esperanza shuffled in from the kitchen with a bowl of beans, grumbling through his flowing, longhorn *mustachios*.

"I don't see why you have to leave now. The whole *estancia* is yours. Everybody's afraid of you. You're the big *toro* of the pasture and nobody comes within ten feet of you."

Cardigan was sitting at the table, wearing one of Esperanza's cotton shirts. "Would've left last night if Pinto was in any shape."

"An' leave the *señorita?*" said Esperanza.

"What does she have to do with it?"

"She don't want you to go."

"What did you do with those?" Cardigan pointed his fork at the beans.

"Those are on foot, *señor*. Boiled. Tomorrow we have them on horseback. Fried. You stay tomorrow and you see why we call them *nacionales*. *Sapodillas*. You should see my *sapodillas*. I make them for *General* Porfirio Díaz himself. Sweet, hollow pincushions of puff paste, *señor*, as frothy as lather from the amole. I fry them in deep grease and make syrup to go over them hot. And *panecillos.* . . ."

"All right, all right, biscuits," said Cardigan impatiently. "Just bring the coffee and forget. . . ."

This time the crash of gunshots did no more than make him jump in the chair. Esperanza stood there, quivering with rage, hands filled with his smoking Colts.

"You don't like my *panecillos?*" he shouted.

"I didn't say tha. . . ."

"You don't like my *panecillos.* I make them for the whole Mexican army, but they aren't good enough for you. What are you, a *hidalgo? Sacramento,* no, just a loco *Tejano* who can't even ride through a mesquite tree without getting knocked off. . . ."

"You want me to slit your throat?"

It came from the doorway, and it stopped the cook. He stood there a moment, staring toward Innocencio. Then he let the Colts drop back into their holsters.

"Madre de Dios, Innocencio, I was just telling him how I cook my *panecillos.* "

"Get back in the kitchen where you belong," said Innocencio, moving on in. He looked at Cardigan, grinning evilly. "Some *batalla* we had last night, no? I never see anybody throw a knife that way. Just a little flip and it goes in so deep Aragonza can't get off the wall for fifteen minutes."

Cardigan shoved the bench back, rising. "Little Indian toss I learned in San Antone. I didn't want you to think you were the only one could use a pig-sticker around here."

Pinto Parker came from the bunkroom, his head swathed in white cotton bandages Esperanza had put on the night before. He stopped a moment by the table to steady himself, grinning ruefully at Cardigan. Then he nodded toward the door. Cardigan followed him out, serpents of ground fog streaming about his legs. Parker stopped by a big cottonwood to one side of the shack, turning toward Cardigan.

"You're leaving on account of me, aren't you, Card?" he said.

Cardigan shook his head. "I'm fed up."

"No," said Parker. "If it was just you, you'd stay. There's something here. I know. But you're leaving because you don't want to let me in for something like last night again."

Cardigan shrugged his acceptance. "Just licking them didn't necessarily convince them you aren't Lieutenant Dixon."

Parker was studying his face. "They were willing to have you killed at the bull-tailing the other day, but they didn't try anything on me. That's because they still thought I was Dixon. What would happen if they found out I'm not Dixon?"

Cardigan's eyes grew opaque. "They might cut *your* cinch."

"And that's why you're going," said Parker. "To get me out of it. They've already tried to kill you, but you'd stay if it was just you."

"It's not your roundup," said Cardigan. "It wasn't from the first. I didn't look at it that way when the thing started. I hadn't known you long and you were just a man I trailed with, and I didn't look at it one way or the other. Now, I've known you longer, Pinto. It's not your roundup, and I've got no right to rope you in on it."

"What if I want to be roped in?"

"We're still going," said Cardigan.

"The girl don't want you to go, Card."

"What's she got to do with it?" demanded Cardigan.

"She didn't interfere last night."

"What cows does that get you?" asked Cardigan.

"It shows you she don't stand solid with Garza," said Parker.

"You're still riding a muddy river."

Parker's voice was intense. "You know what I mean. She wanted your help somehow all along. That's why she took a shine to you from the first. She sensed what I should have known. You weren't my kind. Just because you came in here trailing a bunch of wet beef didn't make you a tinhorn rustler like me. There was something else. She sensed it. She tried to get your help, but you wouldn't trust her because you thought she rode in Garza's wagon. Hasn't she proved different yet? It was only her arriving when she did the first time that kept Kamaska from killing you. She tried to stop that killer bull at Mogotes Oros just as hard as I did. It was her told me something had gone wrong when she saw Garza and the others dropping back and letting you have the bull. And now, last night"—he reached out to grasp Cardigan's arm— "maybe she's in such a position she can't come right out against Garza, Cardigan, until she knows someone else is backing her. You can see how it would be for a gal, all alone like that. You can't run out on her, Cardigan, just because of me."

Cardigan bit his lip, meeting Parker's eyes. "You'll go, anyway, Pinto?"

"The hell I will! What is it, Card? What is it you're after in here?" He was looking into Cardigan's eyes and must have seen it there, for his hand dropped from Cardigan's arm, and he took a step backward, his voice sober. "All right, Card. You don't have to tell me if you don't want to. It won't make any difference. Not after what you did last night. Nothing would make any difference between you and me, Card."

The sound of someone's boots made a dull tap across the hard adobe compound. It was *Tío* Balacar, moving toward them in that pompous, stiff-legged walk, the fringed ends of his silk sash ruffling against his polished jackboots. His face was blotched purple with some kind of local herb Esperanza had smeared on the deep gashes made by Parker's spurs, and one of his eyes was squinted shut and twitching all the time. Aragonza was with him, a pinched, lethal look to his pale cheeks as he stared at Cardigan. His right arm was bandaged beneath the sleeve of his fancy *charro* coat and held in a black sling. Garza and Florida were following, and the woman was watching Cardigan with a repressed desperation in her big eyes.

"Well, *compadres*," said Balacar, and, although his thick lips held that pawky grin, Cardigan could see the corrosive hatred smoldering in his eyes. "That was quite a rodeo we had last night, eh? I haven't had such a *batalla* since my cadet days in the *Colegio Militar*. *Pues*, I understand you *Tejanos* do that every Saturday night just for amusement. I'm sure you're already laughing about it, eh? I understand you're leaving this morning, and I'd hate to have us part with a bad taste in our mouths."

"On the contrary," said Cardigan, and he saw hope leap into Florida's eyes, "we aren't leaving this morning," and saw the hope turn to a fervent thanks, "we're staying."

IX

A butcher bird sat preening itself in the leafless *junco*. Mexicans said this was the only bird that would alight on the bush, for the *junco*'s thorns had formed Christ's crown. It was a somber belief and seeing the bird, somehow, filled Cardigan with an apprehension. He recalled the first time he had felt that, riding the brush this way, just before Navasato had been killed, and turned to look at the rustling mesquite stretching, dark and illimitable, behind him. They had ridden after mustangs again, and it was the first time since they left Hacienda del Diablo that Florida had found a chance to speak with Cardigan. Balacar and Garza had drawn ahead slightly to scout for tracks, and Florida pulled her scarred, little brush horse up to Cardigan's dun.

"I think it was a mistake to come out this way," she said tensely.

"We've got to wait for them to make the first move," he said. "As long as Balacar wants to keep up a pretense like this, we've got to play along."

"It's like sitting on a powder keg," she said. "You can see it under *Tio*'s smile. The way Kamaska watches us. Garza's eyes. Your first slip is your last, Cardigan."

"I think they include you in with Pinto and me now, don't they?" he said, turning toward her. Their eyes met for a moment, and then he reached over and touched her hand. "Florida, if you want to tell me now, I'll tell you."

She grasped his hand and squeezed it with a certain desperate thanks at this evidence of his trust, and her words tumbled out in a swift, tense mutter. "You know who Balacar is?"

"I know he rode with Díaz in the 'Sixties. Turned revolutionist later on. Mixed up with gunrunning down in New Orleans. Packs a lot of pull with the *peónes* for what he did in the army. Is that what he's doing here?"

"Gunrunning? You know it isn't. You know it's more than that." She glanced ahead quickly. Balacar and Garza were barely visible through the chaparral, talking in low tones. Florida twisted back in her rawhide brush-poppers rig. "You're right about him packing a lot of pull with the *peónes*, though. Almost as much as Díaz. What do you think would happen if Díaz showed up here in the brush with five hundred Krag rifles and as many freshly broken horses?"

"He'd have just about that many men to use them within a week."

"The same with *Tío*," she said. "He was a fiery, popular, dashing cavalry leader, and his exploits in and after the war have become almost legendary among the Mexicans of the border. All he has to do is let it be known he's here and needs men to follow him, and they'll come flocking like so many buzzards to a dead horse. He already has the horses. All he needs is Lieutenant Henry Dixon and those Krags. As soon as he lays his hands on those guns, he'll send out word."

"You're a *revolutionaria?*"

"It's no revolution," she flung at him. "Mexican politics don't affect me. And they have nothing to do with this. It'll stay right here in the brasada. Do you remember Cortina?"

"The Red Robber?" said Cardigan. "What Texan doesn't remember him?"

"Then you know what happened when he got going," she said. "He was leading a veritable army before he finished.

241

The whole border had a regular war on its hands. You finally had to call on the United States Army. And it took them ten years to break Cortina's hold down here." She leaned toward him, eyes big and black. "It'll be worse with Balacar if he's allowed to organize, Cardigan. You know what a terrible place this brush is. It's full of men in hiding, and very few law officers who came in after them ever went out alive. Think what it would be with an army in here, under a man like Balacar. Think what a terrible job it would be trying to smoke them out. It would be worse than any of the Indian wars. They could raid any town from here to the Red River. They could rustle cattle till cows stopped growing horns. It could well lead to another war with Mexico. You know how touchy the Cortina trouble left the whole border."

The scope of it staggered Cardigan. "Cortina was a piker beside this bird."

"It's been going on in the brasada, that way, since before Texas broke away from Mexico," she said. "But nobody ever had the nerve to try it on a scale like this."

He glanced around him, realizing what an impregnable fortress this harsh, impenetrable jungle would be for a force like that. "And they want your place for a headquarters?"

"It was the only spot in the brush big enough to corral that many mustangs," she said. "It would have been hard to steal that many horses anywhere, even over a period of time. Besides, rustling such a large number might have given away what Balacar intended in here, and he didn't want that until he was set. They did have to have horses, though. You know half the Mexicans in the brush and along the border don't own an animal. I didn't know exactly what was in the wind when Garza came to me wanting to use my ranch as headquarters for his *mesteneros*. He paid for a six months' lease for the use of my corrals and men. We'd just finished fall roundup and my crew was idle, so I didn't see any harm. By the time I realized something was going on, Garza had won over Kamaska and Innocencio. *Brazaderos* like them would give anything to ride with Balacar. And Aragonza had worked with Balacar before. I couldn't fight them openly, even when I did find out. I tried to reach Masset, but it was impossible. He'd always thought I was mixed up with the rustlers in here. The *nagualismo* business starting about that time didn't help much. Two of Masset's deputies were killed that way and he connected me with it."

"You could have gotten out."

She drew herself up perceptibly. "It's my brasada, Cardigan. My house. My land. Do you think I'd let them take it that way?"

The drum of hoofs turned him in the saddle. Kamaska had remained behind at the Hacienda del Diablo, and his horse was lathered with the hard ride from there as he pushed by them on his hairy mule. He halted by Balacar and Garza, speaking in a hot, breathless way, glancing back at Cardigan. Garza nodded, said something, neck-reined his horse away. Florida caught at Cardigan's hand.

"Quick, you've got to tell me. Who are you?"

"Yes," said Balacar. He had turned back to them through the screen of mesquite. "Who are you, Cardigan?"

"Don't you know?" Pinto Parker laughed from behind them. "He's Lieutenant Dixon's brother."

A dull flush reddened Balacar's heavy-fleshed face, and he controlled his anger badly. "We have found mustang sign. We'll be riding."

He reined his horse in beside Florida, and Kamaska dropped back till he was just ahead of Cardigan, and they broke into a trot through the brush. Cardigan watched for them to come up with Garza, but the man did not appear.

Aragonza was trailing, and kept dismounting to check the sign. They crossed a portion of brush that had been swept by the fire. There was a great stretch of blackened stubble, still glowing and snapping sullenly in places, reaching to a sandy riverbed that the fire had been unable to leap. They plodded through the white sand and into thick brush beyond.

"Evidently a large cut of *mestenos* was driven this way by the fire," said Balacar.

None of them answered, and Cardigan gripped his reins more tightly with the thickening of the sullen antipathy that lay between all of them. Parker was grinning blandly at Innocencio, and the knife man shifted uncomfortably in his saddle, his forehead still red and lacerated where Cardigan had struck him with the table leg. Then a startled, crashing sound broke from the thickets ahead, and Aragonza shouted back at them.

"*¡Mestenos!* Head them off. They are cutting toward you. Head them off."

A mustang with great singe marks blackening his dun hide burst through mesquite with the berries caught like brown bubbles in his mane. His wild eyes rolled white as he saw them, and he turned on a hind leg like a roper, taking another direction through the brush. With a hoarse shout, Kamaska was after him. Another *mesteno* crashed into the open, and then three mares clattered in from the mesquite. Cardigan spurred his dun so that it nudged into Florida's pony before digging into its gallop.

"Don't get separated!" he shouted in her ear, and then was past her.

He sensed her horse following behind him, and saw Parker line out after Florida. Then he was into the chaparral, with the mares making a great crashing before him. Keeping his eyes open, as Florida had told him, was next to impossible.

Every time a clawing mat of mesquite or a hackberry branch thrust itself out at him, his head jerked aside, and his eyes twitched with the violent instinct to shut. Yet he forced himself to keep them open, smashing hell-for-leather into the *mogotes,* and found he could dodge the malignant brush with more ease than before. He ducked under a post oak and, where he would have missed the agrito beyond that if had allowed his eyes to close and probably would have had his leg swept out of the stirrup, he spotted the thorny, crawling spread and swept his leg up to avoid it.

He neck-reined the dun violently to one side and scraped past the thick, shaggy trunk of a hackberry. Then he pulled up and turned the blowing animal, waiting for Florida. It was when his own noise had stopped that he realized there was no sound behind him. He had purposely not gone far, only riding enough to penetrate the first thicket. An insidious fear fingered him. He was just touching his dun's flanks to send it back when the sound came. It stiffened him in the saddle, and he felt the blood drain from his face, and his lips formed the word soundlessly. *La onza.*

With an abrupt motion, Cardigan kicked his dun back through the mesquite and into the clearing. It was empty. He opened his mouth to call Florida, then closed it. He turned the dun, a strange, clawing sensation tightening his vitals. Then it came.

"Card, watch out! Card, watch out! Card . . . !"

There was terror riding the hoarse, cracked shouts, and then agony, as the intelligible words became a wild, shrill scream, and that scream was so imbedded within Cardigan's memory by now that he raked his dun without thought and drove it toward the sound with all the coals on. He exploded through a mass of *granjeno* and ducked flat on his dun to tear beneath a low stretch of *chaparro prieto* and jerked aside from a clawing arm of mesquite. The screams had stopped by now and he had smashed a straight line a hundred yards through the brush before he pulled up his lathered dun, trying to place the spot where the sound had just come from.

The brush was utterly silent, save for his dun's heavy breathing. He tried another tack through the mesquite, going slower. Finally he went back to the original clearing and started circling out from it. He lost track of the time it took him to find Pinto Parker. He pulled through a stand of torn prickly pear into a small opening. Parker was lying face down. Most of his shirt was gone and the flesh across his back was ripped away so deeply the white pattern of his bones was visible, and the ground beneath him was soaked with blood.

Cardigan got off his horse slowly, his face set in a stiff, terrible mask. It didn't matter what Pinto Parker had been. It didn't matter that he hadn't known him long. All that mattered in that moment was the feeling of utter loss in Cardigan. The vagrant, poignant memory of a reckless laugh passed through him, and of a swaggering figure in the saddle, and of a cheerful Texas lullaby sung one night up by the Nueces when the going had gotten especially tough.

It must have been the sepulchral rustle of mesquite that caused Cardigan to turn around. Africano stood there, bare, leprous torso covered with fresh brush scratches, black chest rising and falling heavily. Cardigan drew a sharp breath, turning toward him.

"Africano. . . ."

"Careful, *señor!*" It was a sharp command, but more than that, stopping Cardigan, was the guttural warning of the dogs.

"I don't have to touch you, Africano." Cardigan pulled his gun. His lips were flat against his teeth. "I don't have to touch you to kill you."

Africano was staring at Parker. "You think . . . me?"

"What else?" Cardigan's voice was brittle and he was trembling a little now. "You've been around every time. *¿Nagualismo?* Go ahead. Go ahead and change back into that *onza* before I put a slug through your black brisket. I'd like to see you try."

"No, *señor*, no. I'm not *nagual.* Kamaska's loco. Just because I come from Yucatán? That was a long time ago, *señor*. I was a *niñito*, a baby. Garza is from Yucatán, too. This is my country, *señor*, my brasada. Do you think I'd let them take it, Balacar and the others? I've been trying to help the *señorita*. When you came, I thought it was to get Balacar. I have tried to help you, *señor*. . . . "

"By running around changing yourself into an *onza* and tearing people up?" said Cardigan bitterly.

"No, I tell you I am not *nagual.* Didn't I give you Balacar's letter case when I found it? Didn't I tell you of George Weaver? I was trying to warn you of *la onza* that night of the fire, but I got there too late. I used to work at Hacienda del Diablo, but Garza ran me off when I found out what they were up to and threatened to tell the *señorita* if they didn't leave. They have tried to find me and kill me ever since. And now she knows, doesn't she . . . ?" Africano stopped abruptly, his black head raising, and then shouted. "*Señor*, behind you . . . !"

It was his own whirling motion that saved Cardigan, carrying him partially to one side. The hilt of the *belduque* tapped at his shirt as it hummed past him, driving into Africano's chest. The man made a gurgling sound and fell against Cardigan, knocking the Remington upward with its first shot. The slug shattered through the brush above Innocencio's head, where he stood across the clearing. Before Cardigan could jump away from Africano's body and throw down his second shot, the two dogs had leaped past him, snarling savagely.

"Kamaska!" shouted Innocencio, trying to turn and run—"Kamaska!"—and then the ferocious animals were on him, and he went down with a pitiful shout beneath their snarling, slashing fury.

Kamaska came into the open from the other side, and Cardigan had his gun cocked, and he fired with the conversion held straight out at the level of his hip. The square, ape-like Mexican grunted, and reached out with both arms, and kept on coming toward Cardigan in that heavy, shuffling stride. Cardigan fired again, without throwing up his gun. Kamaska flinched, and kept coming. The Remington bucked with Cardigan's third shot. Kamaska made a sick sound with the impact of that one, and staggered a little, and then put his foot down in another step, grunting with the pain it caused him, and came on, grunting with each step. Cardigan's lips peeled away from his teeth in a grim desperation, and he dropped the hammer on his fourth one. Kamaska made no sound with that one driving through his thick, square belly. He took another step, his hands spastically spread out in front of him. His face contorted with the effort his will was making to drive him on that last step. His foot struck the ground with a solid, thumping sound. His thick, callused fingers touched Cardigan. Then they slid down the front of Cardigan's shirt, and Kamaska's weight almost knocked Cardigan over, falling against him, and sliding to the ground.

"*Señor.* . . ."

It was Africano, trying to raise himself on an elbow, the *belduque* protruding from his chest. The dogs were worrying at Innocencio's body across the clearing, growling and snarling. Cardigan squatted down by Africano, and the man waved a hand at Parker.

"You know . . . you know what this means?"

"It means you got what was coming to you and. . . ."

"No, no, I'm not *nagual*." Africano licked lips flecked with blood. "I mean that they would kill Parker?"

"What do you mean . . . they?"

"They no longer think he is Lieutenant Dixon. They must have found the real Lieutenant Dixon!"

X

There was something strident about the utter silence of Hacienda del Diablo that caught at Cardigan. He hauled his dun to a stop just inside the fringe of brush, searching the compound for signs of life. Africano had died in the thicket with Pinto Parker. The dun was shaking and heaving beneath Cardigan, he had driven it so brutally to reach the spread. It came to him now with a shock that there were no mustangs in the corrals. Neck-reining the dun abruptly into the open, he spurred the flagging animal across the porch. His Remington was in his hand as he swung off the blown horse, and his heels tapped across the flagstones in a grim deliberateness. The heavy door stood ajar. Cardigan slid in with his back coming up against one wall and his gun covering the living room that ran the length of the front of the building. One man was in the room. He sat on the floor, slumped against the wall near the hooded fireplace, legs thrust out before him, head on his chest. The wall above his head was pocked with bullet holes that had dripped yellow adobe down onto his white head. Two big, stag-gripped Colts lay, one on either side of him.

"Esperanza?" said Cardigan.

The old cook had trouble raising his head and focusing his eyes. "Cardigan," he croaked. "I thought you was dead. Balacar sent Innocencio and Kamaska out to kill you and Parker."

"Lieutenant Dixon?" said Cardigan.

250

"How did you know?" Esperanza made a vague movement with his hands, licking his lips. "Dixon came while all of you were gone into the brush. He said the two men who'd been guiding him had been killed almost a week ago by some nigger, just before he reached the Comanche Trail. I figure it must have been Africano. Africano run Dixon's string of mules off into the brush and scattered them. That's how you and Parker must have come across the one Garza found you with. By the time Dixon got the mules rounded up, he was lost in the brush. He tried to find his way alone, but he said this nigger kept trying to kill him and get the mules again. Finally Dixon killed all the mules and cached their loads of Krags and started out alone to find us. . . ." Esperanza trailed off, making that motion with his hand again. "*Agua,* Cardigan, *agua.* These holes in my *estomágo* give a *hombre* a *diablo*'s own thirst."

Cardigan got a clay pitcher of water off the table, and Esperanza slopped it all over his chest drinking, finally pushing it away. "Kamaska lit out to tell Balacar the real Dixon is finally here, and they come back. They had to bring Florida in on the end of a gun. Garza claimed you and Parker had been taken care of, but Balacar sent Kamaska and Innocencio to make sure. He wanted them to bring your head back in a saddlebag. He said he wouldn't believe you were dead till he saw that. He said that's the kind of a *hombre* you are."

"Who let the mustangs out?"

"Florida. She wanted to stop Balacar from getting the guns, I guess. She's been against this from the beginning . . . only me and Kamaska and the others were too dumb to see that. Garza paid us extra *dinero* and promised we'd ride high beside him as soon as they got those guns. We always thought Florida would be with them, but I guess they only wanted to use her till they got the mustangs broke. She got out somehow while Balacar and Dixon were talking and let all the horses loose, and that made them mad. They started knocking her around, and I see what they really had intended with her all along. I'm her *hombre*, Cardigan. I been on *hacienda* with her grandfather and her father and her, and they can't do that. You see what I got for my trouble. Aragonza. I never see a man pull his gun so fast. I had mine already out before he started. *Madre de Dios.*" He licked his lips again, blinking his eyes almost sleepily. Then, with a perceptible effort, he focused them again, reaching up feebly to clutch at Cardigan, his voice a hoarse croak. "You've got to get them, Cardigan. You got to stop them. Once Balacar gets those guns, there'll be no stopping him. He can get mustangs again. That ain't hard. Maybe it'll take him time, but he can get them. It's the guns."

He drew a long breath.

"The whole thing hinges on them. Once they're in his hands, the brasada's going to burn from one end to the other. You think that was a good fire at Mogotes Oros? You wait till Balacar gets going. This whole border country won't be safe for a man like you to set foot in. They'll raze every town from here to Austin. There won't be a cattle ranch left south of the Nueces. And nobody'll be able to stop them, Cardigan, five hundred men with Krags under a soldier like Balacar in this brush. Nobody's been able to clean the brush of rustlers and killers in the last hundred years. What chance do you think they'll have with an organized army? And Florida"—his hand tugged at Cardigan's shirt with a spasmodic fear—"you got to stop them, Cardigan. Before they get those guns. She's with them and Balacar'll kill her as soon as he has the Krags for sure. The only reason he kept her alive was her influence with the *brazaderos* but, as soon as he gets those guns, he won't need her any more. From the description Dixon gave of the place he cached those Krags, I'd say Río Frío."

"My horse is done," said Cardigan.

"There's some old brush ponies staked out behind the cookhouse. They ain't these mustangs, but they'll take you where you need to go."

Cardigan rose, took a step toward the door, then turned.

Esperanza waved him on. "Go ahead, go ahead. Ain't no use waiting to see me sack my kak." He took a gasping breath. "Make it before night comes, Cardigan. I heard *la onza* a while back. Make it before night comes or you'll have the *nagual* on you out there."

"I don't think so," said Cardigan. "I think that's already taken care of."

It was a stringy-backed, hammer-headed gelding no more than fifteen hands high, scarred from nose to tail by the brush, and, once Cardigan touched its hoary flanks, the evil little beast threw itself into a mad gallop, crashing through the brasada as if it hated every thicket personally, throwing itself broadside through *mogotes* of chaparral, driving tumultuously through a bunch of mesquite with its head down and little eyes glittering belligerently, dashing across open spaces in a driving impatience to be at the brush again. Cardigan had taken some wild rides in his day, but this sat the fanciest saddle. It was a constant battle to remain on the horse, ducking flat along its cockleburred mane or throwing himself off to one side, riding its rump, its neck, its flanks, not spending five minutes of the whole time sitting straight in the saddle. Yet, with all its apparent rage at the brush, the horse took him through *mogotes* the dun could never have negotiated, bursting thickets the devil himself would have gone around, penetrating seemingly impenetrable chaparral, crashing prickly pear so solid it looked fit to stop a herd of steers. All the time it was Florida's admonition. Keep your eyes open, keep your eyes open.

There was a post oak that batted his head and left him sick and dizzy and reeling in the rawhide-lashed brushpopper's saddle, and mesquite that caught at his face while he was off to the side and left his flesh torn and bleeding, and agrito that ripped his Levi's to shreds, and nopal that jabbed his hands and arms like bayonets. He seemed lost in a mad nightmare, filled with the roaring crash of brush and the clatter of chaparral and the squashing pop of prickly pear.

Esperanza had said Río Frío, just south of where they had hunted *mestenos* that first time, and the best Cardigan knew was to drive in a straight line with the sun on his left. Soon he was fighting the brush as bitterly as the pony, flinging a curse at each jabbing *comal*, shouting a hoarse execration at every low-reaching hackberry branch. He had gotten the feel of it now and was going more by sense than sight, his swing to the side automatic when a post oak loomed ahead, his jerk upward again instinctive to avoid the clawing arms of *comal* before his face, riding like a drunken man, swaying and cursing and shouting and panting and bleeding.

He crossed a great, blackened stretch, where the fire had burned itself out in some pear flats, and ran again into the thickets. There was no trailing for him; he knew too little of the brush for that. He struck a wet creek finally and knew it to be Río Frío, for there was no other water within miles, and turned down the dribble, fighting through cottonwoods and hackberries festooned thickly with parasite moss, and the constant pop and crash of brush as he burst through it didn't allow him to hear any sounds. He came upon them in this mad rush, tearing through a screening thicket of huisache that grew down into the river, and almost running down Aragonza on the other side.

"Cardigan!" shouted Aragonza, jumping backward.

The man's first surprise kept him from any action, and, by the time he was ready, Cardigan had hauled his heaving pony to a stop and slid off and stood there, swaying and bleeding and panting, his legs spread out beneath him, his torso bent forward slightly. *I never see a man pull his gun so fast!* It was in Cardigan like that, what Esperanza had said, and he was waiting, with the knowledge. *I never see a man pull his gun so fast.*

"Go ahead," he said.

Aragonza went. His right arm was still in that black sling, but Cardigan had seen enough to know the man was as good with either hand, and, when the Durango serape flapped against Aragonza's *charro* vest with his blinding movement, whatever had been in Cardigan's mind was swept from it as instinct and habit reared up from his unconscious in an inundating wave. He felt his whole body sweep into motion, and that was his last conscious sensation till the crash of guns jarred through him. It must have been the jolt of Cardigan's slug striking Aragonza that made the man pull his trigger, spasmodically, for Aragonza had not lifted his gun high enough to be in line. With the smoking six-shooter still pointed at the ground, Aragonza sobbed in a strangled way and fell over on his face.

The brush pony had been spooked by the gunfire and bolted for the mesquite, but the clatter of the men bursting into the open from there caused the animal to rear up and whirl back toward Cardigan. With all his concentration on Aragonza, Cardigan's awareness of Florida had been but a dim one in those first moments. She was standing on the far side of the clearing.

"Cardigan!" he heard her cry, and with the brush horse

charging wildly at him he threw down on the trio who erupted from the thicket behind Florida. He had to snap his shot at the first man he saw, and it was Comal Garza, coming out of the mesquite with berries dripping all over his shoulders, and that Ward-Burton hugged in against his belly as he snapped the bolt. Cardigan's gun bucked in his hand, and he had time to see Garza's face twist, and then the horse's shoulder crashed into him, spinning him around.

Desperately Cardigan tried to keep his feet. He spun into a hackberry, hearing the horse thunder on into the brasada behind him, and then reeled off the tree and went to his hands and knees in the sand, facing away from the hackberry a foot behind his head. He flopped over onto his back with his gun in both hands. In that position, lying there flat with his feet toward them and the gun sighted down his belly through his toes, he saw *Tío* Balacar. Balacar must have been the one to fire that first shot, for he was still coming forward in a stiff-legged run, and he had already thrown his gun down for the second shot. Cardigan thumbed desperately at his own hammer, knowing his head would be blown off before he could ever fire.

He recoiled to the roar of the shot. Then he lay there, his gun still gripped in both hands, not yet cocked, realizing it hadn't been Balacar's gun which had made the sound. *Tío* staggered on forward a couple of steps, his face blank with a stunned surprise, and then a glazed opacity dulled the brilliance of his little, black eyes, and, when he fell forward, one of his arms dropped across Cardigan's leg.

Florida was standing above Garza, with Garza's smoking Ward-Burton still held across one hip. She was not faced toward Balacar any more. She had snapped the bolt of the gun again, and her thumb was still over the breech where she had jammed in a fresh shell. The third man who had been running out with Balacar and Garza was halted, a frustrated rage showing in the way his mouth worked as he stared at the weapon, his hand still gripped on the flap of a holster at his hip, holding it open over the butt of an Army Colt he hadn't been able to draw.

Cardigan got to his feet, stepping over Balacar, slipping the Colt from the man's holster, and it was rather a statement than a question. "Lieutenant Dixon."

"Yeah," said the man sullenly.

"I'm United States Marshal Edward Cardigan, and I'm taking you back for desertion, theft of government property, and fomenting activity inimical to the government of this country, and that's tantamount to treason. They usually hang a man for that."

Florida was staring at Cardigan, wide-eyed, and her words were hardly audible. "Marshal . . . Edward . . . Cardigan . . . ?"

"You can see why I couldn't tell you." He was turned toward her, and it was spilling out now, the way he'd wanted it to come for so long, the way he'd wanted to let her know she wasn't alone. "I didn't know whether you were with them or not, Florida, for sure. I couldn't take a chance. I had a job to do, and I couldn't take a chance. So much more depended on it than just you and me. The lives of so many men who would have died if I'd failed, men like Masset and Weaver and Smithers."

"Weaver was a marshal too?"

"Yes, the first one they sent in to find out what was going on down here. Lieutenant Dixon was in the Quartermaster Corps at San Antone. Balacar reached him. It's usually money, in a case like that. Enough money. Dixon got assigned to a detail transporting those Krags from San Antone to Fort Leaton. At the Nueces, two Mexicans met the detachment, and, with their help, Dixon got the guns into the brush.

Two of the troopers were killed during the ruckus. Our office had word that Balacar was active somewhere north of the border, and, when the Krags disappeared and with the reports Masset's office had been sending in about this *nagualismo* business going on south of the Comanche Trail, the government decided it was time for them to step in down here and try and clean it up.

"After Weaver disappeared, I was assigned. Instead of coming straight in, I figured it would be better if I dallied onto someone who knew the brasada and who would be accepted in here among the class of men who ran the brush. We had tabs on the local rustlers and border-hoppers working out of San Antone and other towns near the brush. In Brownsville I finally tied in with Pinto and Navasato to run a bunch of Big Skillet beef across the border. Pinto never suspected who I was till right at the last. . . ."

He trailed off, and she looked up at him, sensing what was in his mind. "He wouldn't blame you, Cardigan. He didn't. He stuck, didn't he? Even after he began to understand how you'd used him."

"It didn't matter at first." Cardigan's voice was guttural. "He was just a two-bit rustler, and he was just someone who could get me in here. But you know Pinto. After being with him that way, riding with him, camping, fighting, drinking"— he moved his head in a helpless, frustrated way—"I can't help how I feel. It doesn't matter what he was or what he may have done. I can't help how I feel."

"He understood, Cardigan. He wouldn't have had you any other way. You're that kind. Pinto understood what kind you were and admired you for it, and, whatever happened, he never blamed you."

It was the rustling sound that made Cardigan realize how much of their attention had been focused on Dixon. Florida stood in front of where Garza lay, and it had hidden his movement just long enough. Both Florida and Cardigan whirled toward him, but he was already on his feet and plunging into the brush. Florida tried to fire, but she hadn't shoved the fresh shell home hard enough, and the Ward-Burton jammed on her. Cardigan had put his Remington away, and it took him that long to draw it, and then it was Florida, shouting: "Cardigan, look out! Dixon! Cardigan . . . !"

He whirled back, the Remington out, firing after Dixon as the man leaped into the mesquite. He heard Dixon cry out in pain, and then crash on through the thicket. Cardigan plunged after him.

Garza!" called the woman. "What about Garza?"

"Dixon's the man I want!" shouted Cardigan, smashing through some prickly pear. "Garza won't go far with that slug I put through his belly."

He was still shouting when the sound came. He stopped shouting, and stopped running, and stood there, with his mouth open. Bursting through the pear after him, Florida ran into Cardigan, almost knocking both of them over, and then, against him like that, she stiffened, and her fingers tightened on his arm. It rose above the brasada like the scream of a woman in mortal pain, weird, terrifying, unearthly. It was the same sound Cardigan had heard before Navasato, and Masset, and Pinto. He felt a suffocating constriction in his chest, as the cry died, and Dixon must have stopped running somewhere ahead of them, for an utter silence settled over the brush.

"No, Cardigan," whispered the woman, "no, no, no."

"Cardigan!" It was Dixon's shout, shocking them, coming shrill and cracked from ahead. "Cardigan, for God's sake, Cardigan! Help me, Cardigan! For God's sake, Cardigan . . . !"

Cardigan made an impulsive movement toward the sound

that carried him halfway through a lane between mesquite thickets with the woman clinging to him, and then Dixon's screams had stopped, too. Gun gripped in a white-knuckled hand, Cardigan forced himself onward. Sweat was running down the deep grooves from his nose to his lips as he passed the mesquite and forced his way through thickly entwined chaparral. There was an open spot beyond the chaparral. Dixon lay there, face down. Florida stared a moment, then turned her face to Cardigan's chest with a small sob.

"I was a fool," Cardigan muttered thickly.

"A fool?"

"I thought Africano was the *nagual*."

Her face turned upward with a jerk and her eyes were shining up at him in a wide fear. "You mean . . . Garza?"

XI

Night touched the brasada with its ghostly hands, and the *chaparro prieto* stood in sinister silence along Río Frío. From somewhere far off a coyote mourned through the darkness, and nearer, through the mesquite, back in the secretive pear, the sibilant, chuckling crackle of movement through the brush mocked them. No telling how long they had crouched there, above the torn, dead body of Lieutenant Dixon. No telling how long they had waited. It seemed an eternity to Cardigan. His hand about the Remington was aching from its tight grip and his palm was sticky with sweat against the butt. The woman, beside him, was still having those fits of trembling, her breathing coming out in small, choked spurts. She watched him intently with the fear in her big, dark eyes, and her lips kept forming his name, as if it were the last thing she clung to.

"Cardigan . . . Cardigan . . . Cardigan."

He couldn't blame Florida. He was terrified himself. A deep, instinctive, primal fear that rose from the first fear the first man had felt for the night, and the unknown. He licked his lips, remembering the twisted horror on Navasato's face when they had found him.

"Cardigan . . . Cardigan."

He took a careful breath, trying to blot from his mind the picture of Sheriff Masset's bloody, rended body.

"Cardigan."

He almost shut his eyes to keep from seeing Pinto Parker,

lying there, torn, shattered, dead.

"Cardigan."

And still the sound, quietly out there, circling them, stalking them. The rustle of mesquite that might have been the wind, only there was no wind. The faint sibilance of something brushing the curly red grama. The barely perceptible crunch of prickly pear.

And the tracks, Cardigan. Hadn't Pinto said it? *Just like cat tracks. Only they couldn't have been. Cats don't grow that big in Texas, or anywhere.*

He tried to swallow past the thickening in his throat, and almost choked. He felt his fingers digging into the flesh of Florida's arm, and tried to ease the grip. And still the sounds. A sibilant rattle. Agrito? A faint tapping. Mesquite berries knocked from a branch. A scraping whisper. Nopal?

"Cardigan, I don't think I can stand it. . . ."

"*Shh*"—he put his finger across her wet lips—"it won't do us any good to move. It'll just give us away."

And the tracks, Cardigan. A jaguar, perhaps. Too big. Cats don't grow that big in Texas. Or anywhere. What is it, Africano? What is la onza?

There it was again. Mesquite? Oh, hell! He shifted his position to ease aching muscles. How could you tell if it was mesquite? How could you tell anything? What did it matter? It was out there. That's all that mattered.

La onza is a hybrid, señor. A cross between a bull-tiger and a she-lion. There is nothing more deadly. There is nothing more terrible.

"Cardigan. . . ."

He squeezed her arm hard enough to make her wince, lifting his gun a little. It seemed to be nearer now. From the right? He turned that way slightly, cocking his head. On the left? He began to shift back, and then stopped, the mad-

262

dening frustration of it sweeping him. He bit his lips to keep from cursing, or standing up, or crying, he didn't know what. He realized he was breathing hoarsely, and tried to stifle it. Tears were running silently down the woman's face. She was biting her lips, too, and blood reddened the tears as they reached her chin.

"Cardigan!"

It came all at once, the crash of brush and that terrible, screaming sound that no cat could ever make and the woman shouting at him, and the bellow of his gun as he whirled and saw the huge, blurred silhouette of it, hurtling down on them. He caught Florida with a sweep of his free arm, knocking her back and aside, and jumped back himself to fire again, not throwing down this time, dropping his thumb on the hammer from where he held the gun at his hip.

He had a kaleidoscopic sense of evil, little eyes, gleaming green as they were caught in the moonlight and white fangs in a great, velvety snout and the blasting heat of stinking breath as the beast let out another of those unearthly screams, and then he was being thrown back by its terrible weight and impetus, all the air exploding from him in an agonized gasp. He had no conscious feeling of shouting again. With those terrible talons ripping at him, he felt the gun explode somewhere down by his hip.

He tried to get to his feet, crying out in pain as a swipe of the huge paw caught his upflung arm, tearing it away from his face. His impression of the animal was still blurred and unreal, and, still going backward, he gained his feet, and managed a stumbling step on into the thicket, and jerked the Remington into line again to fire point-blank at the huge, snarling face before him. The screaming sound it made deafened him this time, drowning the report of the gun.

A great suffocation gripped him, and after that, nothing.

263

XII

It was a voice. Coming in from somewhere, Cardigan knew that, if he knew nothing else. It was a voice.

"It looks like my *onza* has eliminated Marshal Edward Cardigan now, too, my dear, doesn't it?"

"Your *onza*."

That was another voice, trembling, afraid, yet brave, with the kind of courage a man has who will go out to meet what he fears, or a woman.

"Then you're the *nagual*."

There was a laugh coming to Cardigan through succeeding layers of pain now that spread over him and spun through his brain. "My dear Florida, surely you don't believe that *nagualismo* rot. I'm no more a *nagual* than Africano was. The only rapport I have with *la onza* is that I've had the animal since it was a cub. It will do my bidding as Africano's dogs did his."

"Don't be fantastic. How can you train a beast like that? Even if it did exist."

"It does exist." The man's voice again. "And I did train it. Isn't that more logical to believe than the fact that I change myself from a man into an animal? They train ordinary cats, don't they? They train tigers to obey the whip. You'd be surprised what those Caribs can teach a jaguar. Why not an *onza*? You should see the beast, Florida. You will. It eats from my hand. Anybody else it will rend to shreds. It took time, of course, and patience. But so does a good horse."

"But why? Are you crazy? . . . a sadist?"

"No more than is a man who trains his dog to protect him. You'll have to admit it was an admirable expedient. There have been ordinary murders through this stretch of the brush for hundreds of years, but that didn't keep men from running it. You saw what happened with my *onza*. These Mexican *brazaderos* have enough Indian in them to know *nagualismo*. Even white men. Look at Masset. It kept them out of Cañada Diablo, didn't it? Every new kill by *la onza* was another brick in the wall of superstitious fear keeping the *brazaderos* out of Cañada Diablo, and we could work here in perfect safety till everything was ready."

A growing acceptance was in the woman's voice. "Did Balacar know?"

"Nobody knew," he answered her. "I kept *la onza* chained in those caves south of Río Frío. When we first heard Parker and Cardigan were coming through with a bunch of cattle, I let it out, thinking they were just rustlers. Then, after it had killed Navasato, I found that dead mule and the Krag with his body, and thought it meant one of them was Dixon. Africano had stampeded Dixon's mules, and this one must have been caught by the *onza* about the same time it found Navasato."

Cardigan was trying to squirm from beneath the ponderous weight of the animal lying across him now. He was sobbing with the agony in him. He wrested one leg from beneath the great, white-furred belly, and rolled from under a bloody paw. The man was still talking from the thicket farther on.

"When Kamaska came, telling us the real Dixon had arrived at the *hacienda,* I told Balacar to go on and I would take care of Parker and Cardigan. *Tío* must have sent Innocencio and Kamaska to make sure. He didn't know about the *onza*. If

265

they hadn't bungled it, the *onza* would have had Cardigan there. When I realized Cardigan had escaped, I followed him with the *onza*. I reached you here just about the time he did, didn't I? And now it's just you and me. We can do the same thing *Tío* wanted. We can have an empire here. We can live like Cortina. Did you ever see his *hacienda*, Florida? Even his *peónes* had silver-mounted saddles. Five hundred Krags and the men to use them and the brasada, Florida. Nothing can beat that combination."

"It's already beaten," she sobbed. "One man beat it. Maybe he's dead now, but he beat it. You won't last the night out with that slug Cardigan put through your belly."

"Maybe you'd like me to call the *onza*, Florida."

"The *onza?*" Fear shook her voice.

"It will eat out of my hand," said Garza.

"This one won't eat out of your hand, Garza," said Cardigan.

He must have made a shocking sight, stepping from the thicket. His shirt was torn completely from his torso, claw marks drawing their viscid, red grooves from his collar bone to his belt, his left arm hanging torn and useless by his side, dripping blood off the limp fingers, the flesh ripped in a patch from his forehead.

"Cardigan," gasped the woman, and he had time to see the desperate joy in her face before she had hidden it against his chest, and he didn't mind the pain that caused him, as his one good arm encircled her pliant waist. He looked over his shoulder at the defeat in Garza's face, and he wanted to hate the man, for Pinto, and couldn't because there wasn't that much emotion left in him.

"The guns?" he said gutturally.

"Down by the river," said Florida, her voice muffled against him. "Dixon cached them under a cutbank. We've got to get you to a doctor, Cardigan, we've got to get you to a doctor."

"You'll come, too?"

"Yes, you know I will. You can't make it alone."

"I don't mean . . . ," he began. "Esperanza's dead by now back at your spread. All the others. Half the brush is burnt out by that fire. It will never be the same again."

She lifted her head to look at him, and understanding of what he was asking entered her eyes. What had happened was still too strong within both of them for either to put this in words so soon, yet her answer encompassed all his questions, spoken and unspoken. "You know I will," she repeated.

About the Author

LES SAVAGE, JR., was born in Alhambra, California, and grew up in Los Angeles. His first published story was "Bullets and Bullwhips" accepted by the prestigious magazine, Street & Smith's *Western Story*. Almost ninety more magazine stories followed, all set on the American frontier, many of them published in Fiction House magazines such as *Frontier Stories* and *Lariat Story Magazine* where Savage became a superstar with his name on many covers. His first novel, TREASURE OF THE BRASADA, appeared from Simon & Schuster in 1947. Due to his preference for historical accuracy, Savage often ran into problems with book editors in the 1950s who were concerned about marriages between his protagonists and women of different races—a commonplace on the real frontier but not in much Western fiction in that decade. Savage died young, at thirty-five, from complications arising out of hereditary diabetes and elevated cholesterol. However, as a result of the censorship imposed on many of his works, only now are they being fully restored by returning to the author's original manuscripts. Among Savage's finest Western stories are FIRE DANCE AT SPIDER ROCK (Five Star Westerns, 1995), MEDICINE WHEEL (Five Star Westerns, 1996), COFFIN GAP (Five Star Westerns, 1997), PHANTOMS IN THE NIGHT (Five Star Westerns, 1998), THE BLOODY QUARTER (Five Star Westerns, 1999), IN THE LAND OF LITTLE STICKS (Five Star Westerns,

2000), and THE CAVAN BREED (Five Star Westerns, 2001). Much as Stephen Crane before him, while he wrote, the shadow of his imminent death grew longer and longer across his young life, and he knew that, if he was going to do it at all, he would have to do it quickly. He did it well, and, now that his novels and stories are being restored to what he had intended them to be, his achievement irradiated by his powerful and profoundly sensitive imagination will be with us always, as he had wanted it to be, as he had so rushed against time and mortality that it might be. THE GHOST HORSE will be his next Five Star Western.